Sync

**A novel
By Dan Tyte**

Copyright © 2024. All rights reserved.

Also by Dan Tyte

Praise for Half Plus Seven

"A coming of age novel snorting with energy"- *Daily Mail*

"A lethal cocktail of Bukowski and Mad Men"- *NME*

"Sharp, spiky satire...a masculine and propulsive romantic comedy"- *Wales Arts Review*

Praise for The Offline Project

"An exceptionally funny, well-observed and street-smart book, as self-aware as it is sensitive. The dialogue is as authentic as any I've read this year"- *The Big Issue*

"It's so well written, it's funny, it's intelligent"- *BBC*

"An intelligent, hearty work, full of lightbulb moments. Brilliant, clever writing"- *Buzz Magazine*

"Synchronicity is an ever-present reality for those who have eyes to see" Carl Jung

For R & B & M

Cover design by Mason Francis.

Silence.

Space and time stand still like a Casio gone kaput.

The morning sky is blue, still, the colour clarified by the quiet. Brown and yellow branches. People on the pavement stopped mid-stride. A row of stone cottages, fresh coffee ready to waft through open windows.

On the road, a car is turned 90 degrees. The headlights mid-flash. The driver door flung open. The seats empty.

A bike is buckled around the bumper. The basket emptied. Around the thin frame a collection of open library books, a cracked iPad and six or seven oranges.

In the gutter lay a man. His face turned towards the cold concrete, his form thrown around the floor. Red, red blood connected his head to the drain.

He would never ride the bike again.

Sadie

If this was the height of earthly pleasures, I'd wondered if I'd be better off dead. But that was a stupid thought. This was not the height of earthly pleasures, nor was it professing to be. It wasn't even a game or a way to get back at Stuart. Not that Stuart had committed a crime that needed avenging. He hadn't fucked my sister, or stopped my allowance, or fallen for a teenage prostitute. It was more what he hadn't done. The opportunity cost of a life lost to stretch marks. To charity balls. To family ski holidays.

Over our eight years of marriage, my passions had been dimmed, outgrown like an old haircut in the sepia of a photograph from a summer long ago. I thought of the way Stuart's hair had receded; over time, slowly but surely, regrettably, irretrievably. The person I was, rubbed away at the edges.

It wasn't always like that. I had been political. That was how we'd met, Luke and I. Stuck next to each other on the four hour journey down to London for a march against the Iraq war. Fat lot of good that had done. Ill-fated, just like our relationship, driven to its destiny by the will of something much more powerful than us.

It wasn't an instant attraction. Like a lot of the boys, his face was still fighting off the teenage acne, his talk the usual undergraduate polemic. He'd yet to fill out in the way I'd later watch from afar, his Instagram posts from all around the world filling my feed, always with a different girl, his body broader, his face surer. But something in the mid-distant gaze of his green eyes told me and only me that he was just as lost as he had been on our first day, ripped jeans and 'Bliar' placards.

It'd been a while since I'd thought of him. We

hadn't seen each other since the wedding but we still shared the irregular correspondence of people who had once been close, a long time ago. Not yet fully formed, unsure of the way ahead. Our messages saying nothing: 'Hey', 'Hope you're well', 'Catch up soon', 'Love to Stuart and the kids', but not needing to.

I was on all fours when I thought of him, Graham grunting from behind, his sweaty paunch bouncing up and down on my arse, his small cock in and out like an indecisive house guest. I stared straight ahead at a generic headboard and buried my face in the mass-laundered pillows. Graham was a nobody. He could have been an anybody. He was older than me by a good ten years or so and it showed. I think I'd always thought an older man could provide protection, which seems like just the opposite of what I should have been looking for from an affair.

This was the seventh time we'd done it, the fourth time in this hotel room, and, I'd just resolved, the last time ever. The previous time, after too much bad champagne at a French place way off the beaten track, he'd blurted out that he loved me. That was two weeks ago and I'd avoided his messages ever since. The plan was to call it off over breakfast. A safe option. But I'd always been bad at planning. One for the road.

And then Luke. As my mind searched for emptiness to block out the boredom of the current reality, he danced onto the blank page in my brain. He was wearing a suit, tailor cut, drinking a coffee, sat on a stool in the window of a cafe, staring intently at a newspaper. He always stared intently. Always gave his full attention to the task in hand. My mind's eye was across the street, watching him, wondering if he was alone or waiting for a friend or a lover, passing the time by reading about another war or the reviews of the latest paperbacks. His face looked good, better than the memory it had become. His dark brown hair had been clipped short. His sharp jawline wore a beard hiding where the acne scars had once been. I'd never kissed a man with a beard. Before Stuart, they'd have made a guy look like a geography teacher. Now they were en vogue, my transgressions were more likely to be balding than bearded.

'Oh God,' Graham shouted, slumping out of me. His flabby arm reached around my waist, but I pushed him away.

'I've got work. Get off me.'

I turned around, stepped down from the bed and closed the bathroom door behind me.

In the shower, Luke was with me again. I didn't even notice him on the journey down from Liverpool. It'd been an early start and I'd had a late finish at the bar I worked at. Sleep had been deprived by hard house music pumping through the paper thin walls from the third years next door. Plus my nervous excitement. This was one of those new experiences I was meant to be seeking out. I'd never been on a march before. Our generation were more likely to hit the snooze button than get out of bed for something they believed in. A thick copy of *Paradise Lost* judged me from the bedside table.

We were dropped off close to Charing Cross Station and kettled down a side street. The air hung with hash and hope. I didn't really know anyone on the bus. My male friends tended to be temporary. My female friends non-existent. It was the opposite of what I was used to. At school there were no boys and you were stuck with the other girls, in and out of their pockets, make up bags and menstruation cycles whether you liked it or not.

It was soon apparent that the bulk of my fellow students had come along to get pissed, wind up the police or just to say they had. A group of girls had used the cheap ride to London to hit Oxford Street and had tottered on the bus for the journey back with Selfridges' bags and Starbucks. Luke was different though.

I'd never really been in a crowd before, save for a weekend at Womad with my parents and a handful of childhood trips to Twickenham. As we coursed towards Hyde Park, my Converse lost their footing. The bodies behind me pushed forward oblivious. Doctor Martens and denim crushed me against the concrete. My ribs rattled. The sharp taste of metal filled my mouth. This wasn't what I'd signed up for.

When I came around, I was in a St. John's Ambulance tent. Luke was beside me, my rucksack and a 'Make Tea, Not War' sign in his hands. My heart was racing. My head ached. Luke smiled at me. I felt fine.

'Cuppa something sweet, love?' said a matronly voice.

The air conditioning on the coach ride back was stuck on full blast and I'd fallen asleep under Luke's overturned coat, his body burning next to mine.

He asked me out the following week. We ate falafel at a Lebanese place close to the university, before an Orange Wednesday at the Odeon in town. I forget the film.

'Did you know the architect who designed St. George's Hall built it the wrong way around?'

'Kiss me, Luke.'

Our teeth bumped. The weekend's wound reopened.

He didn't pull away.

You could tell this was his first time. He'd worn too much cologne. He pawed at my bra strap as if he were doing a Rubik's Cube in the dark. He couldn't get the condom out of the foil wrapper. And when I did, he put it on inside out. When it was over, he clung to me like a newborn. For once, I didn't mind.

      The water warmed my skin, washing away the sin. I drip dried and reached into my bag for my phone and typed.
      'I thought of you today. I hope you're well, wherever you are. S.'
      I found Luke's number, pressed send and got dressed.

      'I meant it, Sadie,' shouted a voice from the bedroom.

Ysabelle

My people were very superstitious. It could be hard to go about your day without stumbling into something which would signify untold riches or certain muerte, the end of your days. Whenever we got on a bus and popped our monedas into the slot, the first thing we did was check the ticket number. If it read the same backwards as forwards, you had yourself a bileto capicúa and had better get ready for money in your pocket or knives in your back, depending on who you listened to. If we were in a hole- this happens a lot- we'd be told to throw a coin into a fountain and make three wishes for a ladder out. But however deep the hole was, even if the hunger in your niños' faces scolded your eyes, you must never ever take monedas out of the fountain or someday, somewhere you'd get what you deserved, calavera no chilla, make no mistake.

    Some people thought chicken was unlucky, most people thought eating watermelon and drinking vino tinto together meant you'd die a slow death. Italians like us believed putting monedas under a plate of gnocchi on the 29th would bring greater wealth in the following month. It rarely did.

    A newborn wasn't dressed until they had a red ribbon around their wrist to ward off envy. We believed that if you put your shirt on backwards you'd receive a grande gift. My father tried this every day, but it was no use to try and play a game like that.

    When you lived in La Boca, you'd take any bit of extra luck you could get.

    'Some things like to happen together', my abuela used to tell us. This gave my hermanos free rein to cause murder all across the barrio. And they did.

    'You need to look out for the signs,' she would say,

'don't be a stupid big balled boludo and ignore your dreams.'

One thousand times she had gathered us around the fire in our little tin house with the leaks in the roof and told us the same story. We would listen in silence all the same.

It was the week of the big dance. She was about to turn 15. She had the longest, blackest hair in all of Buenos Aires. It shone against the pinks and yellows and blues of the metal shacks her father Gennaro and the other immigrants from Lombardy had built with their bare hands. They'd painted the corrugated iron bright colours to fight the feeling that maybe this wasn't the brave new world they'd hoped for when they left the old country.

The boys of the barrio had started to follow her around when she made her errands up and down the dusty tracks between the houses. Her friends had already been paired off. Her father had made a gentleman's agreement that she would marry Claudio, the strapping son of La Boca's best butcher, Señor Garcia. Marrying into a food business meant our family would never go hungry. Gennaro was happy as a pig in shit.

He put what little savings he had towards a brand new dress for the dance. Her mother had served the family half portions for the whole week to make up the difference. The dress would be as blue as the sea of the Amalfi Coast. A store in Recoleta would make a special delivery on the morning of the dance. She would be the most beautiful girl in all of La Boca.

The night before the dance, my abuela fell into a deep, deep sleep. In her slumber she saw the most vivid image of La Muerte stalking the streets of the barrio. He was 8 foot tall and his cape was as black as the Boca night. Her screams woke up her three younger sisters squeezed into the bed next to her.

When morning came, the delivery arrived. In the excitement, the dream was left on the pillow. She opened the parcel with care, not wanted to rip the pretty paper she'd promised to her sisters to line their drawer.

But the dress was as black as the coal her father dug back home.

She cried her heart out.

'Claudio will never want me in this dress.'

Gennaro was at work and Recoleta was too far to travel.

'If he has any sense, he would love you in a grain sack,' her mother said.

Later that morning she went with her mother to the mercado. As the eldest girl, it fell to her to help out with the shopping.

Picking over some potatoes, her mother dropped stone cold dead.

She never went to the dance.

She never married Claudio.

She wore the dress for the funeral.

'Don't ignore your dreams niños. The inside has more power over the outside than you can ever know.'

Nina

'Plain Jane
Smells like a drain
Her mam's a slag
And she's the same.'

That's what they'd sung to me in school, those other kids. They say kids can be so cruel, probably didn't help that I was half-caste but it don't stop when their balls drop. In my experience, most men are snakes, rats and toerags, don't matter what age they is. I could count on one hand the number of truthful fellas I met in my life. Make that one finger actually.

The two fellas I did fall for, enough to say 'I do' to, well, the first time it was a room full of people, down at that nice hotel by the prison. Gone now it is. Very handy it was for the guests, his family mainly, real scum they were. Hadn't met many of em until then otherwise God knows what I'd have done. Probably saved everyone all the bother.

After the I dos and you may kiss the brides, instead of confetti all you could smell was wacky backy. Poor mam nearly had a turn. He was so handsome though, looked like an Italian film star. Despite the circus, I felt like a princess that day.

We was together for five years and in that time he only ever sat at the table for his tea once in a blue moon. It was like Elvis had popped in for a cuppa when he did. It was only ever me there, sometimes my mam. I couldn't have kids see, my insides wasn't right. He said it never mattered. It was me he wanted.

Half that time he was being fed at Her Majesty's Pleasure, the other half he was doing the things that got him banged up in the first place. I didn't know the half of what he'd been up to. He never let me come up to the courts but I'd heard it from the other wives that it weren't good. Not drugs or nothing like that, nicking mainly. He'd tried to stick a bookies up with a banana one time. Couldn't keep that from me though, it was all over the Echo.

Still, I'd visit him every week, wherever he was. Regular as clockwork. Take him some bits you know, home comforts, let him fill out a Pools coupon if I could get the screw to turn a blind eye. My skirt usually did that trick.

'Hope you're not dressing up like that all week are you?' he'd say.

'Course not, it's just for you, Jase.'

Then one time, I was going to miss a Thursday. Me and mam was off to Torquay for the week. The English Riviera. She could never say 'riviera', mam.

'River, river, river-ria'.

Had us in stitches it did. Well anyhow, poor mam ended up coming down with the flu.

'In summer, just my luck,' she'd said.

I thought I'd go along and surprise him. I couldn't very well send him a text, could I?

But Thursday morning, after I got out the bath, I had a funny feeling in my stomach. Women's intuition I spose. I left my skirts on the rail and put some leggings on instead.

The whole hour on the bus ride there I felt sick. Imagine it was like the morning sickness the other girls went on about. When the screw let me through the big metal doors and I walked into the room, there he was, sat across from Tina Rawlings of all people hand in hand, a pushchair next to the table.

'What's all this?'

'It ain't what it looks like babe.'

'You cow.'

'You're the fucking cow.'

Turns out her little Ryan, well Jase was the dad. Eleven months old he was and Muggins here knew nothing, the only one on the whole estate who didn't.

They could throw away the key for all I cared.

The second one, well...I think I deliberately looked for someone who was the opposite of Jase. And boy did I find him. I thought Bri was the straightest man I'd ever met, would have went back in the corner shop if he'd had change from a tenner instead of a fiver and gave em the difference. Now I won't lie, I was bored shitless with Bri, but least I wasn't the hot topic anymore. Least he was always home at five for his tea. Didn't even kick up a fuss if I broke a yolk. He was nice like that, Bri. Wouldn't harm a fly.

Or at least I thought. He was always on the computer. That's how we met. I signed up for a course in the library to help get a job. I'd just been let go by the Corporation over something and nothing. Typewriter skills were no good these days, it was all PCs. He'd been the tutor. Well, turned out he'd been in those chat forums or message rooms or whatever you wanted to call em. Teenage ones. Now I don't know if that was teenage legal or teenage not legal but I kicked him out there and then before I had the chance to ask. Mam caught him wanking himself in front of the monitor in the back room and that was the only word she could make out.

I ain't told nobody that. Shit sticks around here.

Anyway, that's all in the past now. Bygones is bygones. I sometimes sees little Ryan about but he don't bother me and I don't bother him.

Things have changed for me. Few years ago I met

this fella at a singles' night. Big, fat fella he was. I wasn't letting him anywhere near me, but, I don't know, he seemed to like me so we'd meet up for a cuppa and that. Old fella he was, had his own firm, an estate agents, houses all over town. I was between jobs just then, the computer thing never worked out.

'Come work for me, Nina,' he'd said.
'And what the hell would I do?' I'd said.
'Just be yourself, love.'

And so I did. I probably should say here, I stopped going by Jane after primary school. We'd moved to a new estate and mam had thought my middle name Nina was harder for the bullies to rhyme with. I'd always daydreamed about being someone else. Think all little girls did. One of those posh women from Cowbridge with the lovely nails and a husband who worked in London in the week. Or Sue Barker on Wimbledon, doing a man's job better than a man, and doing it and knowing that every man who looked at the telly would have dropped everything to be alone with you for just five minutes.

When I showed people around houses, I always pretended they were mine. My galley kitchen, my en-suite bathroom, my spiral staircase.

'Anyone would think this was your house, Nina,' they'd say to me, the nice ones.

Sometimes, they weren't far wrong.

We kept a copy of the keys to all our properties. It was off-putting if the owner stood there, like a lemon at the school disco. It put the viewers off. Couldn't wait to get out of there half the time. I'd get to know which ones were the empty houses, the ones someone had died in, the ones people had split up in, the ones owned by people who lived away. Two or three nights a week I'd stay in one of em, sometimes on my own, sometimes having a bit of fun with a fella. I felt like Madonna, waking up somewhere different in the morning. And why not? I wasn't harming no-one. If anything it meant I could do my work better. I knew which side the sun shone on in the mornings, if the traffic was noisy at nights, if next door's dog wanted putting down.

That's where I met him, Luke, showing him round a lovely little two bed terrace. It was in what we'd call the 'up and coming' part of town. Usually meant it was still about three rungs up from the estate. I'd shown more and more single blokes around. Sign of the times I spose.
'Mrs...not here with you today,' I'd asked him.
'Er, no...' he'd said.
He had a lovely colour on him, just come back from Argentina he said. Said he thought it was about time he'd settled down.
'There's plenty of time for that, young fella like you,' I told him. I asked him what he did for a living and he said he'd trained as a journalist, writing for the papers and that. Told him I found it fascinating. Asked him if he'd met all the stars but he said no, he said he didn't do it no more, said he didn't know what he wanted to do anymore.
'I know how that feels, love,' I told him and patted him on the arm. There wasn't much fat on him. He looked healthy, but tired, if you know what I mean. His hair was neat and tidy on the back and sides, just like Jase used to have, but he had this dark brown sweep over the forehead and tucked back behind the ears. Now I don't think I'd ever thought this before, but he had the most perfect bone structure I'd ever seen. You could of cut glass on his cheek bones.
I'd shown round this house 11 times before so I knew it like the back of my hand. An old fella had carked

it in the bath, heart attack apparently, but one of his kids had been in the trade so had done it up all modern throughout. Lovely it was, had a varnished banister, like nanna used to have in her old house, back in then they were, still are as it goes, polished floorboards too. I think floorboards can make an house feel cold sometimes you know. Nothing I likes better than kicking my heels off after a long day and running my toes through the carpet.

But it didn't feel like that here, I felt really warm, being there with him.

I talked him through all the features, you know, the usual spiel. Built in dishwasher here, power shower there, new combi boiler's just been put in so that'll save you won't it love, skirting boards up and down, but he didn't seem interested, seemed like he was in a bit of a daze, little boy lost. He had these lovely deep green eyes. I could of swam in em.

'So what you looking for, love?'

'I just don't know,' he said.

'That's alright...that's where I comes in.'

And I pounced on him. Didn't give him much of a chance, truth be told. I'd been in The Lion at dinner time. Ange's leaving do. Going off to college she was. Buy two glasses of Pinot, get the bottle for another pound.

Yeah he was younger than me, I don't know, 10 or 15 years, but I liked a younger model. Well, it's alright for a fella to say so ain't it?

So we did it, there and then on the floorboards of the box room. The old fella's kids hadn't put a bed in there. We'd told em it'd make the room look smaller. Me sat on top of him, skirt hitched up, tights pulled down. His jeans around his ankles. He ripped one of my buttons off getting my tits out of my blouse.

'Easy tiger,' I'd said.

He was robotic, but God it was good. I remember

it like it was 10 minutes ago.

He never bought the house.

I think of him every day. Only for 30 seconds or so, usually when I'm showing a couple round a new build semi, or filing away the marketing cards, or when the boss looks at me the way he does and I'm trying to ignore it. He always lifts my day. My mam bought me a keyring once which had on it 'The key to happiness is having things to look forward to'. I gets it, I do, but sometimes ain't it nice to look back too?

I was in the middle of some adding up before my viewings for the day when I thought of him. I'm good at adding up the boss always says, 'human calculator' he calls me. But then I had this bad feeling in my stomach, just how I had it when I was on the bus to see Jase that time.

When I looked back at my columns, all the sums was wrong.

Call it women's intuition but something's up.

Charlie

He'd sent me a DM.

That was how it started.

I'd been well and truly hooked into the social cycle. Facebook, Twitter, Instagram, Facebook, Twitter, Instagram. An addict waiting for the red notification button to pop up, the @ to light, the <3 to flash. Back and forth, round and round. I could lose hours like that, lost in a trance, waiting for a virtual back slap from a virtual stranger. For now, the 'UR GR8's outweighed the 'Where U Bin?'s, just about.

Why did they need new material? I could play a gig in their front room every evening. YouTube was cheaper than Ticketmaster and no-one stood on your shoes. Truth was- because that's all anyone's interested in isn't it?- truth was, I'd do anything to put off writing new songs. Procrastination with a capital PROCRASTINATE. It was hard, and not rock star hard. No-one wanted to hear about rock star hard, when they're stuck in a traffic jam en route to their unfulfilling desk job or unloading the dishwasher on a Sunday morning. Hard? You don't know the half of it, girl. Why don't you fuck off back to your country ranch and your pin-up boyfriend and leave the rest of us normal people to get on with our overdue bills and Value range?

But it wasn't like that. My first album had taken everything; everything I had, everything I was, everything I'd been. An emotional outburst 24 years in the making. The sum total of unplanned childhood syndrome, teenage growing pains, small town suffocation, middle class anonymity and the fish out of water feeling of being a Rather Not amongst the Ra's of Oxford. A 3D print of my head and my heart over an acoustic guitar.

The response had been rapturous.

'The New Joni Mitchell', a Jools Holland

appearance, mid afternoon slots on the second stages of summer festivals, an encouraging chart position, a 3/4 sold out tour of mid-sized venues.

And then nothing.

Nothing to write about.

Nothing to give.

Six months, 12 months, 18 months, two years.

A Heat appearance: 'Spotted! Charlie Ray, remember her? In Waterstones, Oxford Street. Buying a rhyming dictionary, Charlie?'

F5.

Refresh.

Graves

He arrived a good minute after the ambulance.

'Beat ya,' a paramedic said to D.S. Graves.

'Fuck ya,' Graves said back. His taxi had been second from the front at a McDonald's Drive-Thru when the call came in and he was fucked if he was giving up a Double Sausage and Egg McMuffin for a pushbike. It was hardly an armed fucking siege.

The police tape was already up and a crowd gathered around it; mothers, pushchairs, shoppers, runners, as if they were expecting someone to magically appear and juggle fireballs or walk across a tightrope made of dental floss with their knob.

'Alright, Sarge?' said one of the low ranking coppers Graves could never remember the name of.

'Fine and fucking dandy,' Graves replied, 'What's happened here then?'

'Hit and run, Sarge?. One vehicle and a cyclist.'

'Who is he?'

'The driver, Sarge?'

'If you've already fingered the driver, you're on for Employee of the fucking Month...'

'...Jones, Sarge.'

'Jones.'

'Sorry, Sarge. We're looking for the driver. Car was stolen, last night, from Hamilton Street. Reported first thing by a terribly distraught old dear.'

'So, the cyclist?'

'ID says Harris, Luke Harris, Inspector.'

'Age?'

'36, Sarge. He was carried off in an ambulance about 10 minutes ago.' Graves was on his second hash brown. One in the muffin, one on the side. That's how he did it.

'Record?'

'Minor public disorder in the May day riots a few years back, Inspector.

'Condition?'

'Still unconscious, Sarge. Rabaiotti says that-'

'-I couldn't give a rat's arse if he was delivering the Sermon on the Mount.'

'Anything else?'

'He had a press card on him, Sarge, so seems he was a journalist.'

'Wonderful. His heart won't have been beating in the first place then.' Just what we need, Graves thought.

Charles Graves pushed Jones out of the way and limped to the cordon. He'd cut his foot in a bar two nights ago and it still hurt like hell when his sole hit the floor. He approached the tape like an obstacle that had caused him grief once too often, tutted, lifted the calves of his trousers to his knees and ducked under the tape with indignity.

He looked at the scene- a black hatchback, a mangled bike, the blood stains in the gutter shining in the morning sunlight. He sighed. Another day, another dull fucking job.

When he met the women from the dating site and told them he was a detective they thought it was all shootouts and psychological games.

'I might be overweight but I'm not fucking Cracker.'

Worse still, the couch potato ones kept going on about some Scandinavian caper, some brooding alcoholic solving dead blonde crimes in the middle of nowhere.

'Never fucking heard of it, darling.'

They didn't like it when you swore. Best to weed those ones out straight away.

Graves knelt down, put a finger in the blood stains, lifted it to his nose and smelt it. Fuck knows why I'm doing this, he thought. Looks the part for the crowd though.

The ambulance whirred off behind him.

'See ya,' he said, to no-one in particular.

Sadie

It hadn't been like Luke not to reply within a quarter of an hour. I'd time him sometimes…14.56, 14.57, 14.58…beep…there he is.

It didn't matter wherever he was in the world or whoever he was with. I'm not ashamed to admit I got off on the control. I had to get it where I could. I was like a cat toying with a ball of wool, a cat who would never, ever wear the sweater. Unfulfilled potential. Barefoot not brilliant, pregnant not powerful.

The phone rang.

'I'm looking to speak to a Sadie'

I did not have the time for amateur salesmen this morning. Graham had already tried and failed with that.

'Thanks love. I'm glad I've got you."

'Look, who is this and how can I help?'

'That's what I'm hoping to find out. This is D.S. Graves of the-.'

'Oh God, what the hell has happened?' The kids flashed through my mind.

'-South Wales Police. First up, what's your full name?'

'It's Sadie Winchester. Now tell me what the hell is going on.'

'Tell us about Luke Harris…'

'Luke?' I knew something had been up. I knew it.

'Yes, Luke Harris.'

'Is he okay?'

'Mr. Harris was involved in an RTA at around 8.30 this morning.'

'Oh God.' My poor Luke.

'You were the-'

'You mean a crash, yes?'

'Yes, a road traffic accident. Everything's an

acronym these days.' The man on the other end cleared his throat. He had a Welsh accent.

'You were the last person to contact Mr. Harris.'
'Oh...I was?'
'I'd like to see you to ask you some questions.'
'I have work today...' I trailed off, conference halls and teenage memories competing for brain space.
'That makes two of us. Where can I find you'
'...I'll be at the ExCel Arena.'
'Onstage? Not a showgirl are you?'
'What? A showgirl? No, it's the Good Food Show. We're exhibiting there.'
'London, good food, I'm sold.'
'It's £200 a ticket.'
'Put us on the guestlist.'

The man on the other end of the line, DI whoever, hung up. I rarely had the time for calls from withheld numbers, but Dee, a dizzy if determined girl from our PR agency had warned me to expect a call from one of the big trade magazines this morning. I'd almost let the call ring off, repeating our key messages over in my head in the back of the cab.

'Mooments is 100 percent organic, from the udder to the tummy'
'We think people are ready for a homegrown British brand to take on the big nasty corporates'
'Our investors are confident we can be the Innocent Smoothies of ice-cream- and no, we wouldn't sell out to Coca-Cola'

The PR people told us this kind of language made us loveable. I fucking hated us.

But the call hadn't been from the editor of Organic Life, the call had been from some policeman from the sticks. And he'd wanted to know about Luke. Today was most definitely not going to plan. I was running late for the biggest food show of the year. I'd been fucked from behind by our biggest investor. And now this copper was going to turn up in the middle of everything and cause all kinds of confusion.

Stuart could not find out about this. Luke was his blind spot. It'd be too much for his little head to handle, today of all days. He'd spent the night in Devon in preparation for an early morning site inspection at the production facility. These type of things always stressed him out. Country folk to him equalled tweed not tractors. And then this afternoon he was delivering a keynote in the supertheatre entitled 'Time to join the Moo-ment Moo-vement'. His childhood stutter, repressed by prep school bullies and a £300 per hour speech therapist, would be on the tip of his tongue. But it has to come from Stuart, the PRs had said, people want authenticity. And anyway, The King's Speech did Colin Firth no harm.

The taxi trundled through the traffic, cars filled with day trippers here to see celebrity chefs and fill their handbags with free samples. The docklands always seemed post-apocalyptic to me, the gleaming glass towers and spires of the O2 among the wasteland looking like the first bold statement of a dystopian society to my eye. Too much time spent in English Lit tutorials with Luke, perhaps. I'm not sure my 21 year old self would have been in raptures had the ghost of existence future rat-a-tatted on Prof. Spence's window and foretold that I'd become the marketing director for an organic ice cream company.

The only stories my day job involved were the concoction of a mendacious brand narrative, bullshitted together with the help of our PR company. It's all about the provenance, they'd tell me. It doesn't need to be 100 percent t-r-u-e.

Moo-ments Organic Ice cream is born and raised on a microfarm in the rolling hills of the Devon countryside. Four years ago, Stuart, Sadie, Harry, Toby & Hettie inherited the farm from Stuart's great uncle, who'd been running the creamery since before Moo-oses was a boy. As a boy himself, Stuart spent long, lazy summers making homemade ice cream on the farm. So when they took over, his dream was to share this passion with you. Starting with just one flavour- Vanilla- because Stuart & Sadie always say the tr-oo test of an ice cream is in its vanilla. Moo-ments now comes in 17 flavours, from Cookies & Devon Cream to Sinful Scrumpy. And you can indulge at selected supermarkets and farmers' markets across the country. Because they care about our environment, Stuart & Sadie wanted to power the farm naturally. Now 100kw of solar panels do just this, so your Moo-ment is even more natural than ever. If you can think of a n-oo flavour you're dying to try, share your suggestion using #noomooment to let us know.

    Around 65 percent of this was actually true. Stuart hadn't inherited the farm from a great uncle. We'd bought it with his last big bonus before the shit hit the fan. His contacts at a hedge fund helped with the extra investment. The savvy bankers were using the slush funds to diversify, everything from social media agencies to sushi franchises. Fortunately, Stuart has me. If left up to him, he'd have pumped into pumpkins in November. The fact he managed to milk such a living out of his hedge fund says everything I ever needed to know about the banking industry. He'd only ever been to Devon twice before, a childhood hunting trip and a failed interview at Exeter University. If only he'd got in, life could have been so different

    Mooment's solar panels had little to do with his

eco-conscience. It took the government subsidy to sign those off. Money talked, as it always did, but it was a small victory for my dormant inner activist. The production was palmed off on a yokel operation in Paignton, the higher-than-supermarket rates and free ice cream enough to keep their mouths shut. Dee's proactive crisis comms planning was to claim distant blood relations with the Winchesters. But the PR people were right. The truth was what we told them. I'd spent too many of my Wednesdays and weekends over the past five years wheeling buggies around at farmers' markets.

    24 hours had passed by since I'd turned the tap on to drown out Graham's Romeo routine in the Travelodge. A day spent guiltless. A day spent in nothingness. The affair, if you could call it that, was thrillless. It scratched no itch. Graham was in the same industry as Stuart and I. He could have had a face-to-face with my husband with me on his breath and he'd never have noticed. I was a mother. I was a marketing manager. My job done. My present worth negligible. Stuart's mind was forever taken up by product diversification, the EMEA market, our corporate social responsibility. He wouldn't have noticed if my tits shot out laser beams.

    Today was the Good Food Show at ExCel. An aircraft hangar's worth of try not buy tourists and supermarket suits. £6k a pop for a 10 by 12 stand next to an artisan scotch egg start-up run by Lizzie and Chad. Chad would tell you it had been his idea all along, peering his gormless face around the divider, but it was darling Lizzie who had the get-up and gumption.

    My day had been spent finalising the arrangements for the show. Did our stand have WiFi? Had we prepared enough media packs? Was our spring/summer ad on my iMac? Had I printed off the parking pass? If this was emancipation, I wish Pankhurst had been miscarried. My little job, my bra in the boardroom, my fresh face of female entrepreneurship- all it did was mirror the mundanities of motherhood.

Mooments had been born one cool day four years ago in the Tuscan hill town of San Gimignano. As the plane climbed through the clouds over Heathrow, I'd made a pact with myself that this would be the last time I'd sit still and watch the seatbelt sign illuminate with these three other people. The child was intended as my escape, another human to love me unconditionally. But the Indian nurse at the 12 week scan had asked how big our nursery was and Stuart had looked to the screen and laughed 'So it skipped a generation'. The ultrasound jelly turned my blood cold and I knew that the child that was supposed to depend on me would forever have a closer bond with another.

I smoked five Marlboro Lights a day for the next six months but the boys' ruddy physicality thumbed its nose at my last shot at control. Their chromosomes made them strong currency in Stuart's family, a haughty, snorty, inbred, overfed, right of centre, south of interesting blur of red cheeks, corduroy and righteousness.

They wouldn't even notice I was gone.

Stuart worked in a hedge fund and expected me to know what that meant. At dinner parties I'd smile and concede that as long as it paid the bills I didn't mind, before shooting him a doe-eyed laugh and asking what year the Chablis was. The suffocation was signed in my own hand. I'd chosen to marry Stuart. I'd chosen to take my coil out and let him come inside me. I'd chosen this middle England mediocrity. And now, just as decisively, I'd choose to leave it all behind me, on this fly-drive tour of Tuscany which took us no further away from the problems of our everyday than if we'd sat in family therapy for a week.

But I hadn't of course.

As we walked through the cobbled streets, the shade of the towers promising protection from the midday sun, Stuart had taken me by the hand and led me down a hill, through the city walls to the edge of an easel, a wide country expanse. It was here that he gazumped me. He'd been doing some thinking. So had I. Things needed to change. Yes, they did. Work had worn him down. Silence. We needed more quality time together. Like this. Silence. Or like running our own business. Silence. The next Innocence. Organic ice cream. The next big thing. Using the family farm. What family farm? Me, in charge. The face. The brains. Him, the money, the boring stuff. We could retire out here as multi-millionaires. What did I say?

I said nothing.

Fast forward four years to today and we were about to take centre stage at the industry's number one marketplace. And despite myself, I did care about that. I cared about Stuart nailing his sales pitch. I cared about the buyers from the three big supermarkets who didn't yet stock Mooments changing their minds. I cared about making enough money for me, my money, not just half of Stuart's estate. Money to make some big life decisions. I cared about being free.

I got out of the taxi and walked through the crowd, up the endless stairs, these heels killing my feet, towards the glass triangle. Luke picked a bloody brilliant moment to get himself run over. I could hear him laughing at that in my head, one piercing yelp announcing a roar that emanated from somewhere near the pit of his beautiful stomach.

I wondered if I'd ever hear it again.

'Welcome. Name please.'

'It's Winchester, Sadie Winchester.'

'Thanks Miss-' he stumbled over the correct term, '-thanks Sadie. Let me just find you on the system.' His fingers tapped away at an iPad, a lanyard around his neck announcing him as 'Marvellous Jackson'.

'Thanks...Marvellous.'

'My pleasure.' The device pinged. It was the first time I'd been this close to an iPad since an aborted attempt to get Stuart, away on business, to play along with a sexy Zoom call six months ago. His room service had arrived before he'd managed to get it up. I'd hung up, questioning whether it was him or me or both and if we were doomed.

'I'm the third Marvellous Jackson after my father and my father before him and I'm the first to meet the Marketing Director from Mooments. I must say, Sadie, I like your Pecan High flavour more than my grandmother Gracious Jackson's famous Banoffee Pie and if you know me-'

'-which I don't.'

'-which you don't, you'd know that was really saying something. Here's your pass, Sadie. Have a really great Good Food Show.'

He handed me a plastic pass and smiled at me like sunshine.

'Thanks, Marvellous.'

I had pale skin. I hated the sun.

The hall was humongous, a hundred hockey pitches heaving with armchair masterchefs and industry makers and breakers. It took me twenty minutes dodging day trippers and demonstrations to find the Mooments stand. In that time, I'd turned down four free pens, two stress balls and a gluten-free breakfast bar-branded Rubix cube. I had more on my mind.

Stuart hadn't been in touch all morning. This wasn't unusual. He struggled with modern technology, with modern emotions. As far as he was concerned, I'd spent the morning in fitness pilates before working through our social media strategy with Dee. If only I had. This thing with Graham was an unmitigated disaster. It had to end. Perhaps the event would go so well we wouldn't need his investment.

The Mooments stand towered over its neighbours. Dee had convinced me that this was the time to go big, to make a statement to the sector. I'd told her I was sure it had nothing to do with her agency commission on the booking but had agreed anyway. She was right, regardless of the motive. Branded flags and bunting were motionless in the artificial atmosphere of the hangar. The Mooments interactive zone buzzed with brats milking a herd of digital cartoon cattle. The branches of a five thousand pound plastic tree hung with hundreds of hashtagged leaves handwritten with the public's ideas for new flavours. It had been specially made by the company who designed the Daleks for Doctor Who.

'You can't put a price on viral,' Dee had said.

One of her team, who wore the bored look only beautiful blondes in their early twenties could pull off, stood chewing gum at a foam farmyard barrel.

'I'm Sadie,' I announced extending my hand.

'Yes, Sadie, I know,' she said, shuffling a paper in front of her, 'I'm Lena...Dee made us cheat sheets with pictures and names.'

'Very clever. You can introduce me to the cows later.'

'Someone is here to see you by the way,' her cogs visibly whirred, 'oh, that was a joke.'

'Who's here to see me?'

'They left a message saying to meet them in the Go

Green room.'

'What did they look like?'

'I didn't really notice.'

'You didn't notice? Lucky you're in PR and not police work isn't it?' Dee did a special line in lackey idiots. Dee and I needed to talk.

'Look, I am thrilled to have a national brand on my CV so early in my career but I've been stood at this stand under these lights breathing reconditioned air since 6am, so it'd be much better if you were nice to me.'

'A lesson for you, young lady. The world's not nice and the sooner you recognise that, the better you'll do in it.'

Her perfect skin started to rash red into her neckline.

'Look, I'm sorry. You're doing a great job. Well done. Now, what did this man look like? Young? Old? Fat? Thin? Black? White?'

She snivelled.

'Like I said, I don't really remember. Like an old guy. Balding I think.'

'Thank you.'

That could be literally any man I knew. Well, any man who was conscious.

I followed the map on the back of my lanyard to the Go Green room. The memory of Luke was etched on the inside of my mind. I didn't need to close my eyes to see him. He was sitting on the grass outside our 1960s university dorm block, legs lolled to his side, the bottoms of his jeans baggy and blackened from one too many dancefloors. Counterbalanced on the other side sat a pile of books- unread novels, plays, lit crit. We were meant to be cramming before the next day's Elizabethan Poetry and Prose exam. A three hour epic paper sat in the crypt of

Liverpool's catholic cathedral. The Merseyside sunshine, a rarity even in the summer, meant we'd made the executive decision to take our study group outdoors. He had one of the most inquisitive minds I've ever known, probing and picking at the prose or poems in a way that was almost childlike. But his questioning didn't come from a naivety, more a need to know the source of everything he heard, to get to the soul of a situation. With hindsight it became obvious he was going to become an investigative journalist, but he equally could have been a litigator or a psychologist. He wanted answers. He had to know how the world and everything in it fitted together, every cog and wheel. That particular day, it didn't take long for talk to turn from the metaphysical poets to the drinks after the exam, the end-of-term plans, the future. It was our future then, for a little while at least. The sun came down on that day, but as I walked through the crowds to meet this mystery man, uneasy about where the day was going next, where my life was going next, the sense of Luke was scorched onto my soul.

My underarms clammed up beneath my shirt, the dogtooth jacket melting in the corners. The lights, the masses of bodies, the gin I'd needed after Graham. None of these had helped me feel fresh. I was about to face the music from someone, who fucking knew who, and I smelt like an old tennis towel. What a mess.

Until now, I'd managed to prove adept at hiding my transgressions from Stuart. I'd hardly needed to go undercover. Stuart had the emotional intelligence of a toilet brush. He wouldn't have realised I was breaking our vows, my body craving something better than this, if Graham or any of the others slapped him in the face with their dick. But now a single text message put me in danger worse than a hundred hours of hotel sex. Because now I'd been caught. Because now it was Luke.

But why did this matter? Why did I need Stuart? I didn't. Not always. I knew that. I would divorce him. But not yet. I'd resolved to that after he'd blindsided me in that Tuscan town, a personal promise made to stay with the father of my children until the right moment came. Until the majority shareholding in Mooments was signed over to me. If today went right, if the proper people were convinced, we'd be a one hundred million pound company by Q4 next year and with my special powers of persuasion I knew our overweight, undersexed accountant could be convinced to advise Stuart that it really did make fiscal sense to balance the shares in his wife's favour. In his soon-to-be ex-wife's favour.

A toddler started crying from somewhere near the pit of Hades. I turned to find the little shit and tear it off a strip or two, but counted one-two-three-ten. If Dee's interactive zone didn't go viral, mobile phone footage of the Mooments marketing director making a child weep certainly would.

'Could you tell me where the Go Green room is?'

'You're outside it, madam'.

This was it. I checked my phone. Still no sign of Graham and the policeman, whatever his name was. He hadn't called since we'd spoken this morning. But he wouldn't call if he was here would he? He wouldn't want to warn me, to give me time to get my story straight or elope to Brazil. I'd seen all the cop dramas. I knew that narrative inside out.

Surely it can't be Graham? His fund technically did own a sizeable stake in Mooments, so he could feasibly turn up and have a legitimate reason for doing so.

That would be a sick game. If hell had no fury like a woman scorned, what about a middle aged loser?

The Go Green room had been sponsored by an energy firm in need of some corporate social responsibility brownie points. Garish sofas and muted coffee tables filled a space the size of a large reception room, the seats taken by a handful of delegates shuffling nervously before their slot on stage.

'Would you like a goodie bag, Miss?'

'What? No, God, no.' There he was. For the first time in a long time, I was glad to see him.

'Stuart, darling, where have you been all day?' He looked nervous, shifty almost. I'd seen him like this in his last days at the hedge fund. Stuart managed to perfect the adult as clueless infant look.

'You know, prepping for the big one.' He weaved like a boxer as he spoke. It didn't work.

'Who dressed you today, darling? This shirt looks divine on you.' His red, clammy head smiled, distracting attention from the damp patches mapping his linen shirt like an archipelago.

'Let me just tidy you up a bit though,' I took a hankie out of my handbag and mopped his brow, straightened his collar. Deep, deep internal breaths. I was out of the woods. For now.

He cleared his throat.

'I've got a surprise for you, darling.'

'You know I hate surprises.'

What the fuck was happening? Did he know? Had the policeman called him too? It was possible wasn't it?

'You do? I thought you liked surprises.'

His voice sounded hopeful, rather than vengeful. Didn't it? It had to. It had to.

'Stuart,' I leant into his ear, 'I'm a fucking control freak. You know this. Control freaks do not like surprises.' Own the situation, Sadie. Don't let him in. Don't let him win.

'It's just-' I cut him off. He looked like a teenage boy with a ripped up and returned Valentine's card.

'It's just you've got the most important speech in the history of Mooments in t minus 45 minutes and, as the Marketing Director, it's my job to get you ready to knock it out of the park.'

For fifteen minutes the world settled down. We sat next to each other and worked through the speech, refreshing Stuart's brain on our three key messages, honing in on what we wanted people to think, to feel, to do.

I'd noticed it at our feet. The phone vibrating in my handbag.

'Stuart, focus darling.'

It vibrated again.

'Darling, you should get that. It could be the reporter from the Organic Times. We've been on Dee's back forever to get a piece in that mag. You told me so yourself.'

He was right. I had told him. Just my fucking luck that he'd listened for once.

I undid the clasp on the bag and angled the screen towards me so he couldn't see the caller ID.

'It's an unknown call.'

'They always are, the journalist calls, that's what Dee told me when I did the interviews about the low fat range.'

'I'm not answering an unknown call, Stuart.'

'Answer it.' His face turned red. His tone stiffened. What the fuck did he know? I pushed my thumb on the flashing icon of a green handset.

'Oh hello...yes...this is she...really glad you could call...yes...it is a big day...' My eye winked affirmative. Stuart relaxed.

'I would love to tell you all about our big, big plans for Mooments, but I'm going to ask you a favour. If you can give me an hour or so, our MD will have given the speech of his life,' Stuart snorted at my spin, I winked again, 'and I'll be in a much better place to give you the best possible story. I don't want to tell you how to do your job, it could even make the front page...okay, bye now.'

'It was-?'

'It was, darling. I'm going to call back. Right after you've blown that room away.' Stuart smiled, his boyish dimples showing.

My mother always told me to face up to my problems, but she was dead and hadn't done a day's work in her life. If what I'd just done- avoiding the questions of a police officer- was classed as perverting the course of justice, then I think I'd just have to keep ignoring her advice.

Ysabelle

I knew something bad was going to happen to him the moment I saw him. With some people you can just tell.

He was sat alone at a table for four when I took over from Gabriela. She'd always give me the lowdown on the customers with running tabs.

'El Gordo in the corner. He's had four cervezas and slaps my culo every time I walk by.'

'La señora aqui, she's nursed the same cup of mate for three hours.'

Gabriela was from San Telmo and made extra monedas dressing up like a dancer and skimming off the German and Japanese tourists for a clinch and a say cheese hablar queso.

She pointed to Luke.

'Este gringo, he's been in every day for the past week. Usualmente, solo cafe, solo para una hora. Today, he's drunk six Quilmes and been sat there for three hours...anyway, he's yours now. Adios!'

'Gracias chica', kiss, kiss and Gabriela was gone.

The bar I'd worked at for the past 18 months was stuck just off the Gran Via and firmly in the 1960s. The walls were stained yellow, the framed newspaper clippings about Boca games from a long time gone by the same. In the corner was an old American style jukebox full of seven inches by Elvis and Los Gatos. It hadn't seen a peso since the crash.

Tourists didn't really come to Buenos Aires for our shopping centres and if they did ours was generally a bar they'd walk straight past. Our regulars were a mixture of shop boys, construction workers or the loco old men and women who roamed around Gran Via buying nothing. This made the gringo stand out like a River fan at La Bombonera.

I made my rounds through the tables, trying not to look at him more than any other customer, trying to stick to my routine. Check the glasses, if they had less than half left, bring another, no questions asked, no requests taken. If they had two drinks on the tab, take them a bowl of bar snacks, nuts, pretzels, sweet and salty tatuca. Clean the tables. Swill the glasses. Wipe the bar, shine the formica up like a broken mirror. The locals could look but they couldn't quite see themselves in the reflection. With the faces on ours, this was for the best.

His face stood out. I'd not seen one like it in here. A gringo face. A jawline like the strong men from the movies we crowded round and watched on Canal 9. Short brown hair like he'd had it clipped for a role in a World War Two story. His snacks were empty. Time to pull out the presidential treatment.

'Hello chico, don't you know the skins are the best bit for you?'

'What, sorry?' He snapped out of a daze.

'The skins contain all the goodness, the pieces you need to make you big and strong.' His table was a monkey nut graveyard.

'The shells?'

'Shells, skins, there's too many words in your language.' He laughed like he hadn't expected to.

'We say here that a man who drinks too much beer in the afternoon is too sleepy to truly enjoy the night.'

'Really?'

'Okayl, maybe it's just me who says that.'

'Don't let your bosses hear you.'

'They'd have to care enough to be here.' The bar was owned by a creepy old Italian called Rossi who spent most of this time and all of his money blowing coca up his nose and getting blown by mujeres. Señora Rossi worked in the kitchen. Gabriela joked to me how she was waiting for the day when she killed her old man with rat poison in an empanada. We laughed but wondered who would pay our wages then. We didn't know what we could be back then, how women could fly in Argentina. Evita was a half century ago and a million miles away.

'What's an American doing here anyway?'

'No soy Americano. You sound more American than me,' he said, 'your English is very good. Better than my Spanglish.'

'I learned all of my English from Ross and Rachel on Amigos.'

'Wow. The One Where The Argentinian Girl Learnt English.'

'That was only half-true.'

'You're lying to me already?'

'This is a bad sign. You should run now.' He laughed. He should have listened. 'Okay, so I studied languages in school too. My English oral won many prizes.'

'You'd fit in well at home,' he said.

'Where is that?'

'Soy de el Reino Unido.' He seemed very pleased with himself, his eyes smiling at mine, two dimples like small caves in his cheeks.

Typical. The first time we'd had a man in here and he was from the UK. Padre had taught us to hate people from the UK. Maggie Thatcher was the boogey lady in our bedtime stories. We all knew the story. Uncle Claudio had left Buenos Aires to save Las Malvinas from the invaders. He'd joked that father should stay home and look after the women and children while he picked the family the most beautiful plot on the islands. He'd take us there on the back of his motorbike when he'd beat the British away. My brother Mario used to fight me over who would get to sit in the sidecar. I was only four years old but I remember the look on Claudio's face. He laughed a little too hard, a little too forced. He smelt like the old men in the bar, like he was damp underneath his army shirt.

Padre took the whole family down to Estación Retiro to say goodbye. He put me on his shoulders as we saw him off, the cord of his jacket cutting into my bare legs. The heat on the platform was unbearable but he wouldn't leave it at home. 'It always rains in March, chica'. The crowd pushed and pulled and sang songs about victory. I waved to Uncle Claudio but I couldn't see him, his shirt and cap repeated over and again on the train. I wanted to go home. Just before the train pulled away, Claudio poked his head through the window of the carriage. 'Luego!' he shouted.

As we walked back through the streets to our house, the crowds dispersing as they went their own ways, my abuela took my hand and led me away from my father. He'd stopped at a stand to pick up a choripan.

'Did you get a good look at your Uncle Claudio?' she asked me.

'Si, abuela.'

'Bueno, bueno. You'll never see him again.'

'You're going to need something more than monkey nuts to soak up that cerveza. I'll be back.' His green eyes were glassy, like he'd been crying, a little on the outside, a little on the inside. It all came out with the cerveza.

> Oscar was cook that day. Chef would have been too bold for his talents. He was the same age as me but he looked ten years older. It happened to boys in the barrio. Life was tough. He was a sweet guy, too sweet for the streets. Gabriela called him El Conejillo, the guinea pig. The way his cheeks hung from the side of his face, it looked like he stored

empanadas in them in case he got hungry.

'Maybe today is the day chica...'

'Unlikely, Oscar'

'Today is a muy importante day, muy importante. We have worked together for 150 shifts today and I have asked you to join me dancing-

'150 times?' I cut in.

'Is it my lucky number?'

'Oscar, vamos, if you ever listened to your abuela, you'd know that 150 is not a lucky number. In fact, 150 is a very, very unlucky number, mala leche...' He snorted like a hog. I squeezed his cheeks. '...or it will be for you if you don't give me a plate of chorizo and cheese in the next two minutes.'

'Chorizo and cheese. Has Evita herself graced us with her presence this evening?'

'No Oscar, Mrs Peron is not here...' He poked his head around the corner of the kitchen.

'It's not for sad sack at the counter there, no, no, he's not even worthy of the monkey nuts, or the old woman in the corner, yes, she definitely looks like cheese would be too rich for her porteña stomach...oh, I see, I see who the cheese is for,' his eye stopped on the gringo, 'it seems 150 really is my unlucky number. Ysabelle, you've cut my legs off.'

In English, they say the way to a man's heart is through his stomach. Maybe the gringo needed to take the time to digest it first. His eyes seemed trained on the bottom of the glass every time I looked up at him.

'Qué pica toca?' said Oscar, 'I'll ask,' I told him.

I sat down at his table and did as Oscar asked, 'what's your story?'. He looked up from his glass.

'You don't like the chorizo?'

'I'm a vegetarian,' he looked at me like a sorry sheep, 'I didn't like to say.'

'We don't get many of those around here,' I said, 'all the mas chorizo for me.'

He'd done the typical gringo thing and blown a loan on a round-the-world plane ticket. He'd been to places I'd only ever heard about in the movies. Singapore, Hong Kong, Tokyo, Sydney, Australia. Me and my brother Che used to laugh about how Sydney Australia sounded like a human being. Che drew him on the inside of a cereal box, a long tall man with a pointed nose and hair to his shoulders.

'Your brother Che sounds like he has quite the imagination,' he said.

'Oh, he does. He has invented 12 new species of animal, all of which have never left the pages of the zoos of his notebook.'

'Che sounds like a man I'd like to have a beer with.'

'Oh, you can't do that,' I said, but I didn't say why, 'tell me about your brothers and sisters.'

'I don't have any. There's just me. My parents must have been happy with their first shot.' He had the cerveza brave.

'Just you? You gringos are crazy. How do you expect to ever win at football if you only ever have one boy per family to choose from?'.

This made him laugh.

'At last. Your face does happy too I see. I bet Oscar back there that I could make you smile and now I did and now he owes me a beer.' A dramatic groan came from the kitchen.

'You can drink and work?' he asked.

'Yes, I can. Oscar's not getting out of his duties that easily.'

'You know what? I think I like this country more by the minute.'

The next few hours passed by in a flash, the time

blurring by. The memory was as clear today as if I was watching it on TV. He told me how he'd fallen out of a boat in the river in Singapore and had to be fished out by an old woman in a Chinese junk. How he'd spent all his money in cat cafes and karaoke bars in Tokyo.

'What's your song?'

'Well, I'm from Wales...'

'Like Moby Dick?' I asked. His eyebrows shot up his forehead. His eyes came alive.

'No, like the land of castles and magic and wizards and sheep and mountains,' he leaned in and mouthed the syllables, 'Way-ulz.' It clicked.

'Si, si, Wales, England.'

He straightened his chair and crossed his arms.

'No, Wales, Wales.' I looked in his eyes, right, left, trying to understand, 'They say to born Welsh is to be born not with a silver spoon in your mouth-'

'Listen, gringo, here we're born with a wooden spoon in our mouths and we're glad of having something to suck on.'

'We're very similar people then,' he said, 'your people actually speak our language down in Patagonia.'

'The Patagonians are not my people, those Tehuelche wouldn't last dos minutos in La Boca.' The old girl in the corner coughed a lung up into the ashtray. He was not distracted.

'Okay, but as I was saying...to be born Welsh is not to be born-'

'-with a silver spoon in your mouth?'

'Exactly. But with music in your blood and poetry in your soul.' He sat back in his chair like he'd won a prize.

'Very nice. So what did you sing?'

'Tom Jones, of course.'

'Tom Jones? Madre de Dios! You must come at once and meet my madre. She is the biggest Tom Jones fan en todo el mundo.' I looked around the room. The old man was asleep on the bar, snoring for Argentina.

'Oscar, we're closing up...' I shouted to the back. He popped his guinea pig head around the doorway and said,

'Un pelo de la concha tira mas que una yunta de bueyes. Adios.'

'What the hell does that mean?' Luke asked.

'Nada. Nada.' I replied, laughing to myself, grabbing his hand, 'vamos!'

We rode across the city on the 15, stood at opposite ends of the cramped carriage, his green eyes locked onto mine as the rickety bus bumped its way towards La Boca. A veteran got on at el universidad and hobbled through the crowd on his good leg, repeating a plea over and over, his voice robotic.

'Mi nombre es Luco Martinez. I was a corporal in the 4th regiment of the Argentinian army. I fought for our country in the Battle of Mount Harriet and the Battle of Two Sisters and saw 23 of my amigos die. Now my country has forgotten about me. I am not asking for your charity. I am asking for any information you may have which can help me get a job.'

The people on the bus pretended not to hear, pretended to be interested in the floor or what passed by the window.

'Why did they do that?' he asked.

'People here are used to being screwed by the government. That drunk's had it no worse than the rest of us.' He seemed to understand.

'Time to make sure the eyes in the back of your head are open. Welcome to La Boca.'

As we walked to my house, the rain started to fall like God had left the bath tap running. The yellows and blues and pinks of the metal houses shone in the shower and I watched him turn in circles in the street taking the neighbourhood in.

'It's beautiful here,' he said.

'When I was a little girl, I thought houses were painted in pretty colours all over the world.'

'Na, they go for brick colour back at home.'

'It may be beautiful but it's still La Boca. Put your camera away if you want to keep it.' I shooed the kids on the street corner back to their madres.

The last time I took a boy back to my madre's house, she had known his madre and padre, had said 'buenos' to his abuelos in church every Sunday morning since she could remember. He was a Boca boy and this one was most definitely not. I took his arm in mine, partly to keep him safe, partly to feel his body next to mine. He was no polo player but his arm felt athletic next to mine, the hairs on end in anticipation.

'I can't quite believe I'm going to meet your mother and I've known you for all of four hours.'

'If you want to know me for any longer you'd better get ready.'

'Oh, I'm ready.' His hand gripped my waist and turned me towards him, his other arm pulling me against his body and into his open mouth. The rain splashed the inside of my shoes wet but I didn't care. I closed my eyes and could have been anywhere in the world, any of those places he had told me about.

'Get a room, gringo,' one of the street kids shouted, a ball stuck to his ripped shoe.

'Bienvenido a La Boca.'

'I think I'm going to like it here.'

'If my madre saw that, your stay here would have been short, very short.'

'Well, it's a good job she didn't,' he said, pulling me

next to him again.

As soon as I turned the key in the door, my madre turned her stream of consciousness commentary to me, to my lateness, to my dinner on the kitchen worktop and to the fact it was about time a pretty girl like me found herself a good man who could give her beautiful grandchildren.

'Madre, quiet, I want you to meet-'

'-Luke. Buenos tardes señora.' He stepped through the shabby threshold into our modest front room. My madre spat her yerba mate all over the coffee table, her cigarello soaking wet. Luke ran a few paces over to where she sat, trying to help, offering assistance in broken Spanish, not quite knowing what to do, my madre ushering the strange man away while going as red as a gringo in the sun. I followed her to the kitchen while Luke hovered in a state of confusion in the living room. A dramatic argument over a will reached an aggressive crescendo before morphing into the sound of passionate kisses from the thirty year old speakers.

'Ysabelle, qué sorpresa. Why is there a gringo in the living room?' Our faces were a fist away from each other. The kitchen was too small for two people.

'The name of the gringo in the living room is Luke and he is my friend.' She threw the tea towel she had clasped in her gold ringed, wrinkled hand to the floor. She had to wind her arm back in to stop the crimplene of her sleeve rustling in the smoky air. Madre was crazier than a chick with goats.

'Are you pregnant?' she whispered, as loudly as the action allowed.

'No madre, I've only just met him.'

'That didn't stop your cousin Maria.' Her drawn on eyebrows raised right up to the crumbling ceiling.

'No madre, I'm not pregnant.' I hushed my voice,

before realising Luke wouldn't be able to understand us. Even if he caught the odd word my madre and I spoke so quickly he had more chance of winning the loto than piecing our sentences together. Although he must have had an idea. Madres and girls in his country must have had the same conversation.

'You always want me to bring a nice man to meet you,' I said.

'Yes, but not now, not when Carlos has come back from the dead two years after Marina thought she had drowned him and now he's found she's married his evil twin brother Chuco. I am missing telenovela history stood in this box with you.' I laughed but she did not. She took her programmes very seriously.

'I'm sorry madre, we can leave-'

'-no, no you cannot. You cannot bring a man into my home and kick him out onto the street without experiencing my hospitality.' I smiled. She always loved cooking for my brother.

'But Ysabelle, first I must ask you, is the gringo from the United States? Or from England? You know how your padre would react.' Padre looked down on us from a gold-framed photograph in the living room, madre never needing to nag him that his moustache needed a trim any more. He was wearing his best yellow sweater in the portrait, the one he wore at all the big occasions in the lives of our familia. He wore it to my cousin Abril's wedding to the undertaker from Cordoba, joking how the congregation would need some colour with all of the groom's colleagues in their uniforms. And there was the photo that Che used to have hung on his wall next to his posters of El Diego, the four of us at the side of the pitch after he scored the winner in the cup final, madre positioned just in front of a stain from the dulce de leche from the alfajores padre ate constantly. The portrait on the wall was an outtake from the shoot that his workplace arranged every decade or so, every time the head of human resources retired and a new one came in. A tall man with a thin moustache and a hand puppet named Chico had coaxed Che into sitting still for a family shot which hung on the opposite wall, his creepy voice playing in my head every time I looked at madre's perm or the ketchup fading on Che's chin. Padre had stayed behind after we left to have individual pictures taken for company files, security passes and identification. Madre had chosen a picture where he was looking slightly off centre, as if he was trying to listen to something one of his amigos was saying just out of earshot. The look on his face is how I remember him; a man always more interested in what was happening just out of reach.

  I looked back to madre.

  'No, madre, he's not English. He is from Wales, Su país es Gales.'

  'He doesn't look Portuguese,' she looked back into the room, Luke shuffling from foot to foot, pretending to appear really interested in the trinkets in her display cabinet; Che's football trophy, a medal devoted to St. Francis of Assisi.

  'No, su país es Gales, his country is Wales. Cerca de Inglaterra, pero no es Inglaterra.'

  'Oooh.'

  'He knows Tom Jones.'

  My madre may be a small woman who was shrinking smaller as the years went by, but the squeal that came from her mouth could have woken up sleeping babies in Brazil. If the studio panel on Through the Keyhole, which madre loved almost as much as the telenovelas, saw our house, they'd have thought it more likely I was the daughter of a foreign crooner than a porteño. For every portrait of my padre, there were a pile of scrapbooks covering every stage in Tom Jones' career, one yellow sweater versus wardrobes of open necked shirts, glistening medallions and leather trousers.

'This is Tom when he came to Buenos Aires in 1974. It brought the country great joy in a time of great sadness.' Luke was sat next to my madre on our two seater sofa, legs squeezed together, a scrapbook on their knees.
'His music can do that,' he said.
'Things are different now, gracias de Dios, but then was a bad time. Peron was just returned from exile en España and when he landed at the airport his bastards killed 13 people, shot them down dead in cold blood.'
'Luke looked to me, I was in the armchair opposite, the one padre used to sit in and stare at the ceiling from. He'd sobered up completely by now. I had too.
'Come on madre, he doesn't want to hear about this, he's a guest.'
'Si, si, but I met Tom Jones too...at the airport.'
'Yes, you did madre.;
'It was the most beautiful moment of my life, but also, the saddest. I pulled a hair off his chest in the very place those people died. He didn't flinch.' Luke's eyes were stuck on the scrapbook, a yellowing clipping from La Nación the day after the concert, Tom's face glistening with sweat under the lights and the heat.
'I still don't know how I feel about that moment.'
We sat in silence for what seemed like an hour.
'There is a word in English, madre,' I said. They looked at me in hope.
'Bittersweet.'
'Bittersweet,' he repeated and looked back to me.
'Sorry,' I mouthed. Madre was lost in her own mind. She snapped out, jerking the album off their knees and onto the floor.

'Lo siento,' he said, his pronunciation poor, his hands grasping for the pages. Madre looked like she'd had a bolt like Frankenstein, the permed hair electric, her head the size of a mandarin. She stood up, her full height coming up to Luke's elbows.

'Si, si, you're right, we have a guest. A guest who knows Tom. A guest who must eat en mi casa. Ysabelle, prepare la mesa, it's time for my famoso bife en vino tinto.'

'Luke is a-.' She'd scooted to the kitchen before I had the chance to tell her he was not a fan of dead animals.

'I'm so sorry. My madre is an intense lady.'

'It's fine, I'm having fun,' he stopped himself, I gave him my 'really?' eyes, 'Okay, maybe not the government murder stuff, but everything else...I don't mean that disrespectfully.'

'This situation needs cerveza,' I told him, 'if you can humour my madre for the next hour, I promise you the night of your life in Buenos Aires.'

'It's a deal,' he said. I checked the kitchen, the flowers of madre's blouse red and green against the worktop, smoke rising above her head. I pulled him in and kissed him quick, his flip flops clapping the linoleum like a lame horse.

As with everything else in her life, madre put passion into her cooking. Within dos minutos, smoke started to pour out of the door of the small kitchen and fill the living room. The pots and pans she had used a thousand times to feed our small familia were now at work again.

'She's always like this,' I whispered, Luke laughing, 'it used to give my padre the perfect excuse to escape the house to play cards at his friend's house next door. Me and Che used to take turns in dragging him away.'

'I've got to say, the smell's enough to make me miss rotting flesh.' he said.

'Oh Luke, I'm sorry. Vegetarianism hasn't made it to Argentina yet.'

'Don't be,' he said, pulling me in to kiss him me again as the opening bars of *What's New Pussycat?* hummed from the kitchen, out-of-tune through the smoky air of our corrugated iron home.

If Maggie Thatcher had Luke's diplomacy skills, Uncle Claudio would never have had to go to war over Las Malvinas. Madre had got her best piece of ojo de bife out of the freezer, defrosted it best she could under the tap and fried it in enough garlic and vino tinto to drown a street rat. She'd heated up my chorizo and hidden it underneath the bife sauce. Guests always ate first and finest at her table.

I'd tried uno mas, once more, to tell madre that Luke didn't eat meat, but he'd cut me off again, not wanting to cause a fuss and it kind of became like a little game. Che was very good at science at school until one day he got in trouble with the teacher for trying to free the little mouse the teacher was using to show the children how animals learn from changes in their environment. Che tried to change that poor ratón's environment a little too much by picking him out of the maze by his tail and hiding him in his bag. Señor Ramos said it was the cruelest thing a student had ever done but Che told padre mi chupa un huevo, meaning he could go suck an egg and the glint in padre's eye said he might have just agreed. It was cruel, the cruellest thing I admit to doing, but that night, Luke was the ratón in my laboratorio. He ate around his meat for a little while, dipping the patatas in the sauce, sipping the tinto madre had rescued from the dusty drinks cabinet, looking back and forth between his two hosts like he was watching a tennis match on Mars.

But he ate the bife, not all of it, just enough so

madre wouldn't be mad. When I thought about it afterwards, I wondered if this meant he was inconsistent, if he was someone my padre would have warned me about, someone not to trust. But I don't think that. I think he was someone who did what needed to be done. Someone who would go to whatever length he needed to make the best situation. I know that to be true now. And besides, my madre's steak is delicious. I wouldn't have fancied his chances in a fight about leftovers.

The tinto poured and poured. Since my padre died, I hadn't seen madre drink in the house. Drinking was padre's thing. Not like a lacra, a bad person, but like his chair was his thing or his yellow sweater.

'To see your padre without a birra is like seeing Diego without a-'

'-birra,' padre used to cut in, his amigos laughing themselves silly. The men in Argentina couldn't go one round without mentioning Maradona.

Just as madre was trying to explain slowly, loudly, in simple English, a story about her aunt who had never been on an airplane because she was convinced they were the toys of Satan, a story that was hard to follow in Spanish, she swept her hand in animation, spilling the wine across the best tablecloth and over Luke, her sleeve soaked like the Cuerpo de Cristo in Santa Semana, his shorts damp on the front like a drunk from my bar.

'Lo siento, Luke, lo siento,' she had howled, springing from the table to his side, her crimplene sleeves waving manically in the air as she tried to find a remedy.

'Go and fetch our guest some clothes from Che's room,' she said, the hands on the clock stopping for a second. We never went in Che's room anymore. I looked her in the eye and she urged me on. 'Rapido, Ysabelle.'

This night which already had seen tinto, was going to need much more. La noche está en pañales, the night was young.

And that's the story of how five and a half hours after I'd brought a gringo through the peeling door of my corrugated iron house, he was crashed out on the sofa asleep on my shoulder, wearing my dead brother's Boca Juniors t-shirt, the notes of my madre's karaoke machine rendition of *Delilah* still on the air.

I woke up with his warm body next to mine, his smell strong and the light from the TV dim in the room. I felt happy. Contento. I counted to ten. I already knew it wouldn't be long until the shadows returned.

Nina

I'd used a calculator under my desk for the past week. The sums might be right now, but the bad feeling just won't go away. It's like I'm at the opticians and can't make the notice out. I'm trying my best to squint and read, but holding back, more than a bit, because I know whatever the words say, they're going to spell bad news. It's put me off my food too and I haven't been off my food since, well, since Jase. We went out for a meal with work yesterday dinner time, on the boss, only for the 2-4-1 deal at the pub on the corner but it was nice of him all the same. There's only four of us now Ange has gone, so a meal don't go to waste. That made him happy.

  Well, Karen, she had a lamb shank, she's a posh type Karen, or she wants to be. She's from the estate originally, you can tell when she's on her mobile to her mam at dinner time, but she married up, a property surveyor I think she said he is, Sebastian, that's his name. There ain't no one on the estate called Sebastian. She's alright though, wasn't at first with me, but we got an understanding now, since I had a word with her. You gotta do that with some people. Show em who you are, as if she didn't know already. Just a quiet word, that's all it took. She's got my back now, in a work way I mean.

  The other week, I don't know why I did it but I did, I'd gone out on a date with one of those blokes off the websites. Now I know why I did that, I'm not a nun am I? What I meant was I don't know why I did it in my dinner hour. We'd been messaging back and forth, not about anything in particular, I always keeps my guard up, in the early days at least. Well, it turns out this bloke, I won't say his name- just in case, you never knows do you?- he happened to be in the area, he was a salesman, travelling round, office supplies and that kind of thing. He'd been at an office on a business park just round the corner from the estate agents. First off I was a bit fuming at how he knew where I worked, but then he explained it was cos I had a photo of me with one of our boards on my profile, and you know what, I did as well. I'm not sure now if it was cos I'd wanted to give the air of a career woman or whether it was cos my hair looked just right that day, but either way, it was what it was.

    I'd been having the morning from hell- I'd walked in on a fella asleep on his living room sofa, kecks down his ankles, away with the fairies. Worse luck was I had a couple with me, meek as Mary. They wouldn't be coming back to us they said. So I decided, what the hell, treat yourself girl, take a break, it won't harm no-one.

    I'd met him in this coffee shop far enough away from work for the boss not to bowl in for a takeaway sandwich. I'd known right away that he wasn't going to be a take home to mother job, but to be honest, I never had much luck with them anyway. He was bald as a coot, I'd clocked that from his profile pictures anyway, but in the cafe the light seemed to radiate off his head, like he had a 12 watt bulb stuck underneath the skin, or he'd shined it in the bogs just before I arrived.

    He'd started telling me this yarn about how he'd had a big house and a flash car but his missus had stitched him up, been having it away with his business partner, yet it was him who had to stump up the cash when the divorce went through. Sounded like a shaggy dog story to me, it's rarely the women in the wrong in my experience, but he was nice enough and there was no one else on the scene at the moment, so I just listened while he chirped on, just enjoying not being in that living room with the fella in his grubby boxers, just enjoying being sat opposite a bloke again.

    The time just got away with me. One minute my

coffee was piping hot and it was 'nice to meet you', the next I was down to the dregs and he'd talked himself quiet. You know what they say, it flies when you're having fun, don't it?

Karen told the boss a tale for me that day, I'd texted her on the rush back and she'd come up with something to do with an unexpected doctor's appointment. Very clever. He'd grumbled under his breath but nothing more.

Fast forward a fortnight and she could see I wasn't too clever so covered for me when the boss was asking what was up.

'Gone off your grub have you, Nina?' he asked, but I'd bolted to the ladies before the question mark. Karen told him it was 'women's problems'. That shut him up apparently, sent him back to lecturing Taz. He's this youngster we got in, Asian kid, lovely boy really, flash as gold mind you and that's the quality some of the worst of em I've known have had. I think he thinks he's a character on *The Apprentice* half the time.

'He could sell sand to the Arabs' the boss says, but I tells him I don't think you're meant to say stuff like that anymoe.

'Who's is it, Neen?'. Karen was stood outside the toilet door while I threw my guts up.

'You what?' It took me longer than it should have to clock on to what she was saying, trying to catch my breath in between wretches.

'I'm 46 for fuck's sake, Ka.' I hates swearing.

'You look half it and it doesn't matter these days.'

'And isn't it a bit late in the day for morning sickness?'

'I was back and forth the loo at midnight with Steffan, Nina.'

She doesn't know about my insides, Karen. Not

from me anyway.

When I made it back to the table, Taz was tucking himself into the last bite of my Chicken Caesar wrap.

'Didn't want it to go begging did I, Neen? Supply and demand, innit.'

I'd have told him that didn't make no sense, but it was the best I could do to swallow the sick down and smile.

I struggled through three viewings after the pub, but my mind just wasn't on it. I thought I'd had it bad that day I went on the date, seeing that bloke in his undies, but sometimes it's not the big surprises that gets to you, but the little snide comments and fake smiles. If I was looking for a new place and some bird showed me around somewhere I didn't like, that's life ain't it? It's not her fault. She don't own the bloody thing. She never chose the wallpaper or put the lino down on the kitchen floor. But it feels like more and more people you shows round these days holds you personally responsible if the gaff don't live up to their high expectations. I gets it to an extent, I do. It's people's lives ain't it, at the end of the day. Before you open that door for them, anything could happen, a whole new life could open itself up to them. But they got to live in the real world if you ask me. It's as much as I can do not to tell em sometimes.

Well, I had a classic one yesterday afternoon. We'd turned up at this house, a three storey townhouse opposite the park. Nice property if you like that kind of thing, mind you I couldn't cope with all my stuff strewn over two floors let alone three. I has an hard enough time of it as it is in the mornings trying to find my heels and my handbags. But it's not about me, is it? And this couple, foreign types, Spanish or something I think, I can't tell half the time, well, they clearly had their heart set on this house. Stupid thing to do if you ask me, before you've even been inside, but then I suppose I've been guilty of dreaming a dream or two in my life so there we go.

You could hear these voices when I put the key in the door so I'd asked the Spanish couple to wait on the front step while I checked it out. It's usually just the owners, in when they said they wouldn't be. Well, I'd followed the voices through to the kitchen and the owners were there- a fella my age with a younger wife, long blonde hair down to her shoulders, ain't it always?- but so was these two fellas, gay I suppose they were, I don't know why two blokes who weren't up to something would want to share a townhouse. It weren't them I heard first though.

'Hello Nina,' this smarmy voice coming up from behind me, 'the ship's sailed on this one I'm afraid. Another dream realised from the city's number one estate agents, Alvin Edwards Estates...where your home is our business.'

'Oh, hiya Alvin.' Our boss hated Alvin. They used to be partners years ago, before I was on the scene, but they had a falling out over something, the boss won't explain the ins and outs of it. Alvin went and set up on his own, in 'direct bloody competition', I must hear about five times a week.

'They're no competition to us, not a patch on us,' I tell the boss to make him feel better, but a sale was a sale.

'Congrats to you, Mr and Mrs Davies,' I said. It was nice for them after all. A new life on the horizon.

'Thanks Nina, and sorry we didn't cancel the viewing. Alvin got in touch and said a couple who'd come to see it last week wanted to put in a bid and it all went so fast. He's been great, though, Alvin.'

'A cash bid,' Alvin smarmed.

'From us, hiya love,' said one of the vendors, stepping away from the kitchen worktop, a plumpish, bald bloke. He looked pleased as punch, which was more than

I can say for the Spanish couple. They'd crept up behind me, the woman nearly in tears.

'Muchas sorry,' I told her, 'there's plenty more houses in the sea,' tapping her lightly on the shoulder to try and make up for it. She didn't seem to understand.

I still felt sick as a dog.

The next morning, I'd made sure I was in bright and breezy. The feeling was still there when I was in the shower, trying to sing a bit of Aretha to send it back where it came. R-E-S-P-E-C-T. When I was in school, I'd tried to use the song to memorise words for a spelling test the teacher used to make us do. It had worked perfect too. C-R-I-C-K-E-T. K-I-T-C-H-E-N. Q-U-A-R-R-E-L. The music made em stick, somehow, until Sir threw eight letter words in, anyway. I always think that though, how come I can remember the words to a song I haven't heard for years, knowing every oo and ah inside out when it comes on the radio, but ask me to tell you the names of the Kings and Queens of England and I'd lose it after Liz, no matter how long I stared at the paper.

I thought the best way to beat this thing was to attack the day. A bit of positive mental attitude. I'd picked up a bag of pastries for the rest of them from the bakery section in the Lidl. Thought it'd put everyone in a good mood, like. It did too. Taz was chuffed to bits.

'I tell you what, Neen, if it was Ramadan I'd go and eat this in a dark cupboard.'

Karen was a doll and took care of my bookings for me so I tried to lose myself in paperwork in the morning, my calculator resting on my lap so no-one could see. Whatever it was, I couldn't concentrate quite right for mental arithmetic just yet.

It was quarter past three when he called me into the back room. I knows that because the kids had just started streaming out of the school. If I was in the office, their shouts and screams stopped me in my tracks every day, just a moment or two wondering what could have been, before getting back on with whatever it was I was doing.

'Can you come into the office, Neen?' He called it that, but that was like calling my bedsit a palace. It was more of a stationary cubby hole, all told.

'Course I can.'

'I don't know how to say this, love, but there's been a complaint in this morning. I won't go into the details of it but a customer feels like we've let them down. They've been all over that social media since yesterday saying so, too, accursed bloody thing. You know what it's like, Neen, throw enough mud and some of it sticks.'

I'd burst out in tears there and then.

It's a few hours later now and I hate myself for that. When I got this job, I promised myself I'd always project strength in the office. I'd been through enough to know that women didn't have to be forever blubbing every time something didn't go their way. All the things in my life I haven't cried at, have just let pass me by like I was watching it happen on the television, and I go and bawl my eyes out over some stuck up Spanish tart.

Even though there was a couple of hours of the day left, he said I could go home, but I'd worried what Karen and Taz would think.

'Let me worry about them,' he said. He was good like that. He seemed to have a woman's way of understanding somehow. Very different to the rest of the fellas I'd known. He'd tell the rest of em I was feeling a bit under the weather I imagine. No-one argues with the boss, even if they gripe behind his back. Karen was on my side anyway, on the face of it, and Taz was too interested in his hairdo to even notice.

He called me back as I was walking out of the cubby hole, pushing the papers out of the way of where the door should have been.

'And Neen, once you've got yourself some rest, why don't you let me take you out for dinner tonight?'

'But you took us out for dinner yesterday-'

'-and you didn't touch a crumb of that did you?'

'Exactly. I wasn't feeling right.'

He laughed at that, a big one from right down in his belly. That's pretty far down, believe me.

'I didn't mean a BOGOF in the local, I meant a nice place, I know this lovely little Italian place over in-'

'-Hold on a minute now. It's awful nice of you to let me off early today, and to offer to take me out tonight. Now for a start, I don't think I'll be feeling up to it and even if I-'

'-Say no more Nina, say no more. I've overstepped the mark.' He stood up from his makeshift desk at that point, his gut hitting against the edge, pushing some files onto their side.

'You've not. It's me. I just need to get my head down I think.'

I knew that wouldn't do it. I shouldn't have gone down that road. I could have just told him I weren't up to it and been done with it. No need to hurt the poor bloke's feelings.

When my head's not a good place to be, I loves escaping into a good film, something I've seen a million times before, something I can just lose myself in. I imagine everyone does really. Jase had half of my collection off to Cash Converters, the thieving toerag, although that's the least of the bad he's done, that one. It's hardly the family silver, but it still cuts me up that he got the worst part of half a pint for my DVDs. Vietnam War films are the ones for me. They're my all-time favourites. I'd watch them back-to-back when Jase was where Jase was, and I know it sounds silly, but I identified with them all in those films, all the characters. The poor American boys sent halfway across the world to fight, the poor Viet Cong doing what they thought they had to do for their country, the poor village girls, raped and screaming and scared witless. My heart breaks every time. All those films are gone now though, *Full Metal Jacket, Apocalypse Now, Casualties of War, Platoon*, probably picked up for half nothing by some student or scrounger, 50p a disc.

My options were a bit limited so I went for the tried and tested. It's a bit of a cliche I suppose, but I can't help but loving *Erin Brockovich*. To be honest, I model myself on her a bit. Just because I'm showing my legs off doesn't mean you shouldn't listen to every word coming out my mouth, buster. She feels a little bit like a kindred spirit. I'm not saying selling houses is anything like making a bunch of fat cats pay for giving cancer to a whole town worth of working people, but we've all got our own battles to fight in this life, don't we? I forget when I watch it that that's Julia Roberts on screen, not a struggling mum, with no good men and too good kids, but a Hollywood star with millions in the bank and not a care in the world.

I'd resisted the urge to go for my usual glass of wine on the sofa. Before I know it, one tipple becomes three becomes two bottles. It's easy when you're feeling sorry for yourself to cling onto the glass for dear life. My head wasn't right, still. The booze might help tonight, but tomorrow won't look after itself. The cupboards were bare, always were, so I tucked into a packet of curry noodles with melted cheese slices on toast for tea. Proper comfort food, but as I was tucking into it my main thought was about why I didn't take the boss up on his offer. A bit of company might have done me good, take my mind off of whatever it was that was troubling me. He does a lot for me, after all. More than pretty much every other fella I ever knew. But I already knew the answer. Erin was my date for tonight.

The DVD was so worn out by now, the cover had nail varnish spilt all over it, which is probably the only reason Jase couldn't flog it. My favourite bit is where she's in the fancy office with those hoity toity lawyers from the other firm and they're looking down on her. The disc skipped over the line she said to bring the stuck-up bitch down. I knew it by heart and mouthed it at the screen anyway.

'Two wrong feet in fucking ugly shoes.'

But for the first time ever, it didn't make me smile.

I still wasn't a hundred percent this morning but a girl's got to make a living. I'd been showing this old lady round a bungalow, hell of a girl she was. Her husband had carked it and left her a tidy little life insurance sum, which she was presently spending on a Caribbean cruise, nine islands in fourteen days, flying out of Gatwick to pick the boat up in Barbados a week Tuesday. It don't half help to get over him, the thought of palm trees and Pina Coladas, she told me. Wanted to put the feelers out about a new place to call home when she got back. She was halfway telling me about how she'd been brushing up on her ballroom dancing in front of YouTube, when I saw it. A newspaper billboard with the words in bold black letters.

HIT AND RUN IN CITY- MAN, 36, CRITICAL

And right away, there and then, my women's intuition, if you want to call it that, said that's it. That's him. Luke.

The paper didn't say much but it was nice to see his

face after all this time. I'd searched for him online, of course I had, but I hadn't known his surname to find him on Facebook. If I admitted the amount of nights I'd sat there scrolling through the Lukes in the area, I probably would have realised I needed to get a life. To be honest, I wasn't even sure he still lived local. He didn't buy a house from me, did he? It's strange, now I know what was worrying me and now I know where he is, I feel more at peace, in a way. I was watching this TV series the other night, I can't remember the name, and the detective said to the bloke he'd arrested, 'why don't you just tell me what you did? Get it out in the open, you'll feel so much better for it'. And I know I haven't done anything, I know that I didn't run him over, but it does feel better, to know the score like I do now.

I'd started reading the story in the street, but the heavens opened and raindrops the size of ring doughnuts came crashing down, getting the print all wet. I ran to the front seat of my car, the name of the firm in big letters on the side but the sticker peeling, so it says 'Estate gents'. I gets more than one funny look at the lights over that, I tells you. I calls her Wallis, the car. Some people think it's after the shoe shop, but it's not. Wallis Simpson, that's who it's after. I saw her in this documentary on the telly about the Royal Family. She's the only out of the lot with a personality, but she couldn't be Queen just cos she was a Yank and wasn't as stuck up as the rest of them. Everyone names their car, don't they?

Turn to page 5 it said, so I did, but it didn't say much about Luke. Nothing about where he'd been or what he was doing with his life, just his age and that he lived locally. I'd imagined he was about that old by now but had no idea he found a gaff round here. What with him just being back from Argentina, I'd thought he could have been off anywhere. Sometimes when I'd think of him, he'd given the journalism up, and was a coastguard, keeping people safe on some beach somewhere in California, other times he'd kept at it, and was sat at the front in one of those press conferences you see on the telly when a girl goes missing and the coppers and the family are sat at the front, scared stiff and saying 'come home' and 'we miss you' and 'it's all okay' and whatever else.

He looked just like I remember him in the picture they used. It was grainy, blurry on the features like they'd blown it up too big for what it was meant for, like they'd tried to make a billboard out of a photo taken on an old brick phone, but he looked like he did that day. There were mountains in the background and he was looking off to the side, like he was waiting for somebody else to appear in the scene. Now the only thing I knows about Argentina is not to cry for it, but he looks like he's about to. My guess is that's where he is in the picture. Look at me, Sherlock Nina.

The story said he was hit off his bike yesterday and the police was now looking for the driver of an Audi who fled from the scene. They had a few eye witnesses in there, like this woman who said she was running down the street and the bang was so loud she heard it over her headphones. By the time she'd turned around and took them out, Luke was just lying there, his bike all broken from the car, lying in a pool of blood. Some other woman, said she'd been out with her baby, she said the car doors were open and before she could catch a clock of the fella, assuming it's a fella, who did it. What's the world come to when you could hit someone off a bike and then do a runner? It's not like they'd have done it on purpose. You've only got to take your eyes off the road for two seconds and that's it. Bam. Probably a kid paying more attention to his phone, on Facebook or texting some girl rather than paying attention to the road.

Apparently Luke's in intensive care at the Heath Hospital. I was only there two weeks ago to have my, well, actually, you don't need to know what I was having seen to. To think I could have been in the same building as him and not known it. To think I've been living in the same city as him all these years and not known it. We could have been in the same supermarket, the same bar, the same restaurant and not known it, although I doubt he's a regular in The Crown for the buy one get one free lunchtime deal.

It said something in red at the bottom of the story. 'Did you see anything? Do you know Luke? Call us on..,' and then a phone number. I don't know why, but I typed the number into my mobile and pressed the green button. The call wouldn't connect. It must be a sign. What would I have said anyway, 'oh, hello I do know him, I shagged him on the floor of a 'for sale' house about ten years ago. Put that in your newspaper.' I would have had a hard time struggling to hear em on the other line anyway. The rain's still bucketing it down and these mobiles he's got us for work should be in a museum.

I turned the engine on and before I knew where I was going, the car was taking itself off. It was driving the other way, took a left where it shouldn't have, and instead of pulling up outside the office, it's the hospital I can see out of the passenger side window, the big fading daffodil they've got painted on the side looking like it's half-dead.

The indicators took on a life of their own and turned into the car park.

Charlie

'Hey Charlie, that was a wonderful show. Loved the *Free Man in Paris* cover. Every bit as good as the original (honest!). X'

This was the message that had started it all. My manager had convinced me a show at a small venue would be a big F.U. to the critics. Two summers ago, my stage set-up had more musicians than a Hard Rock Cafe wall. He'd assured me a stripped back show in London would show everybody just what they'd been missing. That what the world needed was me and my guitar and nothing else. That was the bit the crowds fell in love with, not the brass and the backing singers, the light shows and the video screens. Me, some space and time and the stage.

I'd needed some talking around but Marcus was good at that, had joked that his card shouldn't say 'Manager' but 'Professional Convincer'. I could think of a few more appropriate things right now. I hadn't spoken to him for seven years. Seven years, two months and 23 days to be precise, the very special anniversary of the day the record label ripped up my contract and somehow had the audacity to ask for £50,000 back. Expenses, apparently. After all the money I'd made those toads. Leeches who couldn't hold a note on a recorder but had made a pact with the devil to create vicariously. All the success but none of the struggle. I should tell the kids to become music industry suits. That'd make their parents happy. A sound return on their investment.

The show was at a venue called the Union Chapel. You probably know it. It's a classic comeback kind of place. Elton John, Suzanne Vega, Tori Amos, Amy Winehouse, Bjork. They've all played there. Not that I'm suggesting they needed comebacks, any of them, not like I did. Their Marcuses probably positioned it as a 'giving back to the fans' sort of show. An intimate platform to share new material. That kind of slippery bullshit. I'd gone for it anyway. I had nowhere else to turn.

I'd not played a show since a festival in Norway two summers before. The sea of bodies stretched to the horizon, thousands upon thousands of other humans together in the same moment of space and time listening to me, Charlie Ray from the UK, singing her little broken heart out to them all. I was in the sundown slot. I'm not sure I quite comprehended at that moment it was setting on my songwriting career.

I guess I needed to prove to myself that I could still do it. To blunt the poison pens of the columnists, to turn off the WiFi on the keyboard warriors. To prove that after 18 months of neurotic breakdown, Charlie Ray could still play.

The Joni song was thrown in as a tease. A reminder of the heights I'd hit with the first album. I'd wanted to show that my songs could stand up next to the best of the best. I'd estimated that the uneducated listener wouldn't notice any difference, might even think it was new material.

It was clear from his message that he wasn't an uneducated listener. It was obvious Luke wanted me to know that he knew. Well done, mate. You know a Joni Mitchell song. Are you meant to have passed some kind of test?

I've still got the message saved on my phone. I'll look at it once in awhile. Somehow it's less painful than looking at old press clippings of my career. My romantic past doesn't seem to hurt as much. Maybe that's the problem. Maybe that's why I'll never write another song.

After Marcus had finally dragged me from backstage into the spotlight, the gig had gone better than I'd expected. I'd never been so nervous before a show. The first phase of my career had seen me put my heart and head on the line in front of much bigger audiences than the 1500 or so who'd packed into the old church, half in wonder, half in hope I'd fuck it up so they'd have a snarky tweet to share. There was no time for nerves last time around. I was on the way to the top. That's what I'd been born for, six weeks early and screaming for someone to listen. Even my wails were loaded with meaning.

But laid down scrunched in a ball on the chaise lounge of the chapel's committee room in my makeshift dressing room, it wasn't my birthright of brilliance that filled my bones. It wasn't my rapturous reviews. It wasn't the gleam of my gold record. It was a feeling, at first, a year back since the first crack broke in. A piano wire on a pyramid. A thought, a suggestion inside that it could be over. Twelve months on, a crowd fidgeting the other side of a church wall, the crack was bigger, brighter, the light let through, refracted against the inside, piercing through the night, beauty through the black. But it was easier to hide in the dark.

I needn't have sweated it.

They were so fucking happy to see me and my guitar again, I could have sang nursery rhymes and they'd have lapped it up.

A shout between songs,

'We've missed you, Charlie,'

and the rest of the crowd clapping in agreement.

Once I was up there, the songs took over. They knew me inside out. Better than I knew myself. They were me, then, but who was I now?

It didn't last.

It couldn't last.

It wouldn't last.

'It's all about engagement, sweetie. The fans want to reach out and touch Charlie Ray.'

That's what Marina had told me, the record label's earnestly cheery marketing exec. She consistently wore a burgundy beanie hat with 'Hype' written in white letters on the front, regardless of the weather.

'Charlie Ray doesn't want to be touched, thank you very much.'

'Then it's your funeral, sweetie.'

But I got it. I'd grown up with the internet. Okay, so I wasn't one of those spare room songwriters who'd TikTokked their way to a million views and got snapped up by a label boss trying to 'listen to the youth demographic'. My route was more traditional. More music industry rite of passage, or so I told myself. I'm not saying I lived in a transit van for months on end, gigging my way around dive bars. That would be a false impression of how I hit the big time. The getting for me was less to do with slogging the motorways and more to do with a one-off support slot. The right place. The right time. Marcus had watched from the bar, his gin and ginger order mid-verbalisation, the calculations underway already. He'd missed the main act and signed me up at the side of the stage. It was just how I'd imagined. He was just how I'd imagined.

By the time I went on tour, I'd skipped the toilet circuit and graduated straight to bigger venues and air-conditioned tour buses, the face of a highly-engineered travelling sales machine, spread-sheeted to triangulate success by the label.

In the early days, I'd followed Marina's advice. #CharlieRaySquad. #TeamFollowback. The community grew, the comments encouraged me on. Their new favourite song, their new favourite artist, their gig of the year, the show to crow about.

'This is a ready-made album audience. C and C, Charlie, charm and convert.'

The album was recorded in the spring. I'd put a stopper on that for two decades, waiting to pour it out in a studio, any studio, and onto record. Marcus had chosen a place in the mountains of Scotland. A long way from London. I'd have flown around the sun. It had the equipment he'd decided would suit the aesthetic agreed on with himself. Vintage pieces, analogue kit that created a crackle. Stuff that looked just right for the album sleeve.

The look was easy enough. I was young enough, slim enough, pretty enough, long auburn hair and sea green eyes, a present delivered at birth from Rachie. The clothes weren't mine or hers but grandma's. An ageing earth mother with a walk-in wardrobe filled with flowing dresses and flouncy sleeves, the doors open to her only granddaughter. Sack the stylist. We didn't need one. We had that sense of the seventies, of how music used to sound, of how musicians used to look.

'This isn't the fucking X Factor. This is timeless.'

Forever Songs.

That's what we'd called it. Ten verse-chorus-verses written in my teenage diary by my teenage heart, but these weren't cliched broken heart boyfriend barf shit. They were songs as stories, sometimes of me, sometimes of people I'd observed over those years. The sadness of a stranger on a train. The strength of a girl afraid. The heartache of a lover lost.

When I write it down like that, it sounds cheesy, but strip away the sound from your favourite song and they don't always make the most sense in black and white. Love Love Me Do for fuck's sake.

My guitar playing was strictly rudimentary, but we

beefed that up in the studio. We weren't cheating people, we were adding depth. Richness. No smoke and mirrors, but surround sound turned up to eleven. People didn't need me to play six minute solos with my teeth. That's not the niche I was filling. Not when I had the voice I did. Soulful and fragile. I'd make a circus strongman cry in a heartbeat. The voice was why these songs worked. Songs forever.

'Humans will be playing this on Mars to the little green men.'

Marcus was prone to hyperbole but I wanted to hear every single syllable.

A few months on and the direct messages from unknown admirers had turned weirder and weirder. Turned from thanks for the follow or guestlist requests to the what are you wearing and where will you be. I'd culled thousands of nobodies on a tour bus ride from Edinburgh to Newcastle. It didn't even cross my mind that this is when I should have been writing songs.

Somehow Luke's message had made it through. I was post-gig high. Let's leave it at that. Marcus was racking up the drinks and I'd checked my phone. It was how I'd spent the past 18 months. F5. Refresh. A hard habit to break. But that night the notes were positive. 'Charlie Ray is back'. 'The lungs on that girl <3'. 'The new song sounded sick'. I'd replied to his message. A thanks xo. He'd responded, instantly. Who was this weirdo? A journalist. Okay. He'd written some interesting stuff about the Middle East, that must be how he survived the cull. He was too shy to come and say hi. I'd manned the merch stand for an hour afterwards. 'Engagement'. Signing vinyl, selling t-shirts, posing for selfies.

'A toast. To us.'

I'd woken up the next day alone and euphoric. Praise be for both of those things. My phone had become a doomsday device but as I pulled it under the covers and read the reviews, it held up the high.

His message was there again.

It didn't take me long. Luke Harris. A journalist gun-for-hire. A freelancer. A stringer, I think they called them. 'What's happened to empathy in politics?' 'The girl from Gaza who's made the promise of peace.' 'Behind-the-scenes at the Burning Man Festival.'

Was this guy that hen's tooth? The non-psycho fan. I mean, what was wrong with liking my music? It was great, everybody knew that, at one time at least.

'You should have talked to me. I don't bite. Well, not always xo.'

In the end, I suppose maybe I did.

In Cupid's grand romantic stakes, sending a DM from the safety of a mobile phone might not quite rank as highly as yomping across the windswept Moors but in that moment, it was the best I had. I wasn't looking for love, and for a long time there, I didn't realise I'd found it.

I'd spent my whole life so focused on striving to be the most successful person in the room- and the room next door to that- that matters of the heart kind of came last. It's not that I didn't fall in love ('love', whatever love is) or that I hadn't fallen in lust, delightfully, disastrously on more than one occasion (unless you've been under a rock the past few years, you'll know what I'm referring to. And for the record, his lawyers screwed me better than he ever did, despite the tabloids falling for his stories).

Rachie would have been happy if I'd married Harry. High school Harry. Not that we were at the same school of course, mine was strictly penis-lite. While the rest of my classmates went wild at the merest suggestion of a stiff one, teenage me was oblivious to the advances of the opposite sex.

I'd met Harry at an Oxbridge study group, a full three years before the entrance exam. Rachie had been concerned about my analytical skills. A teacher had once told her that I had a knack of arriving at the best conclusion so telepathically that she'd suspected that I found it beneath myself to share my workings with mere mortals. (That was unfair. Despite being the top of the class, I hadn't wanted to share my secrets because they were mine.) Ironically, and not in an Alanis way, I'd reached the conclusion that music, my music at least, was the antithesis of this. My one outlet for a showing of the sums, the scribbled increments, the crossing outs and the second drafts of a girl trying to come to terms with her place in the world. None of this was on show to poor Harry, of course, his awareness levels just about managing to cope with the class's dissection of Milton or Pound. Despite his limited skills as a literary scholar, Harry was, to use the parlance of our times, fit as fuck and knew absolutely nothing about it. Rachie liked him because his father had a incredible head of hair. She truly believed our genetic combination would be unstoppable. I told her I was 16 and I'd rather set fire to my own womb than have children. We spoke to each other like that, Rachie and I. After her admission, I'd decided Harry needed to stop fingering me in the back row of the local multiplex. He seemed to understand.

If I'd mainly managed to avoid the cliches about private schoolgirls, I'd made up for it once I became famous. Just another female singer fucking her manager. File next to Celine and Shania. It wasn't a sexual thing, for me at least. He always looked silly, really, in his all black uniform, slacks, roll neck, shoes. The one exception, a statement jacket. 'To stand out for the paps, darling, while looking slim enough for them to care', he'd say, patting his three-pack. Fortunately they didn't, not noticing the on-off-on relationship I shared with my slicked back 46 year old common law guardian.

Looking back- I do that a lot now, I have the time, at least in my head- there's a big moral issue about what Marcus did to me. When you're pouring every inch of your being into an artistic project and someone in a position of power, someone older, always, tells you you're the new this or tomorrow's that and then you are and there's drink and sometimes more, then it's easy to think it's down to them, if only a little, and that you owe them, if only a little. This insight is one hundred per cent hindsight it's worth noting. Only a sociopath could have that capacity for clarity about the whys of a relationship in the moment.

And there was the boy band boy. You'll know who he is. You'll have seen the paparazzi photos from the Caribbean beach holiday. You'll have listened to the album (his, not mine). But Luke, he was the one. The kindest, sweetest man I ever met. That's not what gets the girl, usually. Nice guys finish last. When I'd turned off Harry and onto the rest of the male population, it wasn't table manners that turned me on. My crushes at Oxford, because that's how they generally stayed, they weren't directed at the Ra Ra Ruperts, the Trust Fund Blues, rather the bar man at the Eagle & Child, the caretaker on the Jesus quadrangle, the Saturday boy at Blackwell's. Bits of rough. Normals. Imagined in the moments between stanzas in a stuffy tutorial. Unconsummated affairs of the mind.

Luke wasn't a bit of rough, but he wasn't a Hooray Henry or a Marcus either. He was Luke. But what was that?

I hadn't known at first, of course. We'd met for a coffee the day after the gig, me still high from not fucking it up, him, well, I don't know what he was inside, but outside he was nervous energy, curiosity, ingenuity (yes, really). My phone had rung when he was at the counter. Marcus. We were off, his attention turned to more successful projects. I reached for the red button.

The conversation had turned, somehow, from the gig, to our lives, our influences, our upbringings-

'It's been years since I've been to the seaside.'
'Then let's go.'
'But-'
'-but what?'
'But nothing, I suppose.'
It had been his idea.

We'd walked the pier, skimmed the stones, ate the chips like a pair of giggly teenagers, tearing away from the black and white, if only for a little while. I didn't stop to think if it was him or the sea air or the adrenalin from the on-stage outpouring the previous night. It didn't seem to matter.

Four gins in at The Heart and Hand, a Mod pub untouched since the battle on the beach, Luke stood at the jukebox, his back to the room, my eyes sizing him up.

He sat down, sheepishly, tipsy.
I knew the opening riff instantly.
'You cheeky fucker.'
'Let's Spend The Night Together.'

The bedroom was pink and green, the sunshine sneaking in past the blind. My head fuzzed. I gasped for breath. Panicked. Counting, one, two. There it was. Breathe. Relax. Every morning since the age of seven had been the same. I'd woken up in a dark room I hadn't known. It had been nothing sinister, Rachie and Ray had gone 'raving' (their words) for the night and palmed me off on some friend of Rachie's from her book group. Every night til then I'd woken up in their room. I know that sounds weird now, in this post-paedo world, but it wasn't, it isn't. We were a close family. That morning I realised I was alone. It hit me every morning since, whoever was at my side.

The scene around me this particular morning was unrelenting. The walls were covered with clippings. Chic freaks and the obscene. A room dedicated to the work and life of Leigh Bowery, decorated by his wife. Only in Brighton.

He slept next to me, turned inside, his green eyes closed to a calmness. His dimples rising and falling with every breath. Only a fortune teller could have known what would pass between these two relative strangers. The hopes and dreams. The fights, the tears, the accusations. The two homes. The elation. The depression. The unnamed child.

'Morning.'
'I guess it is.'

*

'Who's your Romeo, Miss?' The class cackled in that particular way only a group of privileged teenage girls can.

'That's a very personal question, Amelia.'

That's the problem with Romeo. Falling in love seems like a great idea until the bloke sends you to suicide.

I wonder what Luke's doing right now, if he ever thinks of me at all.

Graves

'I'm sweating Clark's Pies back here, brother,' Graves had maneuvered his not inconsiderable arse to the edge of the back seat and tapped on the plexiglass, 'any chance of a bit of air con or what?'

The driver slid the plastic open and asked his passenger to repeat his request. He'd been hoping to spend the two to three hour journey catching up with the latest edition of a Somali podcast he was hooked on, but it seemed he had a talker, worse luck.

'I said it's tropical in this cab. Sort it out and south Wales' finest won't be shy with the tip, if you know what I mean.' The driver had expected Graves to laugh at the end of that, but he hadn't, and he wondered if he was a psychopath. A recent edition of the podcast had interviewed an eminent Somali psychologist, one of the world's leading experts in such matters, a female head of department of social and behavioural science at the University of Utrecht in the Netherlands. It was the little things, she said, the little things were the giveaways.

He twisted the dial and the sound of reconditioned air whirred out. There goes peace, he thought.

'Abdullahi Mohammad,' Graves read the driver's ID, his eyes straining from the back of the cab, his pronunciation all rat-a-tat-tat. His eyes were the one part of his constitution which retained the sharpness of youth. He'd have coped with specs if he could shave six inches off his gut. The Lord moved in malicious ways, he thought.

'Servant of God, ay?'

'What?'

'Your name, Abdullahi. Servant of God.' Graves had nicked a Somali kid down the docks years back. He'd suspected him of flashing his bits at al fresco diners at an Italian chain restaurant. There were twenty or so positive

IDs and just as many people put off their carbonara. 'Abdullahi wouldn't do that because Abdullahi is a servant of God,' the kid had repeated over and over until Graves had thought long and hard about giving him a backhander in the chops.

'Servant of you for the rest of the day by the looks of it.'

Graves laughed this time, right from the bottom of his belt.

'Not me, brother, that's not the way to look at this,' Graves had a habit of calling black people 'brother', something to do with his police training and Mod youth, 'you could be stuck outside the station all day, doing your fucking Suduku book for hours. That don't pay a pittance does it?'

'Suppose not.' He was humouring Graves. 91 miles to London. This was going to be a long day.

'And instead, we're a pair of lads going to see if the streets are still paved with gold-'

'-how'd you mean?'

'It's Dick Whittington, brother, nevermind, but don't think of this as work, think of this as a chance to break out of the humdrum and grab life by the big hairy balls.'

Graves had lived in London once, a lifetime ago now. That saying wasn't very accurate was it, he thought, unless the lifetime belonged to someone quite young and tragic. It was the 1990s. Everything seemed a lot simpler then. He'd lived in a rotten flat in Walthamstow, sharing with another copper, an Irish sergeant by the name of McKellen who ate lamb vindaloo three times a week and never bought any toilet paper. Graves wasn't sure who'd rubbed off on who. When he'd moved there, Graves had thought being a cop in the big city would be glamorous, that he'd be a law enforcer at the heartbeat of a metropolis, equally feared by the gangland and city hall. The reality had been different. London was just like south Wales in lots of ways, a collection of interconnected villages. Graves' village wasn't really the home of criminal masterminds, not that he'd got to deal with anyway, but immigrants and petty crimes, drugs and car theft and muggings and a murder, once in a while. One particularly depressing night in the pub, the 'Famous Pig & Whistle of Walthamstow' the sign said ('it's what it's famous for you need to be worried about'), he'd asked McKellen,

'What exactly is it we're doing here in London anyway?'

McKellen had looked at him, all ginger hair and dragon breath.

'I mean it's hardly the fucking Untouchables being a copper in Walthamstow is it?'

'Fuck knows what you're doing here ya Taffy cunt, but there's a lot less fucking bombs then there are in Belfast, so there are. That's what I'm doing here, so it is,' McKellen replied, before necking his lager.

Graves had left London for his hometown of Cardiff a year later, a transfer to the South Wales Police, and had been offering varying degrees of usefulness ever since. This case already had all the hallmarks of being at the shittier end of that stick.

The last time he'd gone back to London had promised a bit more action than today's particular venture. Sally-Anne Davies. Or was it Jones? It was generally one or the other, at least when he was romancing local women. Graves could see her now. She had this long ash blonde hair that looked like she was trying to grow out a perm. Legs up to her armpits. Red lipstick and stilettos. Thinking of her now, staring out at the side of the motorway, a row of pointless trees planted to make the experience more wholesome, Graves thought Sally-Anne looked more like a bird from the 80s really. Perhaps that was why he'd liked her, first off. A taste of nostalgia. The reality was, Sally-Anne was a sort who shined on the early dates, really stood out, but wasn't one you could see yourself plonked next to on the three-piece on a Friday night, putting up with your choice of film and letting you have three-quarters of the Chinese takeaway. No, not there, Graves thought. Sally-Annes were for eyeing up, for parading around, for spoiling and shagging, if you were lucky.

Graves' luck had run out on that trip, as it goes. Best laid plans and all that. He thought he'd surprise her. Felt he'd needed to up his game considerably if he wanted to progress past heavy petting. Their previous date had been in an old Italian restaurant, the kind where they've got plastic vines running over the ceiling and frames on the walls of where the family got on the boat. Graves had bit his tongue and not asked the old dear why they'd left that sparkling coast for this shithole. They didn't like swearing, not all of them, that's what he had to remember.

Sally-Anne had been banging on about how much she'd liked the wine.

'I loves this Pinot Grigio,' over and over.

He'd taken the hint. One of the women at work, a desk clerk whose name escaped him now, had told him about this wine experience place in London. Vinopolis. That was it. He'd gone all out. 'I'll pick you up at midday,' he'd told Sally-Anne. What he didn't tell her was he'd be in a limo, twelve foot long with a disco ball and fully-stocked fridge in the back. 'I know you likes that Pinot stuff but I thought we'd have champagne for the way up.' He could hear himself saying the words now. She'd looked stunning, this tan leather skirt. He hadn't needed to tell her to doll up. Dolled up was her default state.

It had been working a treat too. She'd given him a

hand-job just past Leigh Delamare services and he swore the driver was listening in, the dirty sod. What Graves hadn't factored in was the wine. Beer, he could drink beer for days on end, had too many times to be honest. But wine, he couldn't drink wine for anything. Sent him proper loopy. They gave you all of these tasters as you walked around the place. What he found out later was you're meant to swill them around your mouth and spit it out. It could have all been so different. He'd got argumentative over something, he didn't really know then and he doesn't really know now, but through his drunken fog he knew plain and simple he'd been wronged somehow by someone. Had ended up decking some bloke in an apron. Turned out he worked there. Even if he didn't it was wrong, he knew that then and he knows that now. Sally-Anne hadn't taken too kindly to it. Graves supposed if you treat a bird to a limo ride to London, the last thing she's expecting is a dust-up when you got there. He'd asked the driver to stop off in Chepstow on the way home before realising he was a sad, old bastard drinking in a pub on his own. He'd called his daughter nine times before his battery had died. She'd switched her phone off after the second dial. He hadn't left a voicemail. He'd listened over and over to her six second answer phone greeting, her words hurried and distracted, as if the kid was doing something to grab her attention just out of arm's length. She'd been like that as a kid herself, always grasping for the thing just out of reach. That had been the main cause of all the trouble between Graves and her mother, that's how Graves had seen it. Her mother was always too harsh on her, telling her off real nasty and vindictive, that's what he'd tell her. 'Just because you had a bitch of a mother don't become one yourself'. In retrospect, it might be something else that put her on edge all the time. Graves' moods. Graves' drinking. Graves.

He thought he'd erased that trip to London from his memory, the shitty bits at least.

'Leigh Delamare, that's a funny name ain't it?'

'What was that?' Graves said, Abdullah opening the gap in the glass wider so he could hear.

'I said Leigh Delamare is a funny name. Sounds like a daytime TV detective don't it? "It's just another case for Leigh Delamare"' The driver laughed to himself.

'I suppose it does,' Graves laughed back, even though he always associated it with hand jobs.

'What are you doing in London anyway?'

Graves inched forward again, his boxer shorts riding up his arse.

'I'm a daytime TV detective like Leigh Delamere,' he said.

'I knew you was a copper,' the driver said, 'you can always tell.'

'That's reassuring,' Graves said, 'good to know I've still got it.'

'I'm Abdi, anyway,' the driver said, 'it's easier than Abdullah Mohammad.'

'Servant of God.'

'Servant of God.'

'So you from Somalia or Somaliland then, Adbi?' Graves said, 'I've never quite worked out the difference.' A National Express coach beeped its horn at the cab to change lanes. Abdi responded calmly, checking his mirrors, indicating, pulling right.

'Somalia, Somaliland, it's all the same to me, innit, mate,' Abdi said, his voice like he'd said it a thousand times before, 'tribal shit, that's what it is. Everyone thinks their tribe is the best, don't they?'

'I guess they do,' Graves said.

'We're all the same though, that's how I sees it,

Somalia, Somaliland, one people.'

'That's what we all are, brother.'

'What's the need of a cab all the way to London anyway? You in MI5 or something is you? I got a spy in the back of my cab?' Abdi laughed again, a little like a hyena this time.

'That's four fucking questions, brother,' Graves said, 'I'll take them in order.'

Graves can remember the meeting as if he'd just been kicked out of it. "Driving drunk". He wasn't drunk. "Driving uncontrollably". He was in full control of the car. "Speeding when not in pursuit of a person of interest." Suspects are like rats, you're never more than six yards away, it's best to be on the ball, you never know where the next one is, he told them. "Driving without a seatbelt." I'm a fucking copper, he told them.

"Who the fuck keeps grassing me up anyway?"

Coppers didn't rat on other coppers, that's what Graves had thought, growing up through the ranks. But it wasn't like that for Graves anymore, hadn't been for a while. He'd think about it sometimes, in that hazy hour before the alarm went off, trying to pinpoint the exact moment he uninvited himself from the club. The conversations stopping in the locker room just as he walked in. All that nonsense. If he was a younger copper it might have bothered him, he was different then, greener, keener to make friends and influence or be influenced. The 54 year old Charles Graves was not the kind of man who gave a flying fuck about anybody else, often to his own detriment, but in this instance, in the being out of the force clique, it suited him just fine. He'd seen how the whole sordid shit-show worked. How you had to grease a palm and pray the fuck to God or the devil that was all they wanted. Not now. Not him. No thanks.

Fuck off.

'Answer one, the cab question, well, it's all part of a public sector scheme to put cash back into the local economy, isn't it? You can thank a pen-pusher in the procurement department for that one...' Abdi watched his passenger in the rear mirror.

'You're having me on, mate,' Abdi said, 'I didn't come in on the last boat-'

'-although you are good pirates, you lot aren't you?' Graves butted in.

'That's another story,' Abdi all hyena laugh again, 'you wanna know how I knew you were lying?'

'Go on then,' Graves said.

'You looked to the right didn't you? All proper shifty eyes and that.' Abdi seemed pleased with his analysis, then checked his mirrors again, middle, left, right, middle, remembering he was driving a car at high speed on a motorway and not in a crime lab.

'Very clever that, brother, very Inspector fucking Morse.'

'Who's that? CSI mate, that's where it's from, innit? I loves that show,' Abdi said.

'You sound like one of the-', Graves stopped himself, 'actually don't worry about that, very good Abdi, very good, you busted me.'

'I knew it.'

'I'm going incognito, Abdi' Graves said.

'What? Into London?'

'That's it,' Graves agreed, 'under the radar.' The sign for Membury services flashed by. Graves was dying for a slash. All that coffee he'd had at McDonalds this morning. He'd gone back for round two after taking the call which led him to the back of this cab, hours earlier.

'Nah, you're having me on again,' Abdi told him

from the front.

'But I didn't-'

'-nothing to do with your shifty eyes this time,' Abdi cut him off, 'you don't look like MI5. The spooks are all ordinary looking, that's the thing, so they don't stand out.' Abdi had spent an hour a few weeks back lost in a podcast interviewing a Somali guy who'd spent ten years as a language analyst at GCHQ down in Cheltenham. He'd come over from Somalia at the same time as Abdi, fleeing the civil war. The interviewer had asked him about spies, if Somalians would make good spies, and he answered that the best spies blended in, went by unnoticed, so it depended on where they were doing the spying really.

'And you're trying to say I stand out, are you?' Graves said.

Adbi looked in the mirror at his passenger, his full red beard, his scraggly hair, his overhanging gut, the bags under his eyes big enough to carry Black Friday shopping in.

'You tell me, mate.'

Graves hadn't looked in a mirror with the light on this millennium. His skin tone needed the softer shade of the hall light, the darkness blurring the edges of the man just about holding it together in front of him. He used to care about his appearance, was into it all when he lived in London. Crisp Ben Sherman shirts. Sta-prest trousers so sharp they'd draw blood. Sideburns the size of a small house. Graves was the mod revival a decade late, but then Britpop came along and his look was back where it was at. He hated that shite though, whiney little art college drop-outs most of them. He had Fred Perrys older than the little fucking scroats filling up the bar and the back room in The World's End. He liked that Weller was back though, Weller was god to Graves. The number of times he'd fallen asleep on the Northern Line home, lager burps waking him up in Morden, a world away from Walthamstow and his flat and his mad Irish cohabiter. He'd tried to walk it once but came to in a Shell garage on the Holloway Road. If only he'd had Abdi on call then, he thought, laughing to himself. He caught a glimpse of the outline of his face in the back window of the cab. 'If the Modfather could see this sorry sight,' he thought.

'First time in London, is it?' Graves asked, trying to change the subject his brain had settled on, 'you'll have a bit of time for sightseeing if you like.' He was trying to be positive for Abdi. It can't have been a cake-walk, picking up the call from the rank and realising you'd agreed to take this particular passenger all the way across the bridge and over to the English capital.

'You think because I'm a Somali I ain't never been to London,' Adbi spat back. Graves was used to this tone, used to racist accusations being thrown at him. It was standard schtick for a copper.

'Not a Brexit bastard are you?' Abdi said. He wouldn't normally talk to a copper like this but this was his cab. His rules. And this one looked like he could take it anyway, he thought.

'God no, not at all, not at all, peace and love I say, we're all the same, like I said, brother.' He'd seen enough racists back in his mod days, when the skinheads came in and it all turned a bit dark. His superiors had been on at him to go undercover for a little while there. Despite what Adbi saw now, the assessment of Graves back in the day was that he looked 'authentic', looked like he could mix in with a leery crowd and tickle their underbelly before they knew anything about it. 'No thanks, guv,' he'd said, 'I'm happy where I am. Don't think I've got the stomach for that kind of work.' He wasn't sure if that was a convenient excuse or the truth, still wasn't.

'I think you've never been to London because you been too busy driving this cab and providing for your family. No time to go gallivanting up the M4 in your gladrags.' A picture of two young girls swung from the rear view mirror.

'Exactly I have,' Abdi said.

'Thought as much,' Graves said, 'a family man.'

'I loves those kids.'

'That's honourable,' Graves said, knowing it was, knowing it wasn't always like this.

'Easiest thing in the world to love them,' Abdi said, stone cold serious now, even more than when his back was up, 'You got kids?' he asked.

'I got kids.'

'Then you knows then,' Abdi said, 'then you knows.'

It was Abdi who didn't know, Graves thought, not one percent of it.

'Anyway,' he said, 'you're right, I ain't never been to London. You going to text the Queen or am I?' The hyena was back.

'Coffee stop?' Abdi said.

'Pee stop more like,' Graves replied, just as Abdi slammed the breaks on. Graves jolted forward, his belly bouncing back and forth and back and forth, stretching the button above his frayed leather belt to bursting.

'What the fuck was that?' he shouted through the glass, his hands gripping rips either side in the upholstery.

'Sorry mate, looks like there's an accident up there,' Abdi said over his shoulder.

Fucking brilliant, Graves said under his breath.

'There's nothing like smelling of piss when you're interviewing some bird about a potential murder is there? Just my fucking luck.'

Cars slowed to a stop around them, passengers looking in at Graves, wondering why a Hackney cab with a south Wales sticker was stuck next to them in a traffic jam just outside Reading.

'£40 if you soils the seats mate,' Abdi said.

'You're taking the piss now, brother.'

'That's what you needs innit?' Abdi was enjoying this more than he expected. 'You never answered why I was driving you all the way to London anyway.'

Graves tucked his cock into his balls and tried to hold the sensation in.

'Turn that fucking radio off too will you. Don't go chasing waterfalls, my arse. Just what I need.'

Abdi lost it at this, pack of hyena lost it, turning the dial down but struggling to manage the simple task through the laughter.

'You're the funniest copper I ever met,' he told him.

'Funny ha ha?' Graves asked.

'Yeah,' Abdi said.

'Funny fucking peculiar too, and all,' Graves said, knowing it wasn't the only time he'd heard that.

'The world's a funny place,' Abdi said, 'no use in being the only sane man in the lunatic asylum.'

'Very deep that Abdi, very deep. I didn't realise I'd be getting a bit of front seat philosophy as part of the package. The expenses department will be thrilled.'

'All part of the service,' Abdi smiled over his shoulder, edging the cab forward little by little as he did. 'And you still haven't told me what you're doing in London,' he said.

'Hit and run,' Graves told him, giving up his resistance. It was hard enough trying not to piss himself, let alone keeping the case close to his chest. 'I'm off to question some woman who knew the poor bloke.'

'What, you think she done it?' Abdi asked, his voice

all animation and edgy excitement.

'She'd have had to run him over in a jet plane if she did,' Graves said, 'it only happened this morning.'

'Ah, I see,' said Abdi, cogs turning.

'But she knows something you think, yeah?'

'Who knows? Who knows anything?' Graves said, 'but what I do know, is we're going to London to find out.'

But Graves did know something. Did know some things, actually. One of the drips back in the office had called him an hour ago, before he'd struck up his new found companionship with Abdi. He could do with some more ethnic friends actually, he thought, could do with some more friends full stop, maybe this fella could be his regular cab driver. Only part of that is true, he conceded, he didn't have use for any friends full stop, regardless of whether they were white, black, blue or neapolitan.

The copper on the line had said he's emailed Graves a case file with some updated information on the hit and run. Graves had lied, well, half-lied, and said there was no signal on the motorway to check, but the reality was that his digital capability began and ended with short and generally not very sweet messages on dating sites. And even they had been in capital letters for a year before he worked out how to switch them off. Apparently it had been like he'd been shouting at the women, real angry talk, and he'd discovered that only a certain niche section of the market were into that kind of domination. At his age, he didn't quite have the puff in his lungs for it.

He'd asked his colleague to save him the hassle and lay it out for him and it went like this. Luke was a journalist, but when Graves asked what paper he wrote for, the voice on the other end said the name of some website he'd never heard of.

'Am I the only fucker who still gets newsprint on their fingers?' he'd said. He felt like an anachronism around young people.

Scrolling on your mobile phone didn't beat stretching out a newspaper.

Puffing on a blueberry tampon didn't beat smoking a fag.

He wondered where it was all going to end.

He hoped he wasn't around to see it. The minute he took orders from a robot he was walking into the nearest river with stones in his pockets.

'So he's a journalist, so fucking what?'

'So fucking nothing, Sarge, until you check his social media profiles.'

'And that's what you idiots have spent all morning doing is it? While I'm schlepping it up to London, chasing up a lead, doing proper police work?'

The voice on the other end of the line ignored him.

'It was his last tweet. Two days ago. It said he was working on the biggest story of his life...'

Graves had taken this information in, pausing for a beat while the car crossed the Severn Bridge. The morning sun had hidden behind a cloud, creating a view where all you could see was mist and wonder what secrets the sky hid. Bob Dylan had had his photo taken here on a similar day, in '67 or '68. Scorcese had used it for the cover of his documentary on him. *No Direction Home.* The other mods had hated Dylan but Graves had always identified with that line.

'Say it again, will you?'

'He said he was working on the biggest story of his career-.'

'If he works for www dot whatever that could be a school fete or a giant vegetable, lad.'

'But it's not that, Sarge, this website is big, where all the stories break these days. And he's been what your generation-'

'Watch it,' Graves said.

'..what your generation would call a proper journalist. He's written for The Guardian, the New York Times, Time Out, the lot.'

'Interesting, very interesting,' said Graves, 'still though, two and two very rarely makes murder motive in my experience. You'll find that out as you get on in this job. You can rely on me to do the hard yards and follow up this lead in person. You can't beat seeing who you're talking to.'

'Sorry, Sarge, you're breaking up.'

'Never mind,' Graves said, hanging up.

Abdi had sped through the bridge and passed a sign.

'Welcome to England.'

They'd stopped for a piss at Chieveley services.

'Get me as close to the door as you can,' Graves had said, 'it's gonna go fucking everywhere.'

Abdi had stayed in the car, catching up with messages from his kids. The girls had been playing chess, he'd taught them how the summer holidays before last. His wife had gone nuts, shouting the house down that they were too little, that the pieces'd get stuck in their gullets but he'd just laughed.

'What you laughing at Abdi, it's not funny.'

'It is,' the hyena laugh, 'gullets. You been with those women in the call centre too long, babe.'

The girls had kept it up. Almost nearly beat him last weekend, the older one had. He wasn't one for this 'let the kids win' stuff. They'd only get better if they lost, that was his mantra. No good sugar coating it for them.

He'd received four pictures of the pair of them, dog ears on their faces, mucking around mainly, not taking the chess seriously but having a good time.

'Concentrate on the game,' he'd messaged back, wishing he was there and not on this run to London. The reality though was that it was a good earner. He'd take tomorrow off and treat them to a meal of their choice. They could never decide. Big one wanted falafel all the time. The little one Chinese. He didn't care, it was just being with them that counted. He wanted them to have the childhood he never had. Jobs like this were all part of that plan.

After the jam, the traffic had been weirdly absent, like Graves and Abdi had missed big news and the rest of the population had battened down the hatches and taken to the fall out shelters. The houses seemed bigger along the side of the road, the roads wider. It still looked like Cardiff though, Abdi thought, it all looks the same over here really. The Sat Nav counted down into the single figures and he heard Graves from the back of the cab,

'She's hung up on me, well, well, well,' Abdi had turned back, 'stick your foot down brother, things just took a turn for the interesting.'

Sadie

'Shouldn't you be looking for the man who actually did this?'

I whispered behind my hand, my breath too close to the hairy ear of the stranger sat next to me in the back row of the supertheatre. Detective Inspector Charles Graves, according to the identification card he'd flashed on his thigh. The picture didn't show the attempt at a beard he was growing. He looked even worse than he sounded on the phone.

'That's rather sexist isn't it?' he said. A middle aged lady in front turned around to see what was going on.

'Hiya love,' he said.

'Now, that's sexist,' I said, smiling a marketing director smile, 'men.' Her interest sated, she smiled in agreement and turned back to the stage.

'Keep your voice down, please, our talk's about to start.'

'Ah, the big talk,' he said, reaching for the tote bag at his feet, 'these are always handy aren't they? For your bits.' He turned open the programme of events, his stubby, little fingers grabbing for today's page.

'Stuart Winchester. Your old man is he?'

Fuck, fuck, fuck Sadie. Why did you let on? Why didn't you take him somewhere private? Stuart couldn't know what was going on here. I smiled sarcasm back at him.

'How Moments is-' his finger underlined the words like a child.

'It's Mooments.'

'Mooments! Very clever. I need to watch every word with you, don't I?'

Stuart was shuffling around at the front of the room, waiting for his cue from a Saturday morning TV chef. I could smell the sweat on his brow from thirty rows back. Dee was stage left, fiddling around with the presentation slides. A picture of the twins flashed on the giant screen and back off again. It was the quickest I'd ever seen the pair of them move.

'Look, can we just go somewhere a bit quieter to talk?'

'You get me to trek all the way down the M4 to big, bad London and you won't even let me see the show? I bloody love ice-cream.'

'Yes, I can tell.'

'Very cutting,' his hands made an action like he was pulling a dagger out of his back, 'you could be about to earn your biggest ever fan. Now to me, that doesn't seem to be the actions of a very good marketing director but then in the little time we've known each other, your behaviour has been rather erratic hasn't it?'

The pumping chart music stopped. The lights dimmed.

'Ladies and gentlemen, boys and girls, foodies and fans, it's my absolute pleasure to welcome Stuart Winchester to the stage. If you love Mooment's Cookies and Dream as much as I do, he's going to get a big old Good Food Show round of applause...'

'Follow me,' I whispered, excusing myself down the row. I didn't look back or to the stage once.

*

'Tea, coffee?'

'Green tea, for me,' he said.

'You don't look like you drink green tea,' I said.

'I don't usually,' he said, 'but I've decided today is going to be a day for trying new things.'

I paid the girl behind the counter and picked up the drinks. If I didn't know any better, and frankly, I didn't, I'd say this man was flirting with me. Dates with unattractive men were not a new experience for me, but somehow this was. I needed to keep a lid on whatever was happening. I needed to know how my Luke was.

'Right, well, good for you.'

The walls of the space, a cafe tagged onto the side of the exhibition hall, were covered with close-up images of comfort food. Fish and chips, bangers and mash, a full English breakfast, the congealed black pudding like a warning from a tobacco packet. I found a seat in the corner, balancing the tray through the crowd, and he followed behind me, excusing himself as he passed every second table.

'Is that a cottage pie or a shepherd's pie?' he said, 'I never did work out the difference.'

'Can we just get to the point of all of this, please? This is a very, very important day for my family's business and my husband will completely lose his focus if he finds out I've been talking to a police officer.'

'And he'd be even more pissed off to find out you'd been speaking to a police officer if it was because you'd texted an ex-lover, is that right Mrs Winchester?'

He took a slurp of his tea.

'I suppose you get used to the taste.'

'How is he? Luke, is he okay?' I asked, ignoring his dig.

'He's in a critical condition. Somebody got him real good.'

Oh god. My Luke. For someone so strong willed he was such a wuss when it came to pain. A vision of him sobbing in my dorm room bed, his thigh the colour of Liverpool by night. He'd been roped into playing football by the boys on his corridor. It would be his first and last ever game. He'd got in the way of a speeding football struck by an Irish guy from the rival halls of residence. The same Irish guy that had tried to pull me at the

Christmas ball. Luke hadn't wanted to show weakness, getting up and carrying on over the ooo's from his teammates. But in my room, he was a grade A wimp. His soft centre wasn't localised to the thigh. Papercuts would last for weeks. The electric shocks he'd get from the handle of my room could have killed the Rosenbergs. I suppose not every man could be perfect in every way, could they?

'But how is he? He's not a strong guy, not in that way at least.'

'Funnily enough, he's not said much to me, being unconscious and all.'

'Of course.'

Deep breaths, Sadie.

Get what you need and get this clutz out of here.

'So your text to the victim,' he said, lifting his cup again, 'care to explain that one for me?'

'There's nothing to explain. He's an old friend. I was checking in on him. That's all.'

'That something you did regularly, is it?'

'I wouldn't say regularly, no.'

'Tell us about this big story he was working on.'

'I don't know what you're talking about, I'm afraid.'

'Don't be afraid Mrs Winchester, you've got people like me to catch the bad guys,' he slurped his tea, 'and the bad girls.'

'That fills me with confidence, D.S. Graves, it really does.'

'But you knew he was a journalist I gather?'

'I remember that's what he'd wanted to do.'

Of course I knew Luke was a journalist. I'd lied to Stuart that I hadn't read anything he'd written in years, not since he was on one of the big papers. It had seemed easier, the feigning of a lack of interest. But that wasn't true. I had an alert set up every time he'd send a tweet.

They weren't always but often they'd be links to stories he'd written. Long reads on the Middle East, holocaust survivors, corrupt governments. It gave me life to know that at least one of us was being true to ourselves.

'I mean, I've not seen Luke for a very long time.'

'Does checking in not count as seeing him?'

'No, no, of course not. It was just an innocent message to wish him well from the family. That's what they always were.'

'From the family. Very nice. So your husband,' he reached into his inside pocket.

'Stuart.'

'Stuart Winchester. That was it. The Mooments man. He knew Luke did he?'

'Does he. He's not dead. You're talking about him as if he's dead.'

The thought that Luke would die and I'd be stuck with Stuart forever made me nauseous, more nauseous than I already felt.

'My mistake, slip of the tongue. Old friends are they, Mr Winchester and the victim?'

'Yes, you could say that. My husband is very busy today, you saw that. I really don't want to bother him with all of this.'

'Very well. But you're telling me you don't know anything about a particular story the victim had been working on?'

'I have literally no idea what you're talking about.'

'And do you have any idea why somebody might want to hurt him?'

'I have honestly no idea. I just want you to find whoever did this and for Luke to be fit and healthy again.'

He looked at me for what felt like a minute. His eyes were tired, pregnant with twins tired. The air between us hung dead. The clatter of cups and chatter from the other tables turned down to zero.

'Fine, thanks for your time. If you could avoid leaving the country and going off skiing or whatever it is your lot do for kicks, that'd be appreciated.' He got up to leave, his bulk pushing the table skywards, the cups rattling with the aftershock. I looked away as he tucked himself in, emphasising my busyness by mentioning emails, presentations, missed calls. Dee slid into the cafe, too skinny arms flailing, her face sunburn red.

'You've got to come. It's Stuart. He's collapsed.'

What passed through my head as I ran after our borderline anorexic PR girl through a trade fair wasn't what I might have expected. Which smart arse was it who said 'be careful what you wish for?'. I'm not saying I didn't daydream what life would be like without Stuart; actively dance to the gods for it on some days. But not now. Not here. Not like this.

Off the main floor, I followed through an endless series of connecting rooms, interrupting meetings and briefings of people looking equally as encouraging and terrified as Stuart and I had, an hour or so earlier, apologising as we left through the nearest door.

'He's here,' Dee said.

'Stuart.'

'Hello mother,' he said.

'This is Sadie, Stuart's wife,' Dee said. A man in dress-down Friday clothes offered his hand.

'Hello Sadie. I'm Doctor Ali. Your husband has had a very lucky escape.'

'Thank God,' I said. And I really meant it.

'God had very little to do with it. We had to use that wonderful invention on Stuart,' he said, his eyes looking towards a defibrillator sat on the table. 'Like I said, he was lucky we had one of those here. If he'd have collapsed like he did in the middle of your farm, you'd have lost your husband today.'

Stuart gurned behind him, laid out on a stretcher, his open shirt exposing tufts of red hair sprouting from his chest like the first signs of life on Mars. He looked happier than he did before he went on stage, somehow.

'He called me-'

'-mother,' the doctor finished, 'yes, some of them are like that. It can take a while to get back to sense and sensibility, if you get my meaning.'

'What happened?' I said.

'Your husband has had a very minor cardiac arrest.'

'Oh dear God.'

'It happened on stage,' Dee said. I'd forgotten she was in the room. 'Right after he'd announced the flavour range.'

'Oh dear God.'

'You said you wanted to go viral. You won't have had time to check Twitter-'

'No, Dee, I won't have.'

'-but Mooments is trending. Worldwide. It's already been turned into a meme. They're calling him the James Brown of ice cream.'

'I don't get it.' I said.

'He used to collapse on stage,' Dr Ali said, 'my work here is done. For now. He needs rest. A lot of it. No more big speeches for a while.'

'Thank you. Thank you so much.' He exited through the door Dee and I had left ajar.

'Do you want me to put a statement out?'

'What?'

'A statement. About Stuart. From the Mooments Twitter, I mean. People are hooked on this. You can't buy this kind of attention.'

'Sure, what? Sure,' I said.

'Should we be playful? That's the brand voice isn't it? Something like 'We hope you took the news of our new flavours better than our CEO did. The good news is Stuart is making a recovery and will be as good as moo soon'?'

'What?'

'And probably sign off with an emoji. Maybe a cow or that hospital one.'

'Dee, can I have some time alone with my husband please?'

'Oh, of course. I'll do that then. Playful. People will love it.'

'Dee, now.'

'I'm going, I'm going.'

The silence of the room felt sinister after the white noise of the past few hours, the beep of my phone in the background piercing it for a second before being ignored. Not for the first time today. I mopped Stuart's brow with a hankie. It seemed like the appropriate course of action. Brushing the hair from his clammy forehead, I could see exactly where that gormless look the twins wore most hours came from. He looked like a Ron Mueck sculpture we'd seen in the Saatchi Gallery during our salad days. A giant, overgrown baby. He'd even bought the postcard. His take on art, and life, was always pretty uncomplicated. I'd blanked out the photographic evidence of what he actually looked like as a child. Every time his mother had got his childhood photo albums out, his face a blurred person of interest against backdrop of summers in Cap Ferret or around the Christmas tree. I saw his face every day in those boys.

I must have fallen asleep for what felt like minutes but was closer to an hour.

There was a knock at door.

It pushed open.

'There you are,' he said, out of breath, red and puffy.

'Shussssh,' I'd forgotten all about him, ushering him out of the door to the adjoining room.

'Can't you see I'm busy? My husband needs peace and quiet.'

'They're following you around today aren't they, Mrs Winchester? 'Have you seen,' he paused, 'what do they call it? Twitter? X, is it now?'

'I don't know, what do they call it?'

'The kids in the office told me about it.'

'About what? About Stuart, yes Dee-'

'Dee?'

'Our PR girl. Dee told me about it.'

'I think we're talking at cross-purposes here Mrs Winchester.

'I honestly have no idea what you mean. If you'd like to leave me alone now, I've got to see to my-'

'It's Luke. He seems to have found his voice.'

'He's awake?'

'No, no, he's still as comatose as a call centre worker after Black Friday.'

'You're really going to have to explain what you mean or get the hell out of here.'

'Someone's sent a message from his Twitter account. Hacked into it, we reckon. They're saying it was deliberate. That someone meant to run him over."

Ysabelle

'And that's why we're delighted to officially open this new centre, which we are convinced will give the young people of La Boca the opportunity to make something really special of their lives. For too long the young people of this part of the city have been left to fend for themselves. We're not doing this to tick a corporate social responsibility box. Dunamis Investments really cares about the future of Argentina's young people. That's why today not only are we here to officially open this centre, but we are delighted to announce the launch of the Dunamis Scholarship programme, where we'll be paying for the full tuition of five of the brightest and best students each year to study at Brown University in Providence. The United States. The lucky students- sorry, lucky is not the right word-', the speaker smiled, 'the brightest students will have the opportunity to better themselves in the Dunamis Investment wing, which has just opened on the Rhode Island campus.'

The adults nudged the twenty or so kids into a round of applause.

'Has anyone got the scissors? Let's get this thing officially open.'

Marta scurried to the stage and handed the man in the suit some scissors, blade first to begin with. He mocked a stabbing, belly laughed to himself, and took them in his right hand, slicing the ribbon open.

'Let the celebrations begin!'

Applause again.

'That chulo is pretty pleased with himself.' It was Bruce.

'You would be too if you pulled a two million peso bonus last year,' I said.

'Two million pesos. Ni a ganchos! No way! He's lucky no-one else in the room knows that otherwise he'd really have took those scissors to the stomach.'

'Bruce, that's not funny.' But my laugh made him know it was.

Bruce was a good kid. You couldn't say that about everyone around here. His real name was Lucas but ever since I'd known him, three months más o menos, more or less, he'd been Bruce. He must have been the only Bruce in La Boca. He wore a *'Born in the USA'* t-shirt every day, holes in the back pockets of the cover art's jeans making his pigeon chest look an ass. Apparently the t-shirt had been his abuela's, she'd seen El Jefe play at the River Plate stadium in the 80s on the Human Rights Now tour. Well, you know what Bruce? Some of us are still fucking waiting.

Bruce's case file said he'd been living on his own for the past few months. His abuela had choked on her own vomit and he'd found her there the next morning, the bottle and foil on the floor at the side of the mattress. Nobody knew where his mother and father were. He couldn't really remember them, said his abuela was the only one he remembers being there when he was a niño.

He was 16 now, so technically an adult in the eyes of the government, but he wasn't fully grown. He could look after himself, sure, he had the street smarts. You don't walk around the barrio asking to be called Bruce and avoid a beating unless the other kids know you'd give one back twice as bad. And the things you see by the age of 16 in La Boca, you'd live ten lifetimes somewhere else in the world and not even know they were humanly possible. But Bruce was still a boy, a lost boy, however hard he tried to be the big chabón.

It was being the big man that brought him into my life. He'd kicked some kid's ass, really bad. The other kid was still eating his pancho through a straw if you believed what the boys here said. But to hear Bruce tell it, he was doing the right thing. He'd stepped in when a group of barrio boys were beating on some smaller kid trying to take his new Nike sneakers off his feet. Bruce had known this kid, his abuela went way back with his abuela, although judging by his shoes this one's wasn't a junky. So he'd stepped in to help. Most of the boys had run when Bruce stepped in.

Bruce didn't know his padre but, in La Boca, his reputation went before him.

The story went that he'd found out a rati, a cop, had been taking payments from the owner of a bar to put the squeeze on a rival that had opened across the road. The old bar owner had seen a drop in takings since the new place blew in and took all his customers. The new place had a jukebox and cheap cerveza and these special kind of empanadas that the old place didn't have.

The old bar owner knew the best way to solve his problem was to bribe one of the officers who used to drink in his bar and get him to put sanctions on the new place. To close it down for health and safety reasons or arrest the chef because he was a Colombian without the right papers.

When the drinkers couldn't go in the new bar because it was closed down for the day, red tape outside, a lo siento, cerrado hoy in the window, they went back to the old bar with the higher prices, the no jukebox and the shitty bar snacks. They didn't care too much, they had their cerveza still.

But Bruce's padre had cared.

It was injusticia.

The new bar owner was only trying to make a living, trying to make the neighbourhood better. The old bar owner was a cara rota, a shameless person. Why didn't the old bar owner just make his bar better than the new one? Wouldn't that be mejor for everyone? But that wasn't how things were done in La Boca. The people were less corrupt than the police and Bruce's padre couldn't stand it. It made him sick.

Depending on who you listened to, the officer and the owner had been in the bar when he burned it down. Or some of the old regulars had too, and it had served them right for lacking principles. And Bruce's padre had stood there and watched it flame, laughing to himself, offering his wrists to the police when they arrived. Or he had run, was still on the run, and was in Mexico somewhere. Everyone had their own take on the story. The kids knew it too which was why they ran, regardless of Bruce's pigeon chest.

But he'd got hold of the one kid, hadn't stopped beating on him until a señora passed by and pulled him off.

'It's what El Jefe would have done,' he told me, 'injusticia.'

And that's what put him into the programme. The new centre had opened three months ago but today was the official opening. I think it was the first time someone had worn a suit within the four walls.

The kids were here for a number of reasons. They were all remando en dulce de leche, rowing in the caramel. Either they'd done what Bruce had done. Or they'd sold drugs at school. Or stole the wrong car. Or got the wrong girl knocked up.

I was an abogado, an attorney now. Five long years at the Facultad de Derecho at the Universidad, studying in the day, serving cerveza at night, shooting the shit with Gabriela and Oscar when I should have had my head in the books. I needed the dinero. Actually, it was more like we who needed the dinero. Without padre and Che around, my madre relied on me for monedas. Her cigarellos wouldn't pay for themselves, but tuition at the law school was free for all. There was a way out of the barrio, or at least away from the bad things of the barrio, if only the niños didn't get drawn to the danger and the darkness before they graduated high school.

But it was a big if.

I'd come a long way from the bar, but in some ways I've never left. I was working to serve the same people. Instead of pouring a cold one for the construction worker, I was now helping his son stay out of the penitenciario.

Us porteños had an uneasy relationship with prison, like a River fan marrying into a la Boca family. The sinister twin towers of Caseros loomed over the city, peering down on the poor as a reminder of where you'd end up if you thought or fought for yourself. Everyone had a story about an abuelo or uncle or brother who'd ended up in there for saying the wrong thing to the wrong person, five to a cell and stinking of shit.

But the reality was those ones were harder to disappear. All the political prisoners had to be registered. You couldn't just rub them out. Not like you could with the people in the barrio.

My kids weren't leftist revolutionaries. The only cause they had was staying alive, looking like the big guy. Whoever I was defending, madre would have been beaming.

'My Ysabelle is sticking it to the man, sticking up for the little porteño down at the courthouse,' I'd hear her say, generally to the television.

'You're the first one of our family to wear a suit to work.'

She'd hoped to be able to say that about her hermano. Walter. Just like Uncle Claudio, he'd been born at the wrong time. In the wrong place. Hadn't Argentina always been the wrong place? While Claudio was a fighter, Walter was a thinker. He'd been studying filosofía at the Universidad. Walter didn't just read about the class struggle in books. He lived it in La Boca. He was easy prey for the Montoneros, the left-wing guerillas. Claudio was the tough guy but Walter got drawn in. There were bombings, kidnappings. They shot a politician in front of his daughter. A neighbour saw Walter on the television. They could see his curls creeping out from underneath the balaclava.

And then one day he never came home.

Abuela knew what happened though. Her dreams told her so. Walter was captured and taken to a compound out of the city. He was strapped to a chair and asked a series of questions. To give up his commanders. To give up his familia. He said nothing. He was tortured. Abuela didn't tell the details here, her eyes glassing over when it was clear the picture in her mind was somewhere else, somewhere darker. He was in an aeroplane then, with others. His eyes looked different. He wasn't Walter any more. The door opened and he fell into the sea.

'This would have killed your abuelo.'

Abuela fought back. She was one of the Mothers of the Plaza Mayo, the las locas, one of the hundred white headscarves that congregated every Thursday outside Casa Rosada, holding up pictures of their disappeared, the photograph fading but their resolve to fight back stronger together than ever. They changed our country. In my own way, I want to carry on their work.

My madre though, she was happier with her telenovelas. They say it skips a generation. But my career made her wrinkled cheeks puff with pride when I walked to work through the barrio, through the same streets that our Italian forefathers had built with their bare hands all those years ago. So much had changed, and yet.

'Let's blow this popsicle stand?'

It was Bruce again. At first, Bruce and the other kids hadn't know what to do so had stood around awkwardly while the suits made obligatory small talk. It had now reached the point where they'd decided they'd done their bit, that asking about the aspirations of one barrio kid without really listening to the answer was this year's corporate social responsibility box ticked.

'Where the hell did you learn that kind of language?'

'Oh, I don't know,' he said, making a big fuss out of the words, 'some dumb movie or computer game I think.'

'And you translated it into Spanish all yourself?'

'Más o menos, more or less,' he shrugged, the sound of self-congratulatory suits buzzing in the background.

'Come on, I've got something to show you.'

Bruce was more of a bouncer than a walker, his shoulder blades jagged in and out like a trap in a ghost train house as he urged me to follow him out of the reception and to the computer room. It was where we spent most of the short time we'd known each other. The programme had the idea that rehabilitation was done holistically, so as well as providing legal counsel to the chicos, I got involved in all kind of other things. With Bruce, it was computers. I didn't mind so much. I was meant to be teaching him computing for business, Microsoft Office, how to use word processing and spreadsheets and those kind of things, but mainly he goofed around and showed me little games that he'd coded.

In the first lesson they'd planned in for us, he told me, 'listen señorita, I don't think I'm going to be using Powerpoint in whatever line of work it is I go into,' this cheeky smile on his face, his teeth like gravestones.

Bruce logged onto to his usual machine, his fingers tapping out his password like percussion. Ph1ladelph1a. I'd spotted it on that first day, his digits unsure that time as he worked it out in his head. It had elevated me to some kind of Sherlock in his eyes, the attorney and sleuth all rolled into one.

'So you've got to see this,' his mouth working as his brain navigated around the desktop. Out of nowhere, loud death metal music blasted out from the speakers. The fund had spent muchas monedas on the equipment, it was a room full of the latest specifications, no second hand dial-up modem gear. At that distance my ears hurt like they wanted to bleed.

'Bruce, what the hell! Tranka, chill, you'll wake up the suits with that racket.' He sniggered, all excitement.

'That's not even the best bit,' he said, turning the volume down a touch.

CORRE DEL RATI.

The words punched up on screen big and bold like graffiti from a falling down wall in La Boca. The dot of the i of rati was a police siren, its whirring adding an unnecessary new element to the noise.

'Run from the Police?' I asked, 'what kind of game is this Bruce?'

'Try it yourself,' he said, wheeling his chair from in front of the computer and urging me to sit.

'So you use the arrows to move and press the spacebar to jump. Even un salame could play.'

The keys moved an avatar dressed a little like something out of the movie The Warriors, a kind of tough guy chic as filtered through the imagination of a drama school talent scout. Or in the case of this game, a teenage

Bruce Springsteen fan.

'What the hell am I supposed to do?'

He laughed at me.

'You old people. Ponerse las pilas, put your batteries in. I made this game especially retro so you could win,' he said.

'That's so kind.'

'I know.'

'When did you get the time to make this?' I asked him.

'Oh, you know, I came in some early mornings and late nights.'

'But you're not meant to be in here unsupervised, Bruce.' The hedge fund had been explicit about responsible accompanying adults at all times.

'It's not just you who can watch the fingers and learn an entry code.'

His loco laugh was back.

I made out I was mad with him. It felt like the right thing to do.

'Oh, lo siento, chica. I just wanted to show you how good I was at these things, that's all.'

His eyes started to well a little.

'Tranka, Bruce, chill. Are you going to show me how it works then?'

'It's simple. Super simple. The aim of the game is to cross the road and dodge the police cars to try and get to the other side.' He sat back like he'd just explained the meaning of life.

'And what's at the other side?'

'That would spoil the surprise, chica.' He laughed again.

'Bruce, one thing.'

'Si?'

'Don't call me chica.'

I wondered if maybe Bruce was flirting with me, if I'd let him get too close. There was probably something in the attorney's oath of office about leading on 16 year old kids.

For a little while, I lost myself in the game. I'd never been one for computer games really. Che spent his waking days glued to the screen in our living room killing aliens or stealing cars or beating up on bad guys. I guess it was safer than doing the same out on the streets, but that didn't save him.

My little man could only get as far as the middle of the road before a car full of rati, toting guns and drinking cervezas, ran me flat every time. Bruce watched all proud, loco laughing every time I bit the dust. And then suddenly, the screen jammed, my character caught in a quick-step back and forth, teasing a cop car in a game of chicken.

'Ah, hijo de puta! Pará un cacho, wait a bit, let me sort it out. It does this sometimes.'

He leaned over me, his pigeon chest brushing my side, reaching for the keys.

'Woah cowboy.'

'Lo siento, I just want to fix this.'

I wheeled to the side. Growing up with Che I learned never to get in the way of a boy and his computer. Bruce got on with it, tapping and cursing, and I lost myself in my phone, flicking through work emails. I tried my best to delete the the useless ones, the timewasters. 'Time is money', my boss would tell me, half-joking I hoped. I'd tell him I'm not that kind of lawyer.

'Hey chica, what does this say?'

Bruce had a forum open on screen, scrolling through to find a solution for the broken code.

'It says-' and then it was in front of me, just like I'd felt.

'Click this link, Bruce.'

'But I need to find out how to-'

I pushed him out of the way and grabbed the mouse.

The thread was titled 'Have you seen this story? Run over journalist sends message from his coma.'

It was Luke.

En este momento, in this moment, I realised who Luke was.

He wasn't the strong man from the movie.

He was his gallant friend who went over the top and died.

Nina

I suppose for most people hospitals brings up strong memories. The place where someone you loves or are meant to says ciao for now, or where your little un first bawled their eyes out. I've never had that really, not me. The baby bit you knows about, but the dying, well it happened, mam never found the secret to eternal life did she? She was never an ill women really, not one of those always complaining about this ache or pain or other. When it came for her, it came quick. It's better that way. I'd prefer that for me. No good me bringing everyone else down is there? Not that there's anyone around anyway, not anyone who'd be there at the end anyway. I can't see Taz or Karen visiting me on my death bed. And I hates all that bucket list stuff, you know, the kind of thing you'll see in the women's magazines. 'Docs told me I had six months to live so I did a skydive.' You wouldn't catch me jumping out of a plane even if it stopped a bomb from going off in my gusset. I don't know what it is. I suppose I finds it all too morbid really. All farewells should be sudden I think. Turns out that's how most of the fellas I've known think too.

When I was visiting mam in hospital, we didn't sit there sucking lemons. She wouldn't let you do that, mam.

'You were always playing doctors and nurses, Jane.' She still called me that. She chose it, after all. I was too. I was always the nurse. I don't suppose I thought a woman could be a doctor back then. They're everywhere now though, women quacks. I'm seeing one myself at the minute, on, off. And good on em too. Men have swung their shrivelled dicks round for too long in this country, and we've got it better than most.

'The problem with your nursing, mind love, was that all your dollies used to kick the bucket.'

Oh, how we bloody laughed at that one. Laughed until she coughed. They say it's the best medicine but when you've got a tumour the size of a pork pie on your lung, it don't help in the long run.

'They won't want me in here long, Jane,' 'they'll be sick of the earache.'

She was right too.

She died two nights after they let her out.

'She wanted to be in her own bed, you know?'

The amount of times I must have said that at the funeral. People nodded and smiled, like they understood.

Now the paper said he was in intensive care but I couldn't work out if that was a room in the hospital or just the way they was treating him.

The signs didn't seem to help. Ophthalmology. Physiotherapy. I felt like I was watching Countdown with Bri. He used to love that, was the only thing that got him off the computer. Everyone else seemed to know where they were going, walking round the corridors like they'd done it a million times before, even the ones with grapes under their arm. What was it with grapes? They were the patron fruit of the poorly, weren't they? I suppose it's comforting to suck something sweet when you're not feeling too hot. I'm not sure they would do the trick for poor Luke though. He'd need more than that to get over being smashed by a car.

After walking round for ten minutes like a wet hen I came across a cafe. Posh it was n'all, didn't spot this the last time I was here, although I was more in and out. Didn't want to bump into someone and be put on the spot about why I was there. Now I didn't think Luke had got himself a job whirring up the frothy coffees but I needed a caffeine fix. I was all light-headed after rushing over here like my pants was on fire and then wandered the corridors without any rhyme nor reason, like a dancing drunk in the frozen aisle.

I sat down with my cuppa, spilling a bit over the table and saying sorry to the old fella sat opposite me, and I wondered what the hell I was doing here. You're 46 Neen, not a 16 year old with a playground crush, and you're chasing around a hospital for a fella you had a jump with ten years ago. He wouldn't remember you even if he'd had a packet of Pro Plus and a Lucozade, let alone when he's been hit for six by a Ford Mondeo. And even if he did, wasn't it a bit weird just turning up like this? A bit desperate? Was this what I was now? The kind of woman who clung on to some little good thing she had all that time back? Like some obsessive? Like Glenn Close in that film with Michael Douglas? Lock your bunnies up, boys, Psycho Nina's got the pot boiling.

And just what did I have to say to him anyway? Hiya Luke, it's me, Nina, the estate agent you shagged. Don't know if you're still looking but the asking price has come down by five grand. It's a buyer's market after all. What would he say to that?

Get lost ya nutter, more than likely.

Not that he could talk, I doubt, being in a coma or whatever it was they said he was in.

And what if he had someone else. Just because I'm a single pringle don't mean that a handsome fella like him, brains and just the right bit of brawn, wouldn't be hooked up all this time after does it? He's probably got a wife and two kids sat next to his bed, holding his hand and lighting scented candles in vigil while this deluded old bat is dunking a bourbon into a latte. She's probably one of those wonder women, climbing up the career ladder while rearing two clever, little curly haired kiddies, and doing it all while looking like a bloody supermodel. He don't deserve no less anyway, a bloke like that, not from what I know about him.

I must have laughed out loud at that point because the old fella opposite asked if I was okay.

'Oh, I'm okay love, as okay as I'll ever be.'

And I was. I got it, there and then, totally understood it all. I wasn't meant to be doing this, chasing around after some one night stand all these years later. That wasn't what a respectable woman would be doing, that wasn't what my mam would have done that's for sure. Not acting the silly tart like I was doing. You know what I'd do? I'll go back into work tomorrow and I'll tell the boss that you know what? I would fancy that Italian meal with you, if the offer was still open, throwing him that little smile of mine that got him going. Yeah, that's what I'd do. A nice carbonara, some of those little rice balls maybe, to share, as a starter, anti-pasta they called em for some reason, I never was good at languages. A bottle of wine, between us, not just for me, a nice crisp dry Italian one. And then, who knows? We'll see where the night takes us, where the rest of our lives take us. He's been good to me that boss of mine. Ain't it about time I started being sensible and gave him something back?

That's when I saw him. He was strapped to one of those stretchers on wheels, being pushed by some doctors all frantic. The machine was beeping like a smoke alarm when you puts the toast on for too long. I got up out of my chair and nearly flipped the table over the old fella and started chasing him. They pushed him through a set of double doors and down a corridor, the beeping getting further and further away. Considering the three inch heels I had on, my legs were taking me as fast as they could, but regardless of how fast I was going, it seemed to go in slow motion when I got to him. The doctors moved out of the way and I could see him, lying there like an angel.

He opened his eyes and his lips moved.

'I've missed you, Nina.'

The next thing I remember was the cold of the floor.

Charlie

'Luke, what the fuck are you doing? You're meant to be in bed holding me to your chest. That's what the song would say.'

He was doing it again.

'Look, if I can make you come and tidy the bedroom in the same ten minutes, I'm definitely going to get an album dedicated to me. That's the way I'm looking at it,' he said.

'Who says romance is dead?'

'And that's the name of the album.'

He did it every time. Busying himself after sex, almost like he was trying to pretend it didn't happen. Pacing around the bedroom, picking up crumpled trousers, airing out shirts, pairing socks. Putting the brooch in a shape of a peacock he'd bought me at the antiques market in Lisbon just so. I pretended like I hated it but the reality was, it wasn't so bad. We'd settled on that cosy kind of domesticity. Comfortable living in each other's space fifty per cent of the time, wearing each other down about the little things the rest. A spoon in the wrong groove, a black sock in the white wash. Imagine if the tabloids had got a hold of that?

'Charlie Ray in boring argument in duplex apartment shocker'

I'd drifted off again. That was happening more and more recently. And it was always to those times with Luke. My mind used to be so focused. Attain, attain, attain. Not now. Heat Magazine would not give two fucks about what I was doing right here, right now, teaching in a ten grand a term school in the middle of the Berkshire countryside.

I never gave them the £50,000 back. Marcus was good for something at least. We threatened the label with the most expensive lawyer he could find. 'You've got speculate to save, darling,' that's what he'd say. We settled out of court for twenty. Add the legal fees and we weren't far from where we'd started. 'It's the fucking principle of the thing'. We managed to keep it out of the papers.

So I was skint. Am skint. Present tense. The money from streaming didn't quite cut it.

I tried to write. I really did. Creating a routine. That helps, they said. Up at 7. Yoga. Fruit. Whale Music. Up til 4. Red wine. Stale crisps. Cheap whisky.

Nothing came. No-one wants to hear an album about legal wrangling. About how hard touring is. About red carpet parties. The blank page is an arrogant bitch. Never Songs not Forever Songs.

I'd finally failed and it felt fucking fantastic.

I'm lying. It was terrible. I spent six months stewing in my own juices, rolling round the flat we'd moved into together that fresh, spring morning with all the hope in our hearts. Flicking through channels, scrolling through social, unfinished novels everywhere around me, wondering why Luke wasn't here anymore and knowing the answer.

The Luke Year had seemed like everything at the time, but it turns out it was the in-between bit. The after the comeback gig and before getting screwed by the label year. The Union Chapel show hadn't so much reignited the flame, but scratched the itch. I still had it, if I wanted it. I could have an audience eating out of the palm of my hand. On the first night we moved into the flat, all high ceilings and original tiles, a top two floor penthouse just off Baker Street (he hummed the saxophone, badly, every time we left the front door) an email came in. Luke was tidying, struggling with everything still boxed, the living room christened. The notification pinged in.

'It's from Lucas Hord.'

'The director?'

'The director.'

'Wow.'

'I love him, his work, that film with the scene in the rose garden, the, umm, the-'

'I know.'

'He wants to use Forever Wrong. In his next movie. Oh. My. Fucking. God.'

Luke dropped the book he'd picked up out of a half-open box and came back to bed, holding my head in his hand, kissing my forehead.

'This is quite the day, Charlie Ray, quite the day.'

That deal paid my part of the rent for the year. We should have bought that flat. I had the money then. We'd only been together a month at that point. It all happened so quickly I guess. Luke was like that. You felt like you'd known him forever, like he'd always been there, when the reality was, he kept himself shut away. Assessing our relationship with the clarity that only comes from distance, I feel like I never really knew him, the real him. Did he know the real me? Do I know the real me?

He was working for a press agency when we met. It explained the randomness of the stories he put together. Whatever they could sell into the nationals really. If you've read a newspaper recently, you'll know how full of shit they are. But he always wanted to write about more important things. The Middle East. Corporate corruption. Cybercrime. Rigged elections in the Third World. Injustice wherever it was. These were the things he cared about. It's just that in the early days of our relationship, sometimes he had to write about celebrity tits. He couldn't help it. It paid the bills. His boss had overheads, not least on their Clerkenwell offices and 70s style bar tabs ('who says the three gin lunch is dead?').

'You're just a hack at heart,' I told him. The intention was playful.

He didn't speak to me for three days. He could be an intense son-of-a-bitch and frequently was. I can see it now. I'd made it (and blown it without quite knowing it) by then. He didn't feel like he had. He worked his arse off to get out of that place. Early mornings, late nights. He was never off. I'd tease him that his hourly rate was below the minimum wage.

'Now that's something you should do an expose on.'

When he was working, I was, well, I was, busy doing nothing. I'd tell him I was writing, was trying to write. He didn't push it. I kidded myself that inspiration would strike, and when it did, I'd be ready, pen at the side of the bed. iPhone notes ready to rock. But Luke knew writing came from hard work. Not just sitting around waiting for the muse to strike. Without my teenage notebooks for inspiration, I was creatively done in. Past my peak at 22.

One and done.

While Luke was out on a story, I was broke down a creative cul-de-sac. I took a reiki class to get more in touch with the universal life force but all I got was a repetitive strain injury and a big whiff of bullshit. I realigned my chakra. That actually fucking hurt. I spent three months convinced that learning another language would give me a fresh clarity on the structure of my sentences in English but all my conversational Spanish has been good for is ordering pintxos and rioja.

It was all a wonderful waste of time. In the cold light of how I have to spend my days in the here and now, ticking time away like that now feels like a huge extravagance. I'm a music teacher at the Thornberry

School for Young Ladies. You couldn't write it (well, I couldn't at least). From festival stages to menstruating schoolgirls in seven years. And I am in absolutely no way qualified for the job. I've undertaken no formal teacher training. No Post Graduate Certificate in Education. It helps that it's a school for little rich girls. I'd never get away with it in an inner-city comp in East London. Mr. Pickles. Yes, that's actually the name of the head teacher, although he goes by School Leader (it's important to capitalise it). Mr Pickles hired me in an unedifying display of oneupmanship. The rival school- the Ravenwood Institute- had a member of Shakespears Sister on the staff and Perry (for that is Mr. Pickles first name) was determined to out-do them. The little star fucker. He tells me the hedge fund which owns the school is delighted. In the singular.

    In fairness to him, his grand plan has worked. While my structure-free lessons may ebb, flow and meander the hour away, the little brats enjoy the relative freedom that comes from a teacher that just couldn't give a fuck and on the rare occasion there is a girl with talent, my experience on the frontline of musical fame can really help. Then there's the parents. They're Perry's real barometer. Parents' evening is a doozy. They're queueing around the quadrangle to sit in front of Charlie Ray and tell me how they wore a groove into *Forever Songs*. They're only too happy to sign off on the zeros.

    I'm a big fish in a small pond but the crumbs are all I've got anymore.

    It's not a bad life. It's not a zero hours contract. I'm not flipping burgers for fatsos. The pay is sufficient. My quarters are agreeable. I live in a small cottage in a row of small cottages on the edge of the campus, a wooded walk away from the main building, a 16th century gothic mansion house, all gargoyles and greystone, which acts as the school room and accommodation for the 150 girls. Our houses were formerly the servants' dwellings. How we laugh about that old joke, me and the other masters. That's what we call ourselves. It makes us feel powerful.

My sexual needs are fulfilled by Ted. (Can you tell I've not written a song in years?). Ted is the modern language teacher. Is that a cliche? I should know. I wrote an album full of them and the public lapped them up. Ted has never been in Heat Magazine. Ted does not know what Heat Magazine is. He's more of a El Pais kind of man. My conversational Spanish comes in useful, after all, trying to read the review of the latest Almodovar film or a march for Catalan independence, recognising one word in five.

'Beware false friends,' Ted tells me.

Ted does not tidy up after sex. Ted is glad to be who he is, a 46 year old man, in bed with a 32 year old woman. One who once made FHM's 100 Sexiest Women in the World list. He's handsome enough, in a silver haired Oxford shirt sort of way. He's not who I should be sleeping with at this stage of my life but he's here and so I am and that is that.

The students have broken off lessons for study leave ahead of their baccalaureate exams. It's only my second year as their teacher but already I've created the muscle memory of the troughs of the term. Spring's here and there's a lot of time for sitting and just being. You can't do that in London. Most of my afternoons are spent sat in the garden, looking out onto the woodland, listening to the birdsong or the silence. After spending the first 20 years of my life screaming to be heard, the silence is golden. Damn, someone's written that one haven't they?

Luke.

He's been on my mind a lot recently.

When you're surrounding by children all day long, it can be hard not to think of what could have been. She'd have been six now, little Joanie, little Janis, little Patti the precious precocious unborn child. These names have been given after the event. The thumbnail in my womb did not receive a christening. There were no crustless sandwiches. No Sunday best.

I'd been sick for days. It wasn't uncommon. There were the diet fads. The master cleanse. Juice fasting. Ovo-lacto. Every young woman will know what I mean. It's a sign of our times. Live well, look good. Luke went through it with me.

'Sure, lentils sound delicious.'

But this time it felt like more than that. The devil herself living inside my gut. Again, I was used to this. Ever since I changed pills in my late teens, my periods made me want to rip my insides out and paint propaganda. But this time, there was no bleeding. Had I been taking the pills every day?

Luke bought me the first test. He bought me the second. By the third time, I went to the pharmacy myself. I didn't trust that he wasn't buying a loaded dice.

'If it's meant to be, it's meant to be. I could cope with it. We could cope with it.'

The appointment was made for a Tuesday afternoon. It was performed with minimum fuss and maximum discretion. It was the best I could hope for. The last thing I needed was a minimum wage front desk girl selling the info to a tabloid.

It was always better to talk these things through with the loved one, to anticipate the situation and prepare for the fall out. That's what Marcus had told me, in the early days, when the name Charlie Ray still meant something.

Ha.

Sorry.

I'm avoiding the difficult conversation.

I hadn't told Luke a stranger was murdering the unnamed, unformed thing he'd unwittingly created inside of me, uninvited and announced only with a 'I'm sorry. Did you make it too?'

I didn't.

He'd been working in Essex, posing undercover as a hospital operative trying to build up enough evidence for a sting about lackadaisical and dangerous cleaning methods. I teased him he was a low rent James Bond. He'd been working early and coming home late, the ward shifts and writing copy around them a shitty split shift. We'd barely seen each other, barely touched each other. That was my excuse.

I should have told him.

And that was the end of the end. Fast forwarded through the narrative structure. The verse-chorus-verse.

Fin.

Of course it was. If I stopped and took the time to think about it, I'd have known it would be. I knew then and I know now that Luke is a principled man. It's just I confused that with entitlement back then.

My body. Not my baby. No thanks.

My decision-making style was not collaborative, unless Marcus was making them for me.

The reveal was all matter of fact, a deliberate downplay. A 'so that doctor's appointment I mentioned' over a piece of toast about to split for separate lines.

He moved out the following month. Once he was assured I was stable. Patronising prick, I thought. He wasn't. It wasn't his fault. His capsule wardrobe in a weekend bag. Two small crates of books, the pages of the paperbacks flapping in the summer wind, me stood in the doorway defiant and shit scared.

What does the E stand for anyway? The rest of the country bathes in superfast broadband, streaming virtual reality skin flicks and playing shoot em ups with invisible friends in Tel Aviv and I can't even get 3 fucking G. Not that I need it, that often. It's not like I undertook detailed lesson research or monitored the media for mentions of my name. It's just right now, at this exact moment, I want to know what Luke is doing. I'll search his name every now and again. To know what his last story was. To see if he's on that righteous path. He'd stopped writing for the nationals, last time I checked. Who reads them now anyway? But he was doing real journalism. Investigative work. The stuff he told me he'd do. The stuff he was born to do. Without sounding patronising, I was proud of him. Am proud of him.

I'd hovered my finger over the 'like' button a hundred times, wondering if giving his story a thumbs up from far away would comfort or confuse and never being sure. For once I'd erred on the side of caution. Wherever he was, whatever he was doing, the mother of his unborn child was a notification he didn't need.

The signal was better in Ted's house, but I couldn't be doing with him today. I'd promised myself I'd never ever wake up there- I lived next door for fuck's sake, there was minimal walk of shame potential- but two nights ago I had. Kath and Khalid, two of the other masters, her a mousy Mathematician, him an out and proud world religions teacher, had been there too. A very serious Scrabble tournament. Rioja. Arguments over the validity of the word 'Qi'. Rioja. 'Qi might be a word in Salamanca but it's not in England and I should know because I got a first at Oxford and wrote a number one album so am now the arbiter of all that is right and proper about the Queen's

English.' I was half-joking. 'The vital force that in Chinese thought is inherent in all things'. A grapple in the dark. Waking up there, a blank tile stuck to the inside of my left thigh. After that, I didn't want to knock the door. Could not be fucked with the smalltalk today.

There was a gap in the fence between the two cottages, big enough to get through if I stooped. I stooped. The mud squished my socks wet. All this for some phone signal. Ted was in Exeter for the day, taking a group of girls to a Spanish spelling bee in the university, but I crept along the side of the fence and peered through window anyway. Christ, I needed some excitement in my life. It was all clear. The scene showed some breakfast bowls, a crumpled newspaper, the low hum of Radio 4. Very Marie Celeste.

I sat against the stone wall, my arse getting damp with the dew. At least it didn't have a Scrabble tile on it this time. I didn't care. I needed to know where he was, what he was doing. My phone beeped into action. The signal was stronger in Ted's garden for some reason. 3G. 4G. Messages from my mother. Ignore. I tapped Luke's name into the search bar and choose the news filter. Maybe he'd made his Watergate this time.

The noise the phone made when it cracked against the slate floor wasn't a big bang but felt just as significant. The screen was smashed but I could read the headline.

"Hit and run journalist was working on 'his biggest story yet' reports say."

He was in a fucking coma. Luke. In a fucking coma.
The message from my mother.
"Charlie, call me."
The next.
"Charlie, I'm not sure if you've seen the news but I want you to call me."
And then a voice behind me.

"If you wanted to move into the back garden, all you had to do was ask."

Graves

Looking at him now, you'd be forgiven for thinking it was the history of a different man entirely, but back then Graves had been quite the rising star. After his return from London, his unfussy approach (some said unrefined) had earned him a lot of fans among the higher ups. There was still a certain cache to a boy from south Wales who'd gone east to see if the streets were paved with gold, even if the reality in the case of Charles Graves was that he'd lived in dirty digs in the East End and his police work was no more interesting than he'd encountered in those small Valleys towns. It was when he'd returned home that things had got interesting, even if he hadn't known it quite then.

Graves' name had been on the long list, one of the ones that got thrown into the mix when departmental strategic restructures got talked through. And regardless, he'd move up the ranks of his own accord, sooner or later. That's what had been felt. He hadn't taken the usual path but he had something. That spark. That balls. Those guts. That grit.

And then one day it had all stopped. His name scratched off the list. Deep down he knew exactly why, even if he'd ignored it all these years.

They'd been partners, Graves and Smiler, ever since he'd re-joined the local force. They say you spend more time with your partner than your missus so even if you hated each other's guts, it was best for all concerned if you could at least be civil. Nothing worse than a pair of pillocks more interesting in seeing who's the biggest dick swinger when all the poor old girl wants is to find out who's nicked her Ford Fiesta.

They'd complemented each other, and not in that

TV cliched good cop bad cop way. Smiler was the more considered yin to Graves excitable yang. Part of the reason why he got his name, well, that and the obvious, but his handsome face retained a permagrin when they were out on a job. Good for community spirit, he'd tell Graves, who'd snort and swerve across the road, onto the next call.

He'd nearly choked on his chips when he'd seen it. Graves had mastered the technique of covering the screen of the cash machine with a wedge of his sausage fingers just enough to be able to see the minus or plus poke through at the beginning of his balance. It was rarely the latter. It gave him all the info he needed. A rough framework to know whether or not tonight was a gulp and go or a ten pinter. But on that day, something new happened. The zeroes stacked up past his nails. The Graves of then, 25 years younger, thinner, more hopeful, was forensic in poring over the details of a case. Renowned for it. But he was not an itemised bill man.

'The Milky Bars are on me.'

And they were.

The next morning, Graves had pulled the car off Cathedral Road down a side street and into the lane which ran behind the grand old park that led to the castle.

'Woah woah woah.'

He'd wound the window down, but not quite enough, his vomit splashing over the inside like an autumnal Jackson Pollack.

'The funny thing is, I've not eaten vegetables all week.'

'Sometimes you fucking repulse me, Charles Graves.'

'Not smiling now are you?'

'Fuck off.'

He'd not brought it up. Smiler, that was. But he'd known Graves had come into money. Thinking back afterwards, analysing that night like a fuzzy clip of CCTV evidence, there were too many clues. It was like Smiler was expecting Graves to come back and bankroll the night. He was all a bit too nudge nudgewink about it. Graves hadn't cared then, it was money, probably a banking error like the kind you read about sometimes, like when they put twenties in instead of tenners and had to honour it afterwards, some poor shelf stacker getting it in the balls.

Smiler regularly subbed Graves, Charles earning the same but always seeming to run out of cash by the middle of the month. Smiler was ever ready to pick up the slack, the extra beer, the midnight Indian, the taxi home, the door closed behind his partner's considerable wedge and a word with the cabbie to see him right.

It'd felt good to Graves to stick his hand in his pocket for a change, overdoing it to underline the gesture. The table of chasers no-one really needed, particularly the next morning. Graves was a recent inductee into the world of hangover hell, his teens and early twenties seeing him blessed with the resilience to wake up fresh and go again, a medical anomaly created by a world class liver and a creeping insomnia. It had been the last thing he'd needed that particular morning. Graves had been more used to the grunt work that made up the majority of the working and waking hours of a street sergeant. Petty crime, domestic disturbance, affray, attacks, a rape and murder once in a blue psycho. But the morning of the projectile spew, Graves and Smiler were involved in something deeper, something much more layered than a he said she said handcuffs behind the back slap on the wrist kind of case.

It had begun routinely enough. They'd responded to a six am call from the security guard at City Hall, a white portico centrepiece that wouldn't have looked out of place in Gotham City. The security guard, a middle aged man with an old aged spread, had been doing his hourly rounds, pacing up the marble staircases and down carpeted corridors, counting down the checks, each door closed one closer to his crossword. There were three to go when it happened. The commotion. The 'who's there?'. The bang on the head. The thud on the floor.

'Did you get a look at him?'

'Do I look like I did?'

Smiler had lived up to his name.

'Seems not.'

'He was on me as soon as the wood was out of the hole, black as a panther and twice as strong.'

'Have you ever considered a career in poetry?' Graves had asked.

'Funny you should mention that, I actually do write a few little-'

'Shall we watch the CCTV?' Smiler interrupted.

Graves hadn't suspected anything sinister at the time. Someone had broken into one of the grandest buildings in the city and, looking at the first line of defence, it was hardly Fort fucking Knox.

'Probably trying to half-inch some marble or a fancy painting.'

'Probably something like that.'

It had caused quite the buzz in the town. The Echo had splashed with a still from the security camera on the front page. A blurred man in black stuck in stasis in a meeting room just off the debating chamber.

'Who's the man in black?' the headline ran.

The chief had stepped in to speak to Hopper, a fresh out of college reporter who lucked onto the story because the senior hack was at the Heath Hospital again with cirrhosis of the liver. The station reported 17 crank callers calling in and blasting Johnny Cash down the line at 200 decibels.

Finding him had been easy enough. Cardiff was a small city really, smaller back then, with not enough money to go around. All Graves had to do was lay some bait and a whatever the collective noun was for grasses had bit his hand off. His name was Jason something. He'd banged so many of them up they'd blurred into one after a point. He knew really that he'd just tried to forget this one.

They'd interviewed him together. Brought him into the Rumney station, a 60s style block closest to the St. Mellon's estate where they'd smoked him out. Graves had rugby tackled him down an alley, hadn't had much choice. He couldn't have outpaced him, even then. The suspect had banged his chin on the aggregate floor, blood pissing out like water out of a burst balloon. The station was a bit more archaic than the city centre counterpart, its equipment not always a la mode. The interview hadn't gone how Graves had expected.

'What were you doing there?'
'I don't know.'
'I'll ask you again, what were you doing in City Hall?'
'I don't know.'
'What do you mean, you don't fucking know?'
'I don't know.'

It hadn't made sense. He was used to 'no comment' or 'up yours'. 'I'm not telling you nothing', but 'I don't know' was new to Graves.

'There's something up with this,' he'd said, 'something stinks here, like Ashton's fish counter.'

'He's just a dumb kid, breaking and entering, GBH, trying his luck, simple as,' Smiler had said.

'That's bullshit and you know it. Something's going on here. Why does a kid like that break into City

Hall when there's hundred houses with brand new TVs he can flog down the pub the next day? He wouldn't know a painting if he was fucking in one.'

'Just leave it alone,' Smiler said, and for once he looked at Graves like he meant serious, serious business.

But Graves hadn't wanted to leave it alone. He was stubborn like that. When they'd searched the suspect's house, a new-build council house stuck together with spit and sellotape on the St. Mellon's estate, they'd found a load of listening devices under the floorboards in the second bedroom. His missus hadn't had a clue, playing hell about the new carpets the boys had ripped up.

'It's like a Welsh fucking Watergate,' Graves had said. Smiler had stopped talking to him by this point. He'd warned him off again. Twice. Once nearly coming to blows in the car park.

'Stop stirring it up, Charles. You've had your reward.'

And Graves couldn't make any of it stick. Jason Whatever his face had stuck to his new story. His missus had been laid off by the council and he'd gone to serve up some revenge, mess the place up a bit. Shit in a bin. The microphones or whatever they were, he'd bought job lot off a bloke in the Docks and was hiding them from his missus until he worked out what to do with them. He'd got a couple of years, mainly because of the fuss in the papers and the assault. Graves didn't doubt that he was the kind of chancer who'd be in and out of prison his whole life. But he hadn't nailed him, not properly, and his partner had proved himself a shady fucker and the whole confusing little episode had stunk.

The respective careers of Graves and Smiler couldn't have been more different since. While Graves stagnated, stuck as a D.S. doing the same old shit for the same shit pay, getting older if not getting wiser, Smiler's was a vertiginous ride. After he'd ditched Graves, nominally for a promotion to inspector, he'd not stopped. Chief inspector, superintendant, chief superintendant, deputy chief constable, Smiler was now chief constable Miles. The public face of south Wales' finest. The friend of politicians and policy-makers, business leaders and the BBC. All these years later, Graves was still doing the grunt work. He wondered why he bothered but he had to get the money to send his granddaughter gifts she'd never receive somehow.

He'd met her the once, his daughter just coming back to work after maternity leave, entrusting her six month old to a tea lady at the Senedd while she held a press conference about her company's tie-up with the government, something to do with disadvantaged communities and literacy levels. She'd mumbled, embarrassed and annoyed to bump into her estranged father like this.

'I hope you enunciated better from the stage,' he'd said, regretting it instantly.

But this case had got him keen again. He'd spent the past decade and a half in a series of states of disinterest and, probably, although he'd yet to admit it to himself or anyone (who was there?), depression. He'd done the job long enough to be able to function in first gear. An average day's police work in Cardiff didn't require him to be Hercule Poirot. He had been once, a real investigator, a dog with a bone and the patience to take a fine tooth comb to even the seemingly simplest of closed book cases. That had been a long time ago. But he was sick of the autopilot. What was he doing with his life anyway? He had no-one to share it with. No family on speaking terms. No steady lover. Not even a partner any more. But this case reminded him of that one, the Welsh Watergate. It hadn't seemed like much at first, a simple hit and run. Noble enough, finding the culprit, most likely a scared kid or a pisshead, but no-one was going to give him an award for doing his day job. But now, things looked different. These messages from beyond the coma, well they certainly added an air of intrigue to the whole affair. One he hadn't expected to find. And the trip to London had seemed to awaken something in him. Sure, when he was there, he was nothing but a bobby on the beat, but he'd had lofty ambitions when he'd headed down the M4 at the very least.

'Right then, if you millennial snowflakes can put your phones down for a minute and give me your undivided attention.'

'We're millennials, Sarge. We don't do undivided attention,' said Lake, one of the mouthiest of a new breed of copper, making time in Graves' squad until the job came saving the world from cyber criminals or robot armies. Or so he thought. The other three coppers in the room, similar age, similar outlook, laughed.

'Out.'

'What?'

'You heard, get out, you little shit.'

'What?'

'Do you only respond to TikTok messages or something?'

'But Sarge?'

'Get out, this is serious stuff. If you want to fuck about, go and do it in a chat room or wherever the fuck it is you get your kicks these days.'

Lake sprang up, an uncoiled spring ready to make issue. He looked around for back-up and saw six eyes trained fully on the floor. They'd never seen Graves like this. Yes, he was a sharp-tongued cynic, a stick-in-the-mud, but you could have a laugh with him. Clearly not today. The door slammed behind Lake, Graves missing a beat and going in.

'Good. Are we sitting comfortably? Then we'll begin. So what do we know so far?'

He turned to the board behind him, circling pictures as he spoke.

'Luke Harris, 36, critical in a coma following a hit and run two days ago. Sadie Winchester, 35, the last person to contact the victim. The director of an ice cream firm with her husband, Stuart Winchester, 37, himself now in hospital after a cardiac arrest, and the former college roommate of the victim. She's in the clear, my gut tells me. Him, I'm not so sure. And then we've had a tweet.'

'Well done, Sarge.'

'Don't push it,' a phone beeped but Graves ignored it. He was in his flow.

'A tweet from the account belonging to the victim claiming the accident was deliberate. Rabbiotti, what we got on that?'

Rabbiotti, a second generation Italian-Welshman, who decided a career as a copper beat working with his mam in his family's cafes and now wasn't so sure, said,

'The IP address was blocked, Sarge.'

'In English please, Rabbiotti.'

'Meaning we can't trace where the message is coming from, Sarge.'

'Right, great. So what else have we got?'

'There is something, Sarge.'

'Go on.'

'There's been another message.'

'Well, why the fuck didn't you tell me?'

'You seemed busy, Sarge.' Rabbiotti's flabby cheeks turned rioja red. He handed the phone to Graves.

Graves took it, finding the right distance from his eyeline to be able to read it clearly.

'It's gone off, the phone's-'

'Press the middle button, Sarge.'

'Ah, there it is..."Follow the money", that's what it says. "Follow the money".' Graves looked around the room for an answer.

'What could it mean, Sarge?'

'I don't know. I don't know right now,' he walked around the room, eyeballing each officer individually, 'but we're going to make it our business to find out.'

Sadie

I gave up eating meat on Maundy Thursday. I think now that it was the little repressed Catholic schoolgirl in me, creating my own iconography all these years later. It wasn't intended that way.

Stuart would have understood it more if I'd shaved my head.
'But we're farmers.'
'We're not.'
'And farmers eat meat.'
'That makes no fucking sense at all, Stuart.'
He tried his best to eat my meat-free meals but the reality is I'd have had just as much luck if I'd pulled up the cloche to reveal a steaming turd. Not that Stuart ate at home, ever. It had been part of the pitch in the Tuscan town.
'I'll be at home more. These hedge fund hours are killing us. Me, you and the boys round the dinner table every night like a proper family.'
It was one of the least appealing things he'd ever said to me. It didn't happen, of course it didn't. He tried it for a month or so, a visible effort, a show of willing. Back to the nearest and dearest instead of a late night meeting, dinner at the club, drinks at the hotel. I didn't want that to change and deep down I'm not sure he knew how else to live. The City was like an extension of school for Stuart. A sixth form continuum. The idiots had aged, if not grown. The club as the new common room. He couldn't function in the world he thought he wanted to and I for one was ecstatic. He swapped the hedge fund for a start-up and nothing changed, just this time he was on the other side of the fence. We were bankrolled to the arsehole by his old hedge fund Henrys. If it kept him out of my hair, I

was all for it.

And so it's turned out that chicken livers and cognac are not the optimal diet for a healthy heart. Who knew? Schadenfreude aside, I wasn't mentally prepared for the two men I'd loved, once, to die in hospital beds at the opposite end of the M4 on the very same day. Luke was a hundred miles away, but for now, there was Stuart.

'You'd better hope this doesn't get out, we're meant to be selling low-fat ice cream.' I handed him a glass of water and he gurned like a prefect caught with his hand in the tuck shop till.

'Although saying that, it is out there. Dee, ever the opportunist, assured me you've gone viral.'

'Viral?' he replied weakly.

'Dee, not the doctors. You're an internet sensation, darling.'

'I am?'

'You are.'

And with that, he burst into tears. Wonderful.

'Come on darling, it's alright.'

'Am I dying?'

'We're all dying, darling.'

He burst out again.

'You're fine, you're fine, or at least you're going to be fine. You've just been overdoing it. Rest and recoup are your two new gods, you hear me?'

Florence Nightingale, eat your heart out.

'I'm sorry, darling. I'm sorry,' he whimpered, 'I've let you down. And the boys. The boys.' And the tears came again.

The doctors wanted to keep Stuart in for a few days for observation. A cardiac arrest, however minor, was rather rare in a 37 year old man and while he was recovering as expected, he wouldn't be giving any keynote speeches any time in the foreseeable. He'd baulk at the bill but I'd remind him of his father's maxim that vulgar people knew the price of everything and the value of nothing. He'd like that, even if I was certain the old goat used to look at me when he said it.

At least now I could concentrate on Luke. I couldn't very well go and visit him, not after the doorstop from the police, not least needing to be at Stuart's side, so I'd taken a room at a chain hotel close to the hospital. Needs must. It felt strangely liberating to fade into grey at a three-star. All I needed was a steady WiFi connection and the game of Cluedo could begin. Somehow I didn't think this game would be as easy as the victories of my childhood. Mother was father's third wife, a blond bombshell 35 years younger with one eye on an inheritance and her other on the tennis coach. Or dad, as my youngest brother calls him. Father was 67 by the time I was born, his 8th child and deal-sealer with my mother. After long and distinguished careers in the military and industry, he'd spent my teenage years convinced he was Henry VIII. That should have been a warning to my mother, but she carried on her affairs in plain sight regardless. Some things are hereditary I suppose. With a distracted mother, a demented father and a chorus line of half-brothers and half-sisters too old or young to care, I made it through my adolescence unnoticed and unbeaten in the games room. But today, the option of peeking in the black envelope for the answer was off the table.

The phone rang.
'Sadie?'
'Who's calling?'
'You've hurt my feelings, I thought you'd have committed my dulcet tones to memory by now.'
It was him. That god awful policeman.
'What can I do for you, Officer...Grimes, was it?'
'Very good. Think not what you can do for your

country but what your country can do for you,' he almost shouted.

'I'm sorry. I've not got time for this shit-'

'Swearing at a police officer. Tut, tut. I'll let you off for that, that at least...'

What did he know? He was toying with me. I was the toyer, not a man. Not this man.

'However could I repay you, officer? My best sarcastic voice.

'Well, there is something...'

'Anything.'

'How is Mr Winchester doing?'

'He's fine, thank you.'

Fuck. What did he want with Stuart?

'Well, that's the best news I've heard all day. I'd like to-'

'He's still recovering. The doctors say he's not to be put in stressful situations.'

'Did they now? I wish the doctors would say the same about me. Try as I might, I just can't help finding myself in them.'

'Comes with the territory, I suppose,' I said.

He sighed, like what I'd said had hit a nerve.

'Indeed, Mrs Winchester, only too well. Well, when he does perk up then, that husband of yours, you'll be sure to let me know won't you?'

'I'll be sure to.'

'Maybe feed him one of those fancy ice creams of yours, that ought to do it. Toodle-o.'

'But what about-'

He'd gone.

But what about Luke?

I opened the door to the minibar and surveyed the contents. Chardonnay or Shiraz. I was officially a basic bitch. I reached for both and flopped down on the bed. Dee had strict instructions to hold all calls until further notice but had ignored my order, instead texting me like an excited puppy with opposable thumbs every time an interview request came through for Stuart.

'It's the FT now. Stuart is going to be their 'Person in the News'. They've commissioned a cartoonist to draw him' and a million emojis. *Saturday Kitchen* had already given him an open invite to come into the studio for casual food-based banter. There was a reality TV show winner who'd spent six weeks eating crocodile testes in the jungle who demanded Mooments' Banana Drama as her first meal back in civilisation and was coming on the show in three weeks and wouldn't it be super if Stuart was ready for that?

That could wait.

The boys were staying with Stuart's sister. Not one of his ruddy-faced relations had bothered to come and visit him, a combination of my 'he's fine' fire-fighting and a family sailing trip this weekend, which frankly the twins were welcome to. Thank God, the last thing I needed now was their presence, turning a shit show into a sewage tanker.

I smelt the miniatures, decided the Shiraz was the lesser of two evils and drank direct from the bottle. I took my laptop out and searched for an answer. Luke's last few stories had been for a news site called The Lamplight, who, their Twitter biog assured me, now had more subscribers than all the national newspapers combined. The lead story on Luke's profile on the site was an investigation into the private school system. Anonymous sources were on the record as claiming parents were paying schools to spoil exam papers if a pre-submission assessment indicated the exam board wouldn't give the mark mummy and daddy desired. It hardly seemed like news to me, but it had caused quite the storm in the echo chamber. Shared 21,000 times. 972 comments. 'This is just the start of it' being the general consensus. Yawn. The story had been posted six weeks ago. Hardly a prolific output. But then the first tweet had said he'd been working on the biggest story of his life. Perhaps this explained the radio silence.

Their latest tweet was about Luke. They were offering a reward of £10,000 for anyone who had information about his accident. The next hour was lost in an online pilgrimage throughout Luke's life. His photographs from holidays, work trips, family occasions. Those green eyes. That smile. Unsure then surer throughout the years. It wasn't lost on me how mine had taken that journey in reverse. I searched his name in my Facebook messages and was presented with a life unlived, the vital sentence always left unsaid, the tip of the tongue not typed. A chronology of 'hope you're wells', 'love to the kids', 'you look healthy', 'loved your latest story'. Samuel Pepys eat your heart out. A notification pinged in the top right corner.

'Message requests (17).'

I clicked the link and was taken to a previously unseen inbox, a collection of messages from African princes, persecuted first ladies and breast augmentation clinics. One of the messages didn't fit the formula. I opened it and took a gulp of the wine. It was from a H. Aitch. The profile picture was an X marked in the sand of a beach I could have sworn was in the Caymans.

'Dear Sadie. It's Hamish. Insert usual pleasantries here. Could you send me the details for that journalist you know? Luke something was it?? Forever grateful, H. PS Oh, and don't mention this to Stuart will you? Our little secret (to go with the others!)'

I clawed the top off the chardonnay and dreamed

of room service. Why the hell did Hamish want Luke's details?

Hamish hadn't been like the other men at the hedge fund. There was the most obvious distinction, his sexuality ('but hadn't they all been gay in boarding school?' he'd say) and in the boorish world of the City that did leave Hamish a little on the edges. He'd been glad to be there, and I was too. We became each other's wingman at the fund's frequent social events, Hamish not daring to bring a partner ('half to keep them guessing') and me preferring to stick a hot spatula up myself than chat holiday homes and birth plans with the assorted wives and girlfriends of Stuart's equally adolescent colleagues. We'd wait for the drinking games or Etonian songs to start, and Hamish and I would slip into a smoking room and talk into the early hours. We existed together only in those spaces, the twice yearly events which I'm convinced we only continued turning up at because of each other. I knew nothing of his life outside those occasions and vice versa, although I'm sure mine wasn't hard to guess. Hamish cared about high culture, politics, the things I had burned so brightly for in my former life. Unlike Stuart and the rest of them, the money hadn't made Hamish happy. I'd ask him every time when he was going to get out but he'd only laugh, snort, 'the world's rotten to the core Sadie, darling. It's the least I can do to join in the game'.

I'd told him, one time, Stuart paralytic post-hunt, laid out in the adjoining room, that he'd reminded me of Luke. It was the conversation. The fire. The caring about what I cared about. I leaned across the chaise lounge to kiss him, and he let me, before patting my head and bursting out with laughter. I followed suit, the only thing that could save the tears from falling in that whole sorry situation.

'Dear God, darling, I hadn't realised it was that

bad.'

I'd not thought of Hamish in years. Why did he want to get in touch with Luke? He didn't think Luke, was, well, you know I did say he reminded me of him. But why the secretive profile? He always was an outsider.

'Why would the world want to see what I've had for breakfast?'

No, that couldn't be it. It didn't add up. His message was two months old now but I responded anyway, asking why and linking him to the story about Luke's accident. What I'd give for a drink with Hamish now.

My phone beeped.

It was Dee.

'The tweet about Stuart has had 50k shares and 250k likes. VIRAL!'

At least Dee was happy. I logged into the Mooments Twitter account and watched the notifications roll in, the numbers moving liking a charity telethon.

'Luke Harris has liked your tweet.'

Luke? Luke?

I opened the direct messaging and typed as quickly as I could.

'Luke? Is that you?'

What was I thinking? The police would be monitoring his account and Dee ours and of course it wasn't Luke. He was knocked out cold in a coma in Cardiff.

'Seen 14.42'

Someone had read the message.

My heart nearly jumped out of its cage.

'Typing...typing...'

Ysabelle

'Hey chica, vamos, let's get the hack and get back to the game. You're halfway across the road.'

My hearing was regularly selective around Bruce. It had to be. You'd need the energy of a marathon runner to keep up with him. But en este momento, everything around me was just a buzz in the background. The story said that Luke- was he 36 now? -was involved in a hit and run in Cardiff three days ago. So he made it back to Wales? Madre would be happy with that at least. I'd represented the family of a barrio chico knocked down by a dealer's car two years back. He'd been trying to fish his fútbol from under the chassis of the BMW when the driver had drove over the kid's balls. And I don't mean his fútbol.

We never caught him. The kid had been too clever to rat on the number plate. His familia had received a stash of rolled-up pesos through the door the day we dropped the investigation. The chico's madre presented me with a bottle of vino tinto and muchas gracias for all my help. Not every result was achieved through conventional means in Buenos Aires. I could only hope things were different in the UK.

'Chica, that's spooky, no? This poor chulo's been mowed over, just like you're about to be in my game.'

The loco laugh broke my bubble.

'You would have got on well with my abuela. She dealt in coincidences like that.' I scrolled through the story, too quickly at first, my finger still not yet used to the brand new mouse. It was much slicker than my ancient laptop.

'Give it to the master,' Bruce said, his hand reaching to grab the controls from mine. I gave him the look I reserved for stopping barrio boys in their tracks. I'd borrowed it direct from abuela, her piercing pink stare chilling enough to make the hands stop still. The story said that Luke was a journalist. I'd wondered what he would become, resisting the urge to search him out, the shadows I saw on his soul too stark a reminder of Che. Who would he be by now? He'd be in his 30s now, married maybe, a padre, madre fussing over her nietos, her grandkids, still cursing me for betraying nature. The reason this innocuous story was being hotly debated online was what had happened next. A tweet had been sent from beyond the coma. He'd been working on his biggest ever story.

The accidente was no accidente. He'd been targeted deliberately.

'Maybe he's discovered President Trump is an alien,' Bruce said, 'no, no, maybe he's discovered President Trump is a human.' He looked to me for approval.

'Chica, what's up?' I scrolled back to the top.

'It's okay if you didn't like the game. I made it for you but it's okay,' his dark eyes welled up a little, 'but why do we have to spend all afternoon reading about this poor chulo?'

I took my hand off the mouse and turned to Bruce, six inches away from my right hand side.

'Because I knew this poor chulo. Because I knew this was going to happen.'

The door to the room opened and a group of four men shuffled in, following Señor Garcia. He was the head of the centre and well-meaning enough, but he had to play the game.

'This is our, actually, I should say your brand new state-of-the-art computer room.' The men did their best attempt at humility, which for men like this, rich, gordo, dressed in three piece suits worth three months of life in

La Boca, wasn't very humble at all.

'And this is Ysabelle, one of our very best, one of Buenos Aires' very best abrigados.' I turned and smiled, because it was my job to.

'Ysabelle and the other abrigados make excellent use of the new facilities we're so grateful to you for, teaching the young people administrative skills that will help make them workplace ready,' Señor Garcia said.

'That's exactly what we're doing now,' Bruce said. It was hard to know if he meant it, whether he thought we actually were or that was what they wanted to hear. I didn't bother to close the screen down.

'And this is Carlos.'

'It's Bruce, actually,' he butted in.

'Like El Jefe,' Señor Garcia said, the men laughing.

'He's one of our most talented computer scientists, aren't you Bruce?'

'The most talented computer scientist,' Bruce said. Humility obviously wasn't the order of the day.

'If our IT department ever needs a new technician, we know where to come,' said the oldest and fattest of the men, his head borrowed from a warthog.

'Ah, you couldn't afford me,' Bruce said, and the men laughed again, nervously now, and Señor Garcia led them out of the door.

'Those guys are douchebags.'

'Douchebags who paid for all of this,' I told him. Our eyes turned back to the screen. A picture of Luke clearly taken from his Facebook profile, the backdrop of a Middle Eastern country, his face excited, staring back.

'You put a spell on this poor chulo then?' Bruce said.

'No Bruce, I'm not a witch.'

I told Bruce the story. How this gringo had appeared in my bar one day. How he'd looked like the weight of El Mundo was on his shoulders. How he'd met my madre, and they'd talked Tom Jones. ('Tom who?' Bruce asked.) How he'd fallen asleep in my arms and I could feel the shadows creeping over his soul.

'That's some spooky shit, chica.'

'That's one way of putting it.'

'So what do we do next? We've got to find the chulo. We've got to find who did this to him.' And six thousand miles away from where the British boy I knew for just a short time all those years ago lay, I agreed that we did. For some reason I'd known something bad was going to happen to this man. My abuela always told me not to interfere with the spirits but somehow I had to stop it getting worse.

'Come on chica, this is serious. With your detective skills and my brilliance, we can crack this case wide open.'

'I think you've been watching too much satellite,' I told him. He was grinning like a gato about to get a treat. I couldn't share his enthusiasm.

'Vamos, let's look at what we know.'

I scrolled back to the top of the story and we read again.

'Who's this guy?' Bruce asked, 'Graves. The name doesn't fill you with confidence.'

'Bruce, stop it.'

'But the other way of looking at it is that graves are big business in Argentina.' It took me a second but I got what he meant. Recoleta Cemetary was one of Buenos Aires' most visited spots. Most of the tourists who came through the city spent at least half a day getting lost among the rows and rows of marble mausoleums. The joke always went that the dead did better in Recoleta than the living did in La Boca.

I'd taken him there, Luke. I'd been a hundred times before, the school trip year after year, but I let him navigate his way to Evita's grave, feeling alive, hot kisses in the shade, the taste of salt on his lips, trying to ignore the feeling of inevitability. And now it was here. He'd been pushed to the back of my consciousness over the decade that followed, my daily brain dealing with study, with madre, with the space left by Che. And now Bruce and the boys like him, the boys who deserved better. But he hadn't gone away.

'You can't send the spirits back,' abuela told me, 'they have more power than you can know.'

Detective Inspector Charles Graves had been quoted in the story, the headline screaming out from the WalesOnline website. He didn't say much. The usual police tricks of putting words in a sentence and arriving at no meaning. They were asking the public for information. They would welcome any leads. Policing in the 21st Century regularly threw up new situations and this was one of them. No shit, Sherlock. I'd learned that one from Luke.

'So what do we know about this guy, Graves?' Bruce asked.

'He's not giving much away, is he?' I said.

'Typical rati,' Bruce said, wheeling his chair over to the next screen and logging in, 'we'll find out just who D.S. Charles Graves is right now.'

'Why don't you look for clues on the victim?' Bruce said.

'Si, señor.'

It was already clear who was Sherlock and who was Doctor Watson. I typed 'Luke Harris' into the search bar and pressed enter. The majority of the results were for a fútbol star who'd recently transferred to a big club and had been spotted vaping by the paparazzi on a huge yacht moored up in Monte Carlo. There was also a Luke Harris, CEO at a frozen food company, a recent article saying they'd committed to only using sustainable fishing methods. I'm sure Luke would approve but these were irrelevant to the current task. Perhaps I was no good as a researcher. Aside from the most recent story, it wasn't until the second page that the right Luke appeared, first a story about corruption in British schools, then a week before, an opinion piece on the financial industry and how the City of London seemed to play by its own moral code. The essay contained much hyperbole and speculation but little in the way of facts or supporting evidence. Perhaps that was the big story he was working on now? Who knows, it could be anything I supposed. The Lamplight seemed not to discriminate in the stories they covered. There were sections on topics as diverse as UK social policy to world affairs, the stock market to sports. Maybe he was on the tail of his footballer namesake and the club's Russian oligarch owner had him shot.

'It's ringing,' Bruce said, 'here, through the computer, put the headset on.'

'Ringing who?' I said. What the hell was this loco kid up to.

'The police station...so we can speak to that rati D.S. Charles Graves. You'll have to do it though, your English is, how do you say, more proper like Queen Diana than mine.'

'Bruce!'

He put the headset over my head, my hair tied up in a bun causing the microphone to miss my mouth at first. I shot him my abuela's look but he didn't see. He was in la zona.

'It's ringing, it's ringing!'
'What do I say?'
'I hope they treat the case better than their telephone service. It's been ringing for a minute now.'
'What do I say?' He was ignoring me, not hearing

me.

'I don't know, you're the real detective. I'm just in training.'

'Bruce!'

'Ask him to speak to the D.S. Charles and see where it takes us.'

'Good morning, Cardiff Central Police Station.'

'Oh, buenos, good morning.'

'Yes, how can I help?'

'I, I, would like to speak to a Mr D.S. Charles Graves, please.'

'Wouldn't we all?' the voice said back to me.

'Pardon?'

'D.S. Graves isn't available at the present. Can somebody else help you, madam?'

'I, no se, I don't think so.' Why was I slipping into Spanish now, at this crucial moment?

'Well, would you like to leave a message?'

'I, I, yes, I would.'

'Let me get a pen. First call of the day.' The line went quiet as the man on the other end rustled around. I put my hand over the mouthpiece.

'What should I say?'

'Tell them you know something.'

'I don't.'

'That you knew something was going to happen.' His stick thin arms cut through the air around him.

'Right then madam. Go on...'

'Sorry?'

'Your message.'

'Ah, yes.' I cleared my throat, just like I did when I was addressing the judge in the courtroom.

'This is Ysabelle Vazquez calling from Buenos Aires in Argentina and I'd like to request that D.S. Charles Graves calls me back so I can tell him what I know about the case.'

'You and every other crank in Cardiff,' the policeman said.

'It's true. I knew this was going to happen. I knew Luke was going to be run over.' The line cut dead.

'Brillante!' said Bruce, 'brillante!'.

I'd come out in a sweat not expected by the expensive new air conditioning system.

'What did you do?' I said.

'I hung up.'

'Por qué?!'

His eyes came alive.

'It's so much more suspenseful.' Bruce rocked back and forth on his chair. 'Now let's see if D.S. Charles Graves can find us.' And with that, the lights turned out in the room.

'Vamos you two, it's home time.'

Nina

It was the third time I'd been to the restaurant this year. To be honest, I didn't really have a clue what Spanish people ate before that, was half expecting the menu to be variations on something and chips like it was when mam took me and Jase to Costa Blanca the summer after we got married.

'It's picky bits,' that's what Karen said the afternoon of the first time I went. We were out for dinner ('lunch' she calls it) and I said I didn't fancy scampi as I'd probably have that tonight.

'Picky bits.' Not that I'm sure they were ideal for a first date. The twice before I'd held back, trying to be all ladylike, letting him have the odd prawn. Both times I'd stopped the taxi outside the Chinese on the way home, wishing that's what I'd done in the first place. Why I was here tonight, Lord only knows. Why I went on any of these dates, Lord only knows. I spose I was looking for a bit of excitement really, someone to sweep me off my tootsies and show me a good time. Show me the high life. It had happened, once or twice. The usual sketch from a fella desperate to get a leg over. It generally only lasted until you'd let him. But why I was here tonight was more of a mystery. They'd kept me in the hospital for a few hours' observation, the doctor, young enough to be my boy, asking if I felt up to walking and why I was at the hospital in the first place. Was I visiting a friend or relative they wanted me to inform? No, ta, I'd told him. Since then, I've been stuck like glue to the story about Luke. It's been online mainly, social media, I could kill half the people on the comments sections, making a joke out of what Luke's going through. What we're going through, really. That's the problem with the internet, always some clever dick ready to get a quick laugh at someone else's expense.

Work have been good. When is he not? He's given me a couple of days off. R and R.

'Get your head straight, Neen.' And he don't know a peep about what's really going on.

'Would you like to see the wine list, madam?'

'Er, no, yes, can I just have half a cider? Leave the list here though.' So I could gawp at names I'd never heard of. They never had Jacob's Creek at these places did they?

'Would you like the Andaluscian first harvest or the San Sebastian vintage?'

'Strongbow?' I said.

'Sorry, madam, it's the Andalucian first harvest or the San Sebastian vintage.' And he didn't even look Spanish. Looked like he was from Newport.

'Roll the dice, see where it lands,' I said. I'd had my usual two drink pick-me-up at home, large glasses as you'd expect. You never knew if the fella would be there waiting first, all keen bean and ready to ask you your life story. They wished they never asked when I was sat opposite them. I needed the drink to get me through the stares in the restaurants. A lady of my age sat on her own, the clock ticking. Half the tables taking bets on whether or not he'd turn up at all. He did, this time, but not before I'd had another half of that posh cider. Had a good mind to make it a pint. Apples is apples, after all. I knew it was him as soon as he'd bowled in. A big fella he was, that I didn't mind, most of them knew what to do with it, where to turn the weight to pressure at just the right time. Well, some of them at least. Generally you're left guessing when the door goes, paying more mind than the maytra d, wondering if the weed that just walked in was the adonis the picture promised. This one though, there were no surprises. An accurate likeness. The Ronseal approach. If anything, he looked better in person, up close. His beard had grown fuller than the shop porch chic of his profile. His eyes I couldn't fathom. They were kind at times, all grey and wishy washy, but when things turned, they looked like they belonged sunk back in the head of a thousand year old man, like they'd seen it all and known it all before it even happened.

'Sorry I'm late,' he said, looking like he meant it.
'It's alright, I'm used to it.' He laughed at that.
'Regular at this social club then, are we?'
'Fully paid up,' I told him.
'Me too, same here,' he raised his glass and realised there was no booze in it. Looked like it wasn't his first of the night either.
'Here's to meeting a kindred spirit,' he said.
'I wouldn't be so sure,' I said. Guard up, girl. I hadn't sussed him out yet and it bothered me. The waiter returned.
'This any good?' he said, tapping my glass with his fat finger.
'Aye. If you like that sort of thing.'
'I can almost guarantee that I do.'
'Two of these please, garcon. Hang on, that's French isn't it? Umm..'
'Caña or grande?' the waiter asked.
'Whatever the big one is, we're celebrating,' he said.
'But I've not finished this one yet,' I said.
'Here to help.' The waiter shuffled off.
'Camerero!' he shouted in his wake, 'that's it.' Who the hell was this fella? And what was I doing with him, dolled up on a Thursday night when I could be tucked up with Jean Claude. Still, I was intrigued. I'll give him that.
'So what we celebrating then?' I asked him.
'Oh, I don't know,' he said, gulping his pint, 'life?'
'Ha. Fat chance,' I said, 'it's not been a good week in my life.'

'Okay, well I'm sorry to hear that, I really am. When you've- and I hope you don't mind me saying this- been around as long as we have-'

'You cheeky get-'

'-you'll have learned by now there's good weeks and there's bad weeks.' He was enjoying this. He was right and all.

'How about Thursday then?' he said.

'How'd you mean?'

'Our cause for celebration?'

'I'll drink to that.' He clinked my glass and the cider bubbles burst over the top of the glass. Instinct made me reach and suck them up.

'That's the spirit,' he said. The bubbles went up the wrong tube, sent me spluttering for air like a fifty a dayer.

'I nearly sneezed up apples then.'

'Now that's a talent.'

'Anyway,' I said, 'are you going to give me an explanation for leaving a lady waiting here 25 minutes?' Half an hour and I was off. That was my rule. I'd only ever had to use it twice. In the same pub and all. Wondered sometimes what might happen if I'd stayed. If they'd have turned up and blown me away. If he'd been a doctor who'd stopped for an emergency on his way. Wondered where I'd be now. Probably still sat in that bleeding pub, nursing a half and hoping no-one familiar walks in. Wondering and wishing got me nowhere with Luke, did it?

'Is it a cliche to say it was work?' he said.

'Depends what you been doing. Healing the sick?'

'And feeding the poor,' he said, laughing. His face had more lines than an ordnance survey.

'So what have you really been doing then?' I said. It was the bog standard small talk that started most of these dates. Half expected the voice of our Graham to come over a tannoy system and explain their particulars.

She loved that programme, mam, always said Cilla should have been Queen instead of Liz. Had more in common with people like us.

Some of them said what they did on their profile. I did. I was proud of where I'd got to in life. The estate agents was a proper job, a real career. Making people's hopes and dreams come true. I didn't need a scrounger or skiver bringing me down right now. Not now. Not with my Luke laying in a hospital bed.

'I'm an astronaut,' he said, 'it's a right pain in the arse getting back to Cardiff from the International Space Station at this time of night.'

'And you're a comedian too, I see.' At least he made me laugh. Lord knows, I needed it.

'Come on clever dick. What's the real story?' He looked at me with those big grey eyes and there and then, I felt like I knew him from somewhere. They'd looked through me before those eyes.

'Let's just say I'm a public servant,' he said, 'and I've got a spring back in my step.' He winked at me, picked his pint up and sank the cider.

'Camerero!' He was good company, took my mind off things. I suppose that's all I was looking for. A reason not to think about Luke. I spent the best part of my life being the girl who things just happened to. A proper walkover. But I'd been trying with every ounce I had, less than there used to be thank you- to take back control. To be the honey making money, my best karaoke song, that one. The current situation left me powerless. I could just as well pick up the lucky numbers or ban the bombs as I could bring Luke back to life. To find out who did it to him, that's what I'd really like. To tie the toerags up by their toenails and feed their faces to the rats. That's all they were good for.

'What do you fancy then?' he asked. 'And you don't

have to say me.'

'Well, ain't that a stroke of luck.'

'Could be, could be,' he said, sipping at this pint, more gentlemanly now.

'We could ask that waiter for his recommendations but I think the closest he's been to Spain is watching Real Madrid on Sky TV. How about I order us one of each and we'll see how we get on?'

'Deal.' And we did get on. He had no pretension about him, like a lot of the fellas did, thinking they're someone they're not, someone you don't need them to be. He wasn't all there though. Wasn't giving everything away. But then, was I?

I asked him the awkward question, I don't know why. More to test him really. See if he had a wife and two kids tucked up in a big house in Lisvane and was playing at being a weeknight warrior.

'No, there's no-one around, no-one who's got the time to talk to me anyway.' Should have been a warning sign I guess, but me of all people knows what families are like.

'What's for dessert?' The oldest line in the book but it did the trick. I knew it was going to happen. I'd given into the situation. His charm. The cider helped. We'd been after the same thing. At least I thought we were. Women's intuition. He paid the bill. I'm all for equality, but if you can't be treated like a lady on the first date what hope is there? We walked down the street, not hand in hand, but close enough so I could feel his heat. It was raining, when ain't it, and the stadium opposite sparkled like a lucky bitch's jewellery box.

'Do you fancy one in here?' he said, nodding his head towards The City Arms and before I knew it, fast as a ferret, he was on me, up against the wall, hands everywhere, tongues, the lot.

'Behave yourself, we ain't teenagers,' I told him.

'Is that so?' he said and came in again.

'Okay, Casanova, hold your horses. What about that one you promised?'

The drink was a game, him waiting for it to end, setting the pace, hand on my thigh, me cooling off, little sips, crossing my legs. This was absolute power, if only for a short time.

His place was on Cathedral Road, only about a quarter an hour walk from the pub but I was in heels and he was in heat so we got a taxi. The rule was I never took them back to mine. Wasn't a wise move for them to know where you lived, just in case. Just in most cases as it goes. My place was my place. Course it was small but it was mine, even if the boss did help with the deposit. He'd come in one day, all puffed up like a peacock.

'I've got it, Neen. I've got just the place.' The seller was a young girl, late 20s, early 30s (even though I didn't feel young at that age), looking to shift her flat. She spent all her time at her fella's and was about to burst so was selling up. He drove me to Roath, there's where the flat is, and wouldn't say a word about it.

'Wait til you see it, Neen.' The other places I'd lived had always felt like someone else's- Jase's, mam's, Bri's, but this was mine. Nina's place. Nina's rules.

'If you want it, it's yours, Neen. We won't even put a board up outside. Tell you what, you can even have the commission for the sale.'

'But I'll never get a mortgage. My credit's shot to bits.'

'Leave it with me, Dave could get a dog a fixed rate. He's a bloody magician, that lad.'

I suppose he might have thought it'd be our little love shack, but the truth is he's been in once since he helped me get settled and that was to fix the toilet. I pays him back out of my wages each month, not enough to notice. He's a good man and it's not often I've been able to say that in my life.

'Bollocks.'
'What's up?'
'I've left the bloody buzzer in work,' he said. He pressed a button and a voice came over an intercom. The houses on Cathedral Road were like something out of Little Women. Huge three storey Georgian terraces. You could close your eyes and imagine yourself a hundred years ago, an important lady with important places to go and people to wait on you hand, foot and finger. I'd done it once, last year, we'd had one on the books from some bigwig TV fella who worked at the BBC up the road. I'd only managed the one night there. On my own before you get any ideas. I didn't need anyone else, just me and my imagination.

The door opened and we got let in, an old fella in a uniform coming into the hall, leaving in a hurry when he clocked what was going on.
'Regular occurrence this is it?' I said.
'Far from it,' he said, 'never been kissed, me.' And with that the stupid fool tried to pick me up on the stairs. Managed it too, but he wasn't half out of puff by the top.
'Bit much for you that was it?'
'I'd say I've carried heavier girls up the stairs but you'd get the wrong impression.'
'You might just be the cheekiest fella I ever met.' He wasn't by half, but now wasn't the time for the truth and nothing but. His flat, apartments we had to call them now ('puts 20% on the asking, Neen') was smaller than mine and just as well kept. Surprised me that.

'Where's all your gear?' I asked him.

'I'll be showing you that very soon,' he said.

'Give over, I meant your belongings. Not much here is there?' It had all the hallmarks of a fella kicked out by the missus, marking his time in a let until she saw sense or couldn't cover the rates. I told him as much.

'Sorry Sherlock, you got me wrong. I've not lived with the ex for eight years, four months and, oo, let me see, 271 days now.'

'Not that you're counting?'

'Not that I'm counting. A man doesn't need much to get by. I'm opting out of this age of consumerism. Took my stuff away and set a match to it. Never been happier. Anyway, enough about me. Drink?'

It was the perfect flat for an estate agent to flog. Blank walls, neutral furniture, wooden floors.

'It's easier for the buyer to project themselves there if they don't have to decorate in their dreams,' the boss told us. The only distinguishing feature, or personal effect, was a framed photo. Red haired girl in cap and gown.

'Who's this then?'

'Ah, that's the daughter,' he said, handing me a vase of wine, 'the one without the time to talk to me.' I swear I'd seen her before. Maybe it was the eyes, same as his. You sees a lot of people every day in my line of work.

'She seems familiar.' I sipped the wine, not that I needed it. Not bad.

'She's on telly sometimes,' he said.

'I knew it. Actress is she?'

'No, no, well she can be. My little girl is head of communication at the Dunamis Corporation. You've probably seen her on the news, although she's grown up a bit from this one.'

The sex was better than usual. Some of these chumps needed a bloody YouTube video to find their way around a woman, but this one, he knew what he was doing well enough. The rest of it's a bit of a blur now, too much wine, too much everything, my clothes dropped all over the tiny flat, the only sign of life. Luke was lying in a bed just a few miles away but I needed this. Craved a blow-out. Got my blow-out. It was the next morning it came to me, the booze brain gone, the hangover yet to pounce. He poked his head through the door of the bedroom, whistling and chirpy.

'How do you like your eggs?' I sat up against the headboard.

'I know you.'

'I should hope so,' he said, laughing.

'I mean, I know you from before,' I said.

'Like a past life?' he said, 'I'm not sure I can cope with this one.'

'You're the copper who put my Jase away.'

'Am I?'

'You are, yes, you are. I can see you now, sat in my front room...'

'It does sound like something I'd do,' he said.

'I knew it.'

'Now how'd you want those eggs?'

They already had Jase when he came round. On his own he was, said his usual partner wasn't with him today. Said there was no use in kicking up a fuss about it. Said they knew everything so might as well make it as pleasant as possible so why didn't I put the kettle on? I thought about gobbing in his tea, only for a second. I knew deep down that Jase was the real bastard here, not this fella. Mam was on a day trip to Weston-Super-Mare with the pensioners, thank God. It'd have been too much for her, all this. Too much at her age. She always said Jase was trouble. I took him his tea.

'So, we can do this one of two ways. The first way is I can ask you a few questions, you can tell me the answers and I can be on my way after I've found what I'm looking for. The second way is I come back with a warrant-'

'You haven't got a warrant?'

'-which would mean a team of coppers in full uniform pulling up outside, sirens on, before turning your little home upside down.'

'Now which is it to be? You look like a clever girl now.; He gave me a wink, pure patronising. 'It's number one isn't it?'

'I suppose it is.'

'Good,' he slurped his tea. I still remember it now, that noise. He latched onto me with those grey eyes.

'Did your Jase say anything about coming across a job lot of microphones?' I weighed him up.

'No.'

'Now there's no use keeping it from me. Remember what number two's like. Nee-naw, nee-naw.' Mam couldn't cope with that.

'He said he got them in the pub, was gonna flog them in the market next Sunday.'

'Good.'

'Is that what this is all about?' I said.

'In a roundabout way, yes, yes, I guess it is.'

Charlie

'It's boiled. Regular or decaf?'

'Do you have to ask?' I'd filled Ted in on some minor details, enough to explain why I was in his garden, phone in hand, mouth wide open.

'Here you are.'

'Thanks.'

'Nice pyjamas by the way.'

'Oh, these are-' I cut myself off. I was wearing my fucking PJs, '-loungewear, Ted. I didn't think you'd be in.'

'You don't have to stand on ceremony for me.' I drank up, spinning the cup in my hand to spread the warmth, the Thornberry School for Young Ladies insignia on one side, the Dunamis Foundation on the other, turning until they became one.

'So what are you going to do?' Ted asked.

'Drink this coffee,' I said.

'I'd hope so,' he said, 'but after that?'

I didn't know. Ten years ago, the answer would have spoken itself. A song pouring out on the paper, my thoughts collecting in a verse-chorus-verse. Not now. Not for a long time.

'Get changed?' I said.

'Oh, I don't know. That's quite the look. Imagine it'd earn us bonus points at the owner's inspection tomorrow, assuming they're Charlie Ray fans.'

'And who isn't?' I said, before 'umm, owner's inspection? What's that?'

'This coming as a surprise, I take it?' Ted wore one of his smug looks, rarely seen outside the confines of Scrabble night. 'We've been prepping in the modern language department for a month.'

'Oh.' The music department was more laissez faire.

'Those city boys need to make sure we're still a sound investment. Standard stuff really.' Just what I fucking needed. I'd have to pull out the Forever Wrong lesson plan. If you could call it that. Cross fingers. Close eyes. Hope for the best.

'Did he mean a lot to you?' I was too busy looking through the blank walls for an answer to hear Ted.

'Remind me of his name?' I snapped out of it and shot him a look.

'Sorry,' he said, 'head swimming with jumbled up letters.'

'What?'

'Pernicious. P-E-R-N-I-C-I-O-U-S. Pernicious. Tilly was in bits.'

'Right.'

'I'm sorry. I can see this has shaken you up.'

'Luke. L-U-K-E. Luke. That was his name,' I corrected myself, 'is his name.'

'If he can write a gospel, then he can recover from a bump from a dickhead in a motor car. Anyway, I'm in your way and I'm talking nonsense. I'll head off to HQ to prep for tomorrow. Make yourself at home. There's hobnobs in the tin. Toodle-o.'

He kissed my head and left. So much for not staying at Ted's. The walk of shame in reverse. I got up to swill my cup, catching a glimpse of myself in the window above the sink. Moomin pyjamas. If the paps could see me now. Get the fuck home, Charlie Ray. Hop, skip and stoop through the fence. Run the bath. Pour the wine. Don't check the clock to see if this is acceptable.

It was the telephone which saved me from drowning. Ring ring through the rinse. I'd sailed away to the subconscious. A showreel of life with Luke. It was a mystery what the memory retained. Real life couldn't be condensed into a Hollywood trailer. There was no gravelly voiceover. No tension building tone. No kiss or clinch. No first 'I love you'. Those all happened, of course. Off course. A collage of inconsequentials. A Sunday snooze in front of a re-run. The comfortable silence on a drive to his parents. An argument in Ikea over a coffee frother we didn't need. Ring ring. I pulled the plug. Wet footsteps across the corridor, nearly breaking my neck on the parquet floor.

'Hello.'

'Oh, hello. Sorry to call on a Sunday. You don't know me, but-'

'-Luke. Is this about Luke?' It was a female voice. Young enough, reassuring, confident. His doctor?

'I'm sorry, but I think we've got crossed wires. My name is Melody Jackson. I'm the head of comms for the Dunamis Foundation.'

'Okay.'

'And you're Charlie Ray, I'm hoping. This was the number Mr Pickles passed on.'

'Yes, that's me,' I said, the receiver resting on my shoulder, pulling the towel tighter.

'Very good. Now, I'm sorry to bother you on a Sunday-'

'-it's fine.' She didn't sound sorry.

'-but as I'm sure you know, we'll be at the school tomorrow for the inspection and, well, it's fair to say it was a bit of a coup to have a star such as yourself join an Dunamis school and, so, I suppose, now you've had a chance to, shall we say, bed in, that it's the perfect time to capitalise on your strategic appointment through a media moment.'

'A media moment?'

'Well, yes, in this 24/7 era, you could say the media's full of moments, too many perhaps, but what I, we, mean here is a broadcast opportunity, a little set up to show off the good work you've been doing with the girls.' I heard her clear her throat down the line. 'Without being presumptuous about the results of the inspection, everyone here is aware of the outstanding difference you're making.'

'Are they?'

'Very much so.'

'And we'd like to show you off to the world.'

'And if I didn't want to be shown off. I've had my run-ins with the media over the years-'

'-of course. Understood. I could assure you the piece would be very sensitively handled. 'Charlie Ray gives back to the next generation'. I know the journalist intimately and can assure you of that. Thornberry needs this. Competition is fierce in the fee-paying market. And I'll level with you, frankly Dunamis needs this too. Some good coverage would be a plus point for all of us, I'd imagine.'

'Right.'

'It is in your contract, media appearances that is, but in my experience, these things work best when we're all singing from the same hymn sheet.'

'It is a music department, after all,' I said.

'What? Oh, hymn sheets. Yes. Exactly. Exactly.' She cleared her throat again. Voices in the background.

'And I am Melody,' she said, letting out a little laugh.

'So you are. Melody-'

'Jackson. Blame my father. He was going through a Serge Gainsbourg phase.'

'Great album.' Years ago, I'd cited it as an influence in an NME interview. *Histoire de Melody Nelson*. Had an email from his daughter Charlotte inviting me to a party at her Parisian home. Marcus had me booked into the Plymouth Pavilion. My best interests, he'd said. Keep the fans happy first, he'd said.

'Okay, Melody, that's fine.'

'Perfect. Great to have you on board. BBC Breakfast are arriving at 7am. Just bring yourself, Charlie Ray, to the music room for half past and we'll run through it all. Mr Pickles has already lined up some student case studies. Ones with parents with deep pockets, if you get me. And the journalist is a darling, honestly. Eoghan. Spelt the Irish way. You know him?'

'I don't think so, no.'

'I hope you don't mind me saying so,' she paused and cleared her voice, hesitant for the first time, 'but he was obsessed with your album. As was I. As we all were.' I could hear her smile down the line.

'That's lovely of you to say so.' It always was. Blah. Blah.

'No rock n roll antics tonight then.' She laughed to herself, haughty, relieved.

'Until tomorrow.'

BBC Breakfast. The last time I was on that show was a fucking disaster. Marcus had convinced me to release a concert album. *Forever Songs Live.* He was under pressure from the label for a new release. Something. Anything. This was a filler before the next killer. The killer that never came.

'It's just your audience, darling. The mums and dads of Britain, slurping coffee before the school run.' Viva la revolution. I'd not slept the night before and it showed. Nerves.

Would they ask me about a new studio album?

Tell me they can't ask me about a new studio album?

They asked me about the new studio album.

'...umm...ahh...we...I just wanted to give the fans the opportunity to experience *Forever Songs* in a unique way.'

'So there you have it, viewers.'

The look from the presenter made me sure we both knew I was past it.

But. And a big one. Maybe the TV would be playing in Luke's room. Maybe he'd come round to the sound of my voice. A strange kind of synchronicity. Maybe.

He'd be in the Heath Hospital. That's where I took him that night. That blot on his book. The booze and the tablets. His stomach pumped dry. An anonymous email the apparent trigger. The perils of journalism in the digital age.

'I knew you weren't serious.'

'That's good.'

'Tip for the future- if you're trying to do yourself in, don't use a mixer. It doesn't send the right message.'

A delicate man.

'Can I be put through to the ICU please?' A guess. I'd watched a lot of *Grey's Anatomy* this term. The phone clicked.

'Can I help?'

'I wanted to ask about Luke Harris.'

'Yes.'

'How is he?'

'Who's calling?' His former live-in lover. The mother of his unborn child.

'It's his sister.' He didn't have one. Some keys tapped on the end of the other line.

'He's serious but stable.' Like our relationship, once upon a time. I'd have learned more from Google News.

I dried and dressed, half a mind to fashion show some outfits for tomorrow. But there was no-one to bounce off. No stylist anymore. Luke was out cold. A cardi combo wasn't going to wake him up. That could wait. Pour a wine. My selection more humble than Ted's. Perch the laptop on my knees. But not the old sketch. The hours lost in the social media cycle. That particular addiction was broken. No need for Betty Ford for that one. The notifications on the Charlie Ray accounts slowed to a stop. More Throwback Thursday than Follow Friday.

Right now was about Luke not likes. He was writing for The Lamplight. The new digital frontier in investigative journalism. Maybe it wasn't The Times or The Telegraph but they weren't in hock to an oligarch. They'd been the ones who'd uncovered the story about the environment minister taking bungs from the fracking company. And the fast fashion store shamed over those Indonesian sweatshops. Proper Pulitzer stuff. I was proud of him. A tabloid hack no more.

With that recent history, the tweet about Luke being onto his biggest story yet meant something. Not the prize marrow at the country fayre. The inside scoop on the reality TV cheat. If Luke's current state was the result of rattling a cage, they bit hard. His latest post left no clues as to that, but it got me right in the gut. A longform piece about the selling out of our public schools. Those venerable old institutions- he'd have bit his tongue to blood writing that, ever the egalitarian our Luke- now at the whim of international money men. The pillars of our society sold down the river to the highest bidder. But was something more sinister up? What was the residual effect on our culture if the curriculum was a marketing tool for multinationals seeking legitimacy through buying up 'brands'? Hardly Watergate was it? But the Twittersphere seemed in a tizz. When weren't they? It wasn't the intricacies that interested me. More the theme. Public schools. Did he know where I was now? He was an investigative journalist. Thornberry School for Girls was hardly the Tora Bora Mountains. He knew. Was this a message to me? It had been seven years. Time had passed. We'd grown. I knew he knew I was thinking of him. I can't explain it but I just knew. Instinctively. If you've ever lost someone you'll know what I mean. The soul knows. It was a message.

It was pitch black and I tip-toed across the room. The chime of the empty bottle of wine. Unsure if this was real or dream. The light switched on. My mind searching while trying to remember, the words turning over and over. The melody muscle memory, a classic already. There'd been no need for a notebook and pen at my bedside. Not since *Forever Songs*. Not for so long. I turned the page, the shopping list to blank, and sang softly as the words took shape.

>Synchronicity
>Just because the past is past
>we don't have to let it be
>Synchronicity
>Coming back to you
>to rediscover me

Graves

Graves hadn't slept this soundly since his daughter had stopped talking to him. There was a school of thought among coppers that if you had suspects banged up for a crime, the perpetrator was the one you had to wake up the next morning. They knew they were screwed. Why not get some kip? If Graves was guilty of anything today, and he was frequently, it was getting his groove back. There was proper police work to do today but he was going to keep it close to his chest. He'd pass some of the grunt work off on Lake and Rabbiotti but the gumshoe stuff, the shoe leather on the asphalt bit, that was all his.

But first things first, it was fried egg sandwich time. He had four left in the box. Turned out his date had scrambled herself when she'd worked out where she knew his face from. Despite its capital city status, the opera house and cup final stadium, Cardiff was really just a big village. Throw in Graves' line of work and his current methodology for finding a jump, and it was a wonder that kind of coincidence didn't happen more often. Still though, Graves wasn't purely mechanical. He still believed in the sweet mysteries of life. Nina turning up when she did, well, he couldn't just chalk that one down to coincidence, he respected the universe. Something else was at play. Something he was determined to get to the crux of. On that morning, the sun streaking through the half open blinds of his blank bachelor flat; it felt like his destiny.

The first two yolks split in the pan.

'You've got to break a few eggs to make an omelette.' That was a favourite of Smiler's. His stock phrase for a waste of time lead chased down. How many eggs had Smiler smashed by now? Graves bit through the wholemeal bread, along with the green tea, one of his concessions to balance, the yellow and brown sauce oozing down his chin, and said aloud to no-one in particular, 'let's find the fuck out'.

First on the agenda was a visit to see his old pal Gwilym down in H.F.D. The Historic Files Department. Everything was a fucking acronym these days, he thought, the meaning squeezed out of plain speaking until the residual words were opaque enough to keep people who might ask questions out.

His carriage awaited.

'Abdi, what's happening, brother man?'

'What's happening is I'm driving you around all day apparently,' Abdi responded.

'Very dry, brother, very dry,' Graves said, 'I promised you a good time when we went up to the Smoke, today I'm guaranteeing you a fucking hoot. The fare of your life.' Graves' face was pushed up against the gap for the intercom, his fat arse perched on the edge of a pull-down seat. Abdi couldn't recall being promised anything other than the fare when he got stuck with Graves last. But that was enough. He wasn't after a new best friend. He had his passenger marked down as a manic depressive or schizophrenic, one of the two. He'd need to relisten to that specific episode of his favourite podcast again to confirm his diagnosis. He seemed prone to bouts of real elation, like the one he was in the slipstream of now, and huge slumps. His passenger had spent the way back avoiding phone calls and crying in his sleep. When he woke, he'd apologised saying he never slept at night so had to grab it while he could, before inviting him for a pint.

'Just two rules from me today,' Graves said, 'one. It's my music all the way and two, keep that shutter open so I can hear the thing.' Abdi took the CD from Graves' hand and inserted it into the slot. The opening beats of a Weller classic played out of the tinny speakers, all joyful velocity.

'Turn it up,' Graves shouted. Abdi obliged.

'*A Town Called Malice*. Ain't that the fucking truth, brother man? Next stop the central pig sty, please. And don't spare the horses.'

The Historic Files Department was in the basement of the central police station. Graves hadn't been in there for decades. In that time, he just hadn't cared enough to go digging through old box files. Most of the crimes that came across his desk didn't warrant it anyway, his indifference regardless. A litany of open and closed cases. The petty squabbles of a growing city in a changing world. CSI Cardiff it wasn't.

This time it was different, could be different. The lift didn't go down to floor minus two so Graves took the stairs. It was dark and dingy enough to extinguish even his new-found enthusiasm for the case. He was sure they smelled of cats' piss and wondered how. He blew the dust off the handle and pushed open the double doors to the H.F.D. An ageing copper was asleep at the desk. Rows and rows of shelves spread out behind him, locked away like an ancient library.

'Wakey, wakey,' Graves said, banging his chunky fist against the wooden counter. He was lucky not to get a splinter.

'I didn't touch her,' the old copper shouted through his sleep, red curls around a bald pate, crusty sunken eyes opening to his unconventional alarm clock.

'Charlie, is that you?' What the bloody hell are you doing down here?'

'As I live and breathe.'

'You on fire warden duty, is it? Who'd you pee off to get that gig? That what you doing down here is it? Alarm gone off, has it?'

'Not likely,' Graves said, 'and we both know I'd leave you burn anyway.' Gwilym sat forward, his half-moon specs slipping down his nose, steadying his bag of bones on the chair still set to recline.

'Aye, sounds about right that, kiddo. Neither of us are likely candidates for responsibility like that.' The light flickered above Gwilym's counter, an old filament in a building of LEDs.

'They never got around to changing down here, did they?' he said.

'Seems so,' Graves said, 'how'd you end up down here anyway? We're meant to steer clear of responsibility, remember?'

Graves didn't have to ask. He'd first met Gwilym when he got back from London. Gwilym had felt 20 years older, a going nowhere kind of copper. Just a job to him. Graves wondered if that's how the next generation saw him. Not for long. The sands were shifting. Gwil had a head full of red curls then, and the nose to match. They'd worked the town beat together more than once, spending most of it in a late night steak and sawdust Portuguese place, up the stairs and out the way of work. They'd brought out the worst in each other. Graves fighting and failing the mild arrogance of a Welshman who'd conquered the big city and came back home, Gwilym glad of a new drinking partner. It didn't last.

A call had come in on a serious assault at a nightclub just as Gwil's t-bone had hit the table.

'It can wait,' he'd said, Graves falling into line.

'I can go on ahead,' Graves had said, 'suss it out.'

'Like hell. That chop of yours is a tenner a pop,' Gwil said, 'if we were paying,' cutting through the meat with a wink.

Graves had left him to it. Got there just in time. Fella's head had been caved in by more than one Cuban heel. The bouncers couldn't give a fuck, weren't have none of it. Graves called the paramedics. They saved him. Just. Smiler had turned up when the kid was laid out in the back.

'Where the fuck is Gwilym?'

'On the cheeseboard by now, I'd imagine.'

He hadn't lived it down. They couldn't fire him. His alibi had been tight enough. A domestic broke out in the restaurant, he'd made the call to send Graves and stay and sort it out. Graves had corroborated his story. But they'd known. Smiler had made sure of that. So now, and since then, this is where he was, Gwilym. The H.F.D. And now Graves needed him.

'When you've wiped the sleep out of your eyes, I need you to dig out a file for me.' Gwilym looked at him like he'd told him he'd won second prize in a beauty contest.

'Charlie, you've gotta be shitting me.' Graves gave him the details of the case. For all his previous incompetence, Gwilym had served to master an elaborate indexing system in his fifteen years in the hole. Graves had known him to take pees longer than it took him to put his hand on the file.

'Here you are, Charlie. Don't leave it so long next time. I'll be chasing the sandman over there if you need me.'

Graves walked through the manmade corridor, all yellowed cardboard and musty paper from a thousand long gone cases and pulled out a chair from under the table at its end. He undid the elastic bands and spread the contents out like a collage. The South Wales Echo front page. CCTV images. The statement from the security guard. A mugshot of Jason Tyler, Nina's old man. Yeah, he could see them together. Wondered if he'd see her again. Wondered if he wanted to. He read over the notes from Jason's interview again and again.

'What were you doing there?'

'I don't know.'

What did he mean? It didn't add up. Smiler had warned him off, told him they'd got their man. But there was more to it. Wasn't there? His eventual excuse, some story about his missus being binned off and wanting to catch her bosses at it was stab in the dark bullshit. Why would a no-mark crim from St. Mellons be bugging City Hall?

How much time had passed when Rabbiotti tapped him on the shoulder, Graves didn't know, but what he did know was that he jumped straight out of his skin.

'Shit, Rabbiotti, don't you knock?'

'Sorry, Sarge, there wasn't a door. Just some old ginger fella snoring his head off on the front desk. I jumped over the gate because that's what I thought you'd want me to do. Use my initiative, like.'

'Well, yeah, very good Rabbiotti. 10 out of 10,' Graves said, 'so what you find?'

'Depends which way you look at it, Sarge,' Rabbiotti said, 'Christ, it stinks down here don't it?'

Graves ignored him.

'Go on then.'

'Okay, so the big stories about the council that year were about bin collections-'

'-it's not that.'

'-umm,' Rabbiotti hesitated, 'and something to do with the boundaries of the city expanding into the, uhh, green belt, whatever that is-'

'-getting even colder.'

'-okay, and something about, what was it,' Rabbiotti searched through the photos on his phone, 'streetlights-'

'-fucking hell, son, I wasn't after the parish

newsletter. Is there anything else? Anything more grown up than that page 7 two column nonsense?'

'There was something, Sarge, but I didn't really get it-'

'-go on.'

'Something about,' he scrolled again, reading the words out parrot fashion, 'a row over tendering for public sector infrastructure projects.' he looked up at Graves, recognising he hadn't been interrupted and might be onto something.

'New hospitals and that. A few local firms kicking off for losing out to some big corporation. Went on for a couple of days. A running story, they call that.'

'Alright, News of the World. Go on.'

'That's it really. Bit of a fuss. Few letters from angry know-it-alls for the next week or so.'

'What was the name of the corporation? The one the local lot lost out to.'

'Hang on Sarge,' his fingers pinching in on the screen, 'Dunamis....hang on, doesn't your daughter work for them?'

Graves stood up, his chair crashing to the floor.

'And what the fuck has that got to with anything?'

'Nothing, Sarge, just saying was all.'

'Well, don't just say. I'd prefer you to say what you did next.'

'Ah, yeah,' he said, clocking on, 'you'll like this, Sarge. I called up my contact on the paper to see if the journalist who wrote those stories was still around. The same fella wrote all of them, see.' Rabbiotti looked pleased with himself now, a pup waiting for a treat.

'And?'

'My contact didn't know, Sarge, she's only been on the paper two months.'

'Brilliant. Great work. What was his name?' The

fingers pinched again.

'Merlin Williams, Sarge.' Graves' face showed the maths of his mind.

'Want me to track him down another way, Sarge, look into the records?'

'Don't bother. He's dead.'

Merlin Williams had been a wonderful writer, all frustrated prose wasted on tomorrow's chip paper, a fine investigator and like many journalists of his generation, a just about functioning alcoholic. It had made it easy enough to explain away his death from drink driving. An open and shut verdict from the coroner and a footnote on page 3 of his employer's daily record. Maybe there was more to it, Graves thought, maybe he was onto them, a prequel to the current case, spared the chance of a coma that time. Maybe. Maybe. Maybe.

Graves had asked Abdi to sit outside the station. He'd booked him all day.

'And if you're lucky, some of the night too.' That didn't sound like luck to Abdi, but he couldn't deny the money from a day's work on the meter helped but his conscience wouldn't let him sit there clocking up the pounds for hours on end. He cared about the public purse even if Graves didn't seem to. He'd agreed an all day fare- £200 in the city limits- more if they travelled. Graves had been vague about the today's destination

'It's all about the journey, brother man.'

Abdi hated that at first, all the 'brother mans', but now found it comforting. An outward sign of the cosmopolitan nature of the city. An attempt at acceptance, assimilation, even if it was a misguided one. The world needed more of that, he knew that for sure.

Graves had told him he'd be an hour or two. The

decision to leave the cab was made on a whim, an instinctive parenting decision. His eldest Sadia had a test in the morning. In the grand scheme of things, it was nothing serious, not an entrance exam or a future definer. No mark on the permanent record. But, all the same, she was eight years old and her context didn't share the father's foresight. He should be there tonight to help her preparations, but with an all day fare and a passenger as unpredictable as Graves, he wasn't counting on it.

Abdi rushed through the crowds, past the castle ('isn't it so great they built it so close to the shops?' a tourist fare said to him last year) and into the Victorian arcades opposite. The arcades ran a historic central nervous system through the centre, their wood and glass boutiques an antidote to the gleaming malls that surrounded. Abdi arrived at the store, an antiques dealer on the upper balcony.

'Abdi!' the owner greeted him with genuine warmth, his long beard almost stereotypical of his trade.

'Mr. Hughes.'

'Time for another one?'

'Two today actually.' Over the past year, he'd been collecting a set of 19th century chess pieces, hand-carved as soldiers from the Welsh regiment, complete with a three inch high ceremonial goat. The old man disappeared through a curtain and Abdi let his eye run over the shelves. Relics from a simpler time. He knew that wasn't true.

'There we are, all wrapped up. One for each girl, I presume?' Abdi nodded.

'You've got a king and a pawn there.' Abdi paid the dealer and ran back to his cab, all the time wondering which he was.

'Tuna mayonnaise any good for you?' Graves said, throwing a clingfilmed bap through the gap between front and back seats.

'Can you get halal fish? I should know that, not much choice in the cop shop canteen I'm afraid.' Abdi peered back at his passenger, wishing he'd quoted twice the price.

'It's okay, I'm not hungry,' he said.

'Stick it in your glovebox then, brother man. You will be by the time we get there. Next stop, London.' Graves winked and pointed to the open road. Abdi got into gear and cursed himself for not buying the full set.

Sebastian Snook was not so much simply the editor-in-chief of The Lamplight but its chief architect. He'd joined the site five years ago as international affairs editor after taking voluntary redundancy at one of the broadsheets. 20 years in and none of the old bastions of the truth had got their head around the digital world. Sebastian Snook couldn't deny that they wrote well enough (creating 'shareable content', as it was called nowadays) but someone had to pay for the privilege. His ideas on how didn't get him far in his old place. There was always someone else more qualified to deal with business matters. Snook's job was to write the stories. But at The Lamplight, he'd had earned that freedom. And he'd created something truly groundbreaking. A new way. It wasn't just him who said so (although he did frequently), the framed front covers and glistening awards that adorned his office told him every single day that he was fucking wonderful. A journalistic genius. A publishing messiah. If people paid for streaming services they could never find anything to watch on, wouldn't they pay just as much to a news organisation that would hold the new world order to account in a new world way? And they did. One million subscribers in 32 countries worldwide. And the best thing? The content was all free. That was part of the mission. If you were on the Upper East Side or a pay-as-you-go mobile in west Africa, you could read what The Lamplight thought you needed to know about the powerful people who pulled the levers that controlled your life. He made people care enough to pay even though they didn't need to. Maybe Snook was a genius, but he was a uniquely 21st century version.

    He'd hit it off with Luke at once. Two years ago, Luke had arrived unannounced at The Lamplight's Hackney headquarters. Snook didn't know the man but knew his byline, their stories appearing side-by-side in old media over the preceding years. A rare gap in the diary meant Snook gave the instruction to wave Luke straight to his office. He thrived off the confrontation with broadsheet hacks, teasing and testing to see which side of the digital divide they sat on. A sport spurred on by his own perceived sense of rejection from the establishment. Snook hadn't needed to poke Luke for long. Kindred spirits in cause if not self-appointed confidence. He'd hired him on the spot. Head of Investigations. Snook had performed that role up to now but Luke's arrival meant he could put more energy into growing the brand. Schmoozing the advertisers. Hitting the lecture circuit. Spreading the gospel. Luke had filed his first story by the end of the day. A manifesto piece. No question unanswerable. Delivering the answers the world demanded, even if it didn't know it yet. Subscribers had spiked at 15% more than the average daily uptake. Snook patted himself on the back, again.

    With Luke lying in a coma and the mysterious tweets that followed, The Lamplight's web traffic had taken an upward trajectory even Snook's reports wouldn't have predicted. The advertisers would be ecstatic. What they did next would define their future. For once in his career, Snook had pressed pause. Luke had been working on something huge. He knew that. He'd asked at the beginning to see the files. Luke had given him the outline but insisted he waited until he'd uncovered a fuller picture. It wasn't his choice but his whistleblower's prerogative. They'd wanted Luke and Luke only. The documents were kept on an encrypted localised drive. Luke hadn't wanted The Lamplight's servers to come under a cyber attack. The story was that big, that far-reaching. Snook had stood down. He trusted Luke. He thought of the attention and the awards. His next TED talk.

The appointment in his diary that afternoon was one he'd been waiting for. A three o'clock with the officer leading the case. Calls had come in from a few rank and file and he'd been oblique in his answers but today he'd lay everything he knew bare. Well, most of it.

'Think Wikileaks big,' Sebastian Snook said, rocking back on his chair.

'And what does that mean in English?' Graves said. Snook's face scrunched around the eyes, unsure at first what this anachronism sat opposite him in his warehouse-style office meant. .

'Okay, well imagine the ins and outs of decades of corruption laid bare, original files and all. Voice recordings. Bank statements. Minutes of meetings that never happened, secret deals. But this time focusing on one multinational company, one whose reach is so long they get involved everywhere, all over the world, every government, and whose claws are so sharp they draw blood wherever they go.' He rocked back again, before leaning in, his spindly elbows uncomfortably resting on the untreated wood of the desk. 'Well, that's what it means in English.'

'And which company are we talking about here?'

Graves asked.

'Luke was very proud of his work and very protective of his source.' Graves' left eyebrow, an unruly thing with rogue grey hairs like antenna, raised. A trick he'd learned at the back of classrooms in his distant youth.

'The whistleblower,' Snook said, 'he had a man, a person, on the inside who insisted it was only him who knew the-'

'- so he did all of this on his own?' Graves said.

'In a way, no. He had the full support of the team here. This was...is...a huge undertaking. The story of a lifetime. Pulitzer level...,' Snook's blue eyes lit up, ' but technically, yes, it was only Luke who held the smoking gun.'

'Meaning?'

'Meaning it was only Luke who knew which company we were investigating,' Snook sat back, paused, looked to his framed front covers on the walls. Graves didn't follow his eye, 'but-'

'-but what?' Graves said.

'But there's only one company this could be,' Snook said.

'Dunamis,' the unlikely pair said in chorus.

It hadn't taken them long to track him down. Rabbiotti had attempted to explain the whys and the wherefores of just how the police's tech wizards had handed an address in Ealing to Graves by tracking the IP address of the device which had sent the messages from Luke's Twitter account, but his superior officer had cut him off mid-flow. Graves wasn't the type who needed to see the reckoning to believe in something. He wasn't interested in the workings of the card trick, the inside of the engine. Instinct and information or on your bike. Or in your taxi. As you were.'

'Bit of luck that, huh, brother man? Our latest stops being a few miles apart.' The cab was stuck in bumper-to-bumper traffic on the north circular. A white man with rank dreadlocks wearing a 'Marley Lives' singlet was body popping to the right of the driver door, snaking through the space between the vehicles with a bucket and scraper in his hands. He stopped in front of the cab. Abdi turned the windscreen wipers on. Graves made the wanker sign. He body popped off to the car in front.

'Brother man, turn that CD on will you?' Abdi looked in the rear view mirror, the traffic slower than a push bike with two punctures.

'Sorry, looked like you needed some thinking time.'

The Ealing street was not dissimilar to the one Graves lived on, all three storey Georgian houses with cleaned stone and sympathetic doors, the asking price five times that of his Cardiff street.

'That's the problem with London, brother man,' Graves said, sensing Abdi's tiring eyes in the mirror. 'Not only is it full of cunts, but it takes fucking forever to get anywhere to see them.' Abdi nodded, more in politeness than agreement. His daughter would be home from school now. He hoped she was studying her books and not the television. This was turning into a long day. He turned around to Graves.

'Maybe they need the hyperloop sooner than we thought,' he said. Graves looked at him as if he didn't have a clue.

'You might as well be talking Martian there, brother man. Tell you what, why don't you tuck into that tuna cob and then grab yourself forty winks. I'm off to do some proper police work. To smoke the rabbit out of the hole. Don't wait up.' Abdi would have seen Graves wink at him if he'd been paying attention.

There were three doorbells to the left of the front door. Graves pressed each of them in turn and the door pushed open before the ring had rung. The price tag might be higher but there was no concierge here, he thought. Just what he needed. The flat he was looking for was on the first floor. It was registered to a short-term let company who'd pleaded client confidentiality when Rabiaotti had asked for the tenant's name. No bother. He'd made a career out of door-stepping. He'd got in easily enough. He'd bust through enough flimsy doors to know where to push, where to press, how to lift and turn your way in almost anywhere. The second this one swung open, Graves wished he could put the wood back in the hole. It smelled like an estate's worth of black bin bags boiled in the midday sun. Like the inside of an intestine factory left to rust and ruin. The stench of death, and of something much more rotten besides.

The body slumped in a roll top bath, the porcelain stained red from the wrists. The man, early to mid 40s, was greying, naked, wearing a look of resignation, of the unsaid remaining so forever. Graves pulled the sash windows open and drank in the air.

He called the office.

'Get some local here sharpish. The whistle's had his shrill taken.'

Sadie

The typing from Luke's account decided against pressing enter and sharing a message from beyond consciousness. Nothing. It wasn't long ago that I'd been able to count Luke's messages to me, on the dot, as expected, one, two, beep. My fretting was fruitless though. It was likely one of that gruesome police officer's colleagues (I doubted he could type with those fat fingers) and if it was, then they'd know I'd messaged Luke. I didn't care. There was more in play right now.

My stay at the three star hadn't lasted long. Stuart, home from hospital and as wet as a Romaine, had been released under doctor's orders for round-the-clock care and attention. I'd lasted 72 hours. If I had to make him another cup of Lady Grey, I'd choke him on the tealeaves. It was the longest time we'd spent together uninterrupted in years. Stuart was unappealing at his best, but his current state was unprecedented. He'd tried twice already to sit me down at the end of the bed for the Tuscan talk mark 2. It was all I could do to keep away from pulling the pillow from under his head and going full-on Swiss clinic. But that would have been unwise. Homicide aside, his resurrection could be capitalised on to take Mooments where I needed it. Media coverage equalled sales equalled share price rise equalled bye bye. But for the meanwhile, my role was as matron and mother (not to the twins, their skiing trip had been extended due to the darling conditions. The easy freedom of the rich and carefree.)

Stuart's tummy was sore so today's demand was French toast with just a suggestion of syrup, apparently a dish his house parent would serve to comfort him in that first term of school when the bullies hadn't yet had the direction from parents to leave a Winchester be. I turned the kitchen TV on, a classless concession, but a lesser evil that proved soma to the twins. Their father needed to perk up. Dee had agreed he'd appear on *Saturday Kitchen* in a little under 48 hours.

'I've spoken with the doctors and they've said it'd do him good. Mooments is hot and we've got to strike before we're, well, you know, not. I hope you don't mind.' I didn't mind. The sooner I could check him out of Nurse Sadie's care the better. And if the lights, camera, action proved too much for his dicky ticker, well then I couldn't help inheriting everything now could I?

Some of the shell from the Burford Brown floated in the mixture and, as I fished it out, the words on the TV screen stole my attention.

'The Lamplight offers £10,000 reward in coma case.'

Luke. I reached for the remote and turned the volume up. A man around my age, desperately trying and failing to look younger, slick back hair and polo neck, was talking to the camera.

'...which is why we've done this. It fits fundamentally with our values here at The Lamplight to shine a torch on the truth wherever the powerful collude to keep the citizens of the world in the dark. That's what Luke believed and that's why we won't rest until we get the answers the world deserves. If anyone out there knows anything about what happened to Luke, anything,' his eyes fixed on the camera at this point, 'we want to hear from you.'

He spoke with a powerful smarm I'd not encountered too many times since Stuart left the City. But, if he cared about Luke, then he was alright by me. For now.

What was his line about the powerful colluding all about? This was a hit and run, wasn't it?

'Poor little Luke.' I jumped out of my skin. Stuart was stood behind me, all plaid pyjamas, bed hair and arrogance.

'What the hell are you doing out of bed? I turned to face him, his paunch peeking through the unbuttoned top. 'And what the hell did you say?'

'I said, where's this French toast? Gone to the Dordogne for it, have you?'

'Sorry?'

'And anyway, I've got to get the circulation going. Doctor's orders. I'll be broadcast to an audience of millions come the weekend. Can't go on with bed sores, can I? Dee would be cross.'

'I said,' feeling the red rising, 'what did you say?'

'I told you,' he said. 'About Luke,' shouting now.

'Well, darling,' he said, 'if you play with fire, you're going to get bloody well burned at some point.'

'And what the holy hell is that supposed to mean?' He looked at me, just for a split second with pure contempt, before the mask readjusted.

'I mean, you know these investigative journalists, who knows what kind of stuff they get mixed up in. Poking their nose in where it's not wanted, that sort of thing. It's no wonder-'

'It's no wonder what?'

'Oh nothing, darling, nothing. Now am I going to have to cook this-'

'Say what you were going to say.'

'Do we need to get into this, darling?'

'We're in it, Stuart, and don't call me darling.' Stuart was red now, but his colour was down to discomfort, not rage.

'Well, if you going to poke your nose where it's not wanted, sooner or later someone's going to cut it off. And it'll do more than spite your face.' I couldn't believe what I was hearing. I'd got so close to Stuart in the confrontation that I needed to step back, the clarity of distance. That and to avoid headbutting the little scrotum.

'So let me get this clear. You're saying that somebody put Luke in a coma deliberately...'

'No...I'm merely speculating is all...' Stuart busied himself with the whisk. As if he has a clue what to do, '...you know, just putting two and two together...'

'And does two and two make five, Stuart,' I said, 'or does it make four?'

'I don't know, do I? I was just-'

'You made a career out of figures so you tell me.'

'Luke has always been your blind spot.' The name stuck in his throat. He couldn't look at me. '...ever since university.'

'And blind spots deserve to be in comas do they? Your blind spot is everything in your line of sight. You're such a clueless, clueless excuse for a human being. You can stick your French toast up your sweaty, ginger arse.'

I'd have preferred to boil my own kidneys, but I'd promised Dee I'd meet her in town to talk strategy. After the insight Stuart had just given, as I drove into the congestion zone past Buckingham Palace, I gave serious consideration to letting Dee in on my strategy. Not the PR one, the life one, although the two were tied in a marriage of convenience. How very fucking appropriate. Inconvenience more like. She was an ambitious woman, one who'd spent time with Stuart. She'd get it, wouldn't she? Maybe having her on the inside would help me get there- wherever there was- quicker. Stuart's comments shouldn't have surprised me. He'd had a secret voodoo doll in the image of Luke ever since we'd met. His birth and background bred into him a survival of the richest. To damp down the downtrodden, to sneer at the infirmed. No, I shouldn't be surprised my husband, the father of my children, was a vindictive prick, but was that just it? Or did he know something else? Was there more to it?

I'd been checking for messages from Luke my entire adult life, but since the mystery typing it had intensified. Notification sounds rang through my sleep.

When I arrived at the coffee shop, the usual brushed concrete and Victorian light bulb job that masqueraded as chic in London these days, Dee waved me in. She had her earphones in, hands signing, head nodding and then disagreeing, her eye motioning me to sit at the bench opposite. She reached for a napkin, searched the table and wrote 'SK' in lip liner on a ripped half, all the time one 'ahuh' for two 'yahs'. I left her to it and joined the queue, a far too young barista called Sanchez asking what I felt like tasting today and me telling him I really wasn't quite sure.

'Sometimes blood tastes like metal, if you get where I'm coming from Sanchez.'

I'm not sure he did. He turned his attention to the giggling blondes behind me. Laugh it up while you can, girls. You've got it all to come. I could never be those girls again. But I had a chance to be something stronger, something surer, the scars hidden on the inside rather than open for the wind to get in.

'That was them.'
'Who's them, Dee?'
'*Saturday Kitchen.*' She looked overexcited, on edge, like the wrong word could bring the whole house of cards crashing down. I turned on listening mode.

'It was Poppy, the producer. They've asked me to be honest with them,' her drawn-on eyebrows arched.

'Do we honestly think Stuart is fit and well enough for the live studio atmosphere. She used those words exactly.'

I nodded.

'So, do we?'

'What do you think?' I asked.

'Well, yes, of course.'

'This is our moment isn't it, Dee?'

She looked less sure.

'Our Mooment,' I said, coaxing a smile through her fillers.

'Yes it is...it is.'

'That's what you told me, Dee.'

I took a slow, deliberate sip of my coffee.

'It's just my reputation, you see. PR is all about reputation after all, and-'

'Yes, Dee.'

'I don't want Stuart to wipe out and completely trash mine. I worked hard on winning the trust of these TV people.'

'And you wouldn't have had the opportunity if Stuart didn't have his attack. Remember?'

'You're right, I do.'

'We went viral, remember?'

Her eyes engaged at that word, like remembering a secret crush.

'We did.'

'And if he does crash and burn, won't that increase our talkability. Same for *Saturday Kitchen*. These shows have to work hard for attention these days, Dee. Cut-through, remember.'

'Cut-through,' she said.

'And anyway, Stuart is healthier than I've ever seen him. This whole thing has taken years off him.' I enjoyed the ambiguity of the sentence.

'That's great.'

'Now all you need to worry about, Dee, is-'

'The ad isn't it, yes, the ad,' she cut me off. It wasn't the ad I was thinking about. The recent spotlight hadn't gone unnoticed with our funders and we'd received 150% of our investment round six months ahead of target. If fate had decided I was a lost cause after choosing Stuart over Luke, then something good might just come out of the shitstorm. Maybe this eternal loser was her due her day at the track.

The vibration of my phone against the wood of the table interrupted that thought. Dee seemed relieved it wasn't hers.

'You should get it. It could be that Organic Times journalist at last.'

I gave her my best underwhelmed eyes. In this run of unknown calls and mysterious messages, could it really get any worse?

'Hello.'

'Is it me you're looking for?'

'Very unlikely.'

'But it is you I'm looking for. Funny that isn't it?'

'Not really.'

It was him again. That fucking copper.

'How's your day going?'

'It was about a six out of ten until you called, but you've got a knack of making average days awful.'

'All part of Her Majesty's Service.'

Dee was lost in her emails, her nails rat-a-tatting against the screen protector.

'Can you just get on with it or fuck off? I've got a particularly stressful day ahead and could do without your charm offensive,' I took a sip, the coffee cold now, 'and I mean that in the worst possible way.'

'You've hurt my feelings there,' he replied, all

pretend boo-hoo, 'but maybe that's for the best. Only a very brave man would get close to you, Sadie.'

'And what exactly do you mean by that?'

'Well, you've got a habit of turning up in dead men's messages.'

'Dead?'

'This one certainly is.'

'Which one? Which one?'

'Not lover boy Luke. He's fine. Well, you know.'

'I don't actually.'

'And I'm sure I've caught you in the middle of mopping your husband's brow, devoted wife that you are, so you don't need me to update you on his progress.'

'Are you going to get on with it?' My heart felt like a bottle rocket. The coffee. This call.

'I'm sure I'll see you soon and you'll look ravishing in black, but, first off, if you could tell me all about your relationship with Hamish Spencer and what these recent late night messages are all about, then we can just enjoy the buffet at the funeral.'

The lights flashed red. I balanced my phone between my thighs and speed searched the number, checking the crossers as the page loaded. The lights turned amber into green. The phone rang. That same regional accent answered.

'Luke Harris, please.'

'He can't come to the phone right now.' She laughed at her own joke. Poor taste.

'I gathered that.'

'So how can I help?'

Machines whirred in the background.

'How is he doing?'

Papers shuffled.

'Um, can I ask who's calling?'

The friendly joker had vanished.

'It's his sister.' Think on your feet, Sadie.

'And would that be the same sister who called yesterday?'

'I-'

'-and the same one who called the day before that. Related to the great aunt from Australia who calls every hour and the long lost brother who has a message he simply must pass on.'

'I-'

'This is a busy hospital, not a switchboard for the lonely. Thank you.'

'But I just want to know how Luke is.'

She'd hung up. Luke would laugh if he knew all it took to turn the tables and have me on strings was to be comatose. But all I could do was, well, not cry. I didn't cry. Not what we do, mother told me. Not what we do.

The airbag felt like the pillow I'd needed since birth. Forgiving in a way I'd never known. I waited for the taste, and it came, the metal like mother's milk. The sound happened around me, in another dimension. The hum of the march, the animal sounds of the delivery room, the first cry of the twins, the light applause of the conference hall. The deep draw-in of breath that Luke made after laughter.

My eyes closed, awake, open, and counted to one, two.

Ysabelle

'If Dios wanted us to fly, he'd have given us wings like the angels.'

That was my abuela's take on flying. I'd never been on an aeroplane before. It wasn't that I couldn't afford it now. The salary of an abrogada, even one working for the good guys, meant I could give money to madre and put some aside each month. My colleagues liked to use their money less as a bargaining chip and more as a status symbol, wearing fine clothes and eating at the places to be seen, but I still lived like a girl from La Boca. I didn't have that gringo desire to see the world with a bag on my back. I was happy Luke was different. But this was a trip worth taking.

'Ladies and gentlemen, a warm welcome aboard this Airbus 737 for this British Airways flight to London Heathrow. My name is Captain Jonathan Marsh and joining me in the cockpit today-'. I turned my headphones up. I'd seen enough of aeroplanes on the TV to know that Jonathan Marsh was a handsome man, a smooth operator who had our comfort and safety as his guiding principle. I was trying not to think of the television show *Lost*, trying not to scan the aisles looking at the other passengers, trying not to think that if the plane went down, who would be the strong willed leader of the survivors, who would be the evil traitor, who would be my lover. Madre liked that show almost as much as her telenovelas, even if the subtitles made her eyes hurt.

'Por favor.'

I smiled and moved my legs to the side as the man next to me pushed his way past. I shot him a look that said I understood. He smelt of stale sweat and padre's cologne. It was true that things always looked bigger on the television. We were used to cramped conditions in La

Boca but this was something else. Only 6,000 miles to go. Vamos.

The strangest thing I found about the flight was the collective suspension of disbelief from the passengers that being this high in the sky in a long metal tube wasn't completely loco. We were all bought into acting as we would if we were down on the ground. Polite, bored, tired, hambre, hungry, all pretending we weren't 30,000 feet over the sea, one thrust at the door that would see us spinning into the heavens, madre de Dios. All of that at the back of our minds, locked away in a little box without a key.

The airline had tried their best to copy Argentine cooking but the carton of chimichurri that spilt all over my legs when I pulled the plastic cover off tasted like the flotsam of the falls of Iguazu. The back of the chair in front of me had a screen. It was almost as big as the one madre watched her telenovelas on, sat as close as I was now, or else pacing up and down our pequeño room, her hands clutching her old wooden rosary beads when her favourite character found out his wife was also his hermana. But then I was back in that room, madre cooking, me sat at the table and Luke next to me, lying on a hospital trolley but wearing the uniform of my uncle Claudio, a rip in his blue Armada jacket where his heart stopped beating. The crucifix padre had hung above the table, hammering his thumb one time for every inch into the wall, seemed bigger than before, Jesus replaced by Tom Jones, his lips moving not with the words of one of madre's favourite songs but with a warning.

'Comfy there?'

'Lo siento, oh my dios.' I'd fallen asleep on the shoulder of the man next to me. His eyes smiled like he didn't mind.

'Bad dream?'

'You could say that.'

'You know your dreams have more power than you ever know...'

'Mi abuela used to say that-' and with that the soothing voice of the capitan came back over the speakers.

'Ladies and gentlemen, we'll shortly be arriving at our destination, London Heathrow. We'd like to thank you for flying with us today and wish you a safe and pleasant onward journey.' I had no promises mine would be either of those things.

I'm not sure if it was the tiredness or the different air but the lights above the giant hall which the passengers queued in seemed to flicker one second on, one second off. It was like a game we'd play when they wouldn't get out of bed to make breakfast on a weekend, Che pressing the switch in and out, dark then light, padre asking for 'solo, dos minutos, niños', madre snoring unaware. I took my phone out of my bag to check what time it was here, the satellite searching for signal like it was for everybody else around me, waiting patiently for the message of a loved one to arrive. The hopeful kind you sent when someone close to you was on a flight that may never land. The best I had was a text from Bruce.

'Have you met Paddington yet? Tell that chulo hola from me.' I dropped my phone to the floor. It cracked against the tiles, the protective case in the wastepaper basket of the computer room because Bruce told me cases were for losers.

'Oh, I'm so sorry, so sorry.' The girl in front of me in the queue, a Canada flag stitched to her backpack, turned around to face me. She sounded like Mariah Carey but looked like she hadn't had a shower for a week.

'It's no problem.'

She smiled and waved as she walked up to the

window. I picked up my phone, checked Bruce's message again and saw it was my turn.

'How long will you be staying in the country?'

'I, I'm, not really sure.' The man had white hair and a yellow moustache. I'd watched enough detective shows to know this made him a big fan of smoking.

'You're not sure.'

He said it more like a statement than a question.

'Si, it all depends.'

His eyes looked straight through me and back at my picture, my face half in a smile, Bruce outside the booth in Falabella, trying to make me laugh by telling jokes like a padre.

'It does all depend, yes, you're right. It depends on the information you give me now, Miss,' he looked at the passport again, 'Vazquez.' I swallowed before telling my story, the ant-sized bean of toothpaste in the aeroplane bathroom not quite masking the taste of the bad vino tinto.

'It depends on when mi amigo, my friend, recovers. He's very sick.'

At the Facultad, they told us that if we were defending someone we really believed in, then we should think of the saddest memory we could. That'd make us seem very emotionally invested in the defendant and fool the jury into rooting for the poor chulo in the dock. Too many sad things had happened to me and I didn't need to think about them then and I didn't need to think about them now.

'I'm here to make him better.'

He looked at me again, then back to the passport. I could feel the impatience of the lady behind me, dramatically stretching her legs out after the flight like a gordo after a gym induction, the sound of her stepping onto the ball of each foot louder and louder.

'Welcome to the UK,' he stamped the page. 'You've

been granted a 90 day stay in the country. If you need to extend your stay for a further 90 day period, seek advice from your embassy.' The hint of a smile broke out under his moustache, the burnt yellow of his teeth matching his facial hair. He looked like a Boca coach from the 80s. As I walked through the doors into the arrivals hall, I opened my passport and saw the ink from the stamp had already begun to fade. I wondered if it'd be gone by the morning and if I was really here at all.

I'd expected the arrival lounge to be just like the one from *Love Actually,* familia and friends embracing after long journeys, their eyes filled with tears of joy. We'd watched that movie over and over. Madre always laughed at the characters wearing big Navidad jumpers.

'Baby Jesus was born in a swimsuit in La Boca,' she'd say. Anything else would have been loco. It was 30 degrees at Christmas for us.

Nobody reached out to hug me but a man holding an iPad with my name on it scanned the travellers as we walked in through the double doors.

'Hola, it's me.'

'It is?' he said, turning the iPad around. The screen had gone dark.

'You need to push this button,' I told him.

'Ahh,' he said, laughing off the issue, 'technology, hey? My kids couldn't live without it. Me? I can take it or leave it.' He turned the screen to portrait and moved it away from his eyes.

'Ysabelle Vazquez?'

'Si.'

'Welcome to the UK.'

The man helped me carry my bags to the car.

'I'm Abdi, by the way,' he said.

'Hola.' I tried to shake his hand. I'd seen that was

how people greeted each other in this strange land. He let go of the handle of my case, the bag falling to the floor. He was my age or a little older, wearing a denim jacket that looked like El Jefe wore it onstage in the 80s, a cap on his head with a dragon on the front.

'Your hat is for Wales?' I asked him.

'My hat?'

'The dragon. Or maybe *Game of Thrones*?'

'The dragon. Yeah, yeah, I'm sorry. I'm a bit slow today. Gone straight from helping my daughter out with her maths homework to driving up the M4.'

I smiled. He seemed kind.

'But what am I on about? Banging on about me. You've just flown all the way from Argentina.'

'I slept like a baby all the way here,' I lied. I'm not sure why.

'I don't know why they say that. Slept like a baby,' he said, 'if our babies were anything to go on, that means being up all night screaming.'

'I don't know why you say a lot of things in English,' I told him.

'Tell me about it,' he said, 'you probably guessed I'm not from there originally. Somali, Somaliland, whichever. Somali Welsh warrior now though,' he winked, 'hence the dragon.'

'Here we are,' he said. We'd reached the car, a black people carrier which looked like it was from the future.

'Sorry she's a bit of a banger,' he said.

'A banger?'

'Oh, sorry, an old car, a wreck.'

'That language, again.'

'Aye.'

'Trust me, where I'm from this would be fit for the

queen.'

'Oh, I had her in earlier,' he said.

'You did?'

He laughed, a little like the loco cats from *Jungle Book* with the Beatles haircuts.

'No, no, I didn't, can you imagine? It's my Somali Welsh sense of humour that's all. Always taking the mick.'

'Like Jagger?' I asked. I was even more confused now.

'Sort of,' he said, 'sort of.'

'You okay in the back?' he asked me.

'Si, yes, it's just I'm more used to being on a bus or the Subte. I do feel like the Queen.' His eyes smiled in the rear view mirror, the same look as a picture of two girls on the dashboard.

'Are you a policeman?' I asked him. I wasn't too sure how this all fitted together, a combination of jetlag and very brief instructions.

'Oh ya allah, no. What is it you'd say? Dios mio?'

'Dios mio, muy bien. Your Spanish is-'

'-isn't very good,' he cut me off. 'Learned off Pablo Escobar documentaries, mainly.'

'I see. Everything about this situation makes me want to say Dios mio.'

'Is my driving that bad?'

'No, no, it's not that, it's this whole situation.'

'Well, I don't know anything about that,' he said.

'If I told you, you probably wouldn't believe me.'

'Oh, I probably would,' he said, 'I've seen some things and heard about more,' he looked left and right, pulled up to a roundabout and turned over his left shoulder to face me, 'add that crazy copper into the mix and I'd believe almost anything.' Like your dead abuela's dreams foretelling strange happenings? Like seeing the shadow of death over the shape of a man you'd only just met?

'I won't even start to tell you then,' I said. I felt like I could trust this man. He seemed warm, kind, the first to greet me in this land I'd seen so many times on madre's television.

'I don't know why I'm saying this but he's a decent man, D.S. Graves. A crazy man,' he laughed again, 'but a decent man. I do believe that. Might not seem it at first but stick with him.'

'It might take more than a decent man to sort this problemo. It might need Sherlock.'

The Beatle hyena was back.

'Sherlock he ain't.' He changed lanes and the traffic came to a standstill around him.

'Busy even at this time,' he said, 'welcome to London.' I couldn't see the Queen's house yet.

'There's a saying my grandfather used to tell us boys back home. Roughly translates as oh father, save me from the small one and the rest-'. His front seat wisdom was cut off by the horn of the car behind us.

'Don't know what Jimi Hendrix would have made of this,' he said, 'anyway, on request of my paymaster, this evening we won't be driving to Wales for whatever business you have there, but to London. So sit back, relax and before you knows it, well, before London traffic permits, we'll be at the hotel.'

'Is that normal police procedure here?'

'Na,' he said, 'but he's not normal police.' I guess my new friend was right. He'd paid for my flight too.

The sound of an academic from Mogadishu played over the radio, something about tectonic plates and dinosaurs, I think. I didn't stay awake long enough to find out. I closed my eyes and the shadows came.

Nina

He was in there on his own when it happened. Had said after dinner time that I could go home and get some shut eye, women's problems it was, sending me funny halfway round an apartment viewing. That's what we calls it, even if it's a flat in old money. The way the couple looked through me when I nearly fainted on the metro tile floor tells me they weren't buying no flat.

It was about 7 o'clock and he was finishing up the reckoning, tidying up the figures so the books were good and proper before the accountant came in tomorrow. End of year coming up, always put him on edge.

'You're like my old man in Cheltenham week,' I told him yesterday, but I'm not sure he was paying that much attention.

Lucky he was in the office out the back cos the pane shattered right through. Mayhem everywhere, like a glass of vodka in a beer garden on a hot day, just without any of the enjoyment.

He was putting a brave face on it. Fellas did, didn't they? Apart from the ones who wanted to cry on you and they were twice as bad, but I knows he was shook up. I should be too really. It was meant for me after all.

'Shut that grass up', that's what it said in biro on an A4 sheet tied with an elastic band round the brick. He sent me a message on my phone, but all I got was the little arrow which tells you there's a photo there but you can't see it, like a bonus round on a quiz show and you gotta guess what it is underneath. Texted him right back to say I hope he wasn't sending me no pics of funny business. Not that he would, not like some of those fellas on the websites, a hello, how are you, here's my old boy.

He called up all upset, but I told him I was only messing with him and that's when he told me.

'I don't know anyone who'd want to throw a brick through our window, Neen,' he said.

'And I do, do I?'. He didn't have to say anything. If anyone had a problem with Taz they'd probably give him a clip in person, and Karen, well, she wouldn't be seen with anyone who'd get their hands dirty these days. I knew it was for me. Yeah, you guessed it, a warning from my women's intuition.

Problem is, it's on full time these past few weeks. I'd got used to the butterflies, the rollercoaster guts. Whoever it was ain't really done their research either. Jase wasn't my grass to shut up, not anymore, not for a long time. I still cared about him, I spose, deep down there somewhere, but I had other things on my plate. Luke. Timing's off though, I tells you that. Or on, depending on which way you looks at it.

Whatever Jase was mixed up in now, it didn't take him much to be over his head. It's the situation, he'd always tell me. Wrong place, wrong time. I've worked out by now that some people are always in the wrong place. Wherever they are is where you don't want to be. The place he's in now, I don't know. I've blocked out the whispers on the wind, hard as that is. It's all everyone lives for round here, worse now Facebook's round, all the idiots getting involved in a he said, she said, but I'd avoided Jase, Tina and the not so little one for longer than I cared to remember. The job helped.

Last time he was in trouble, well, last time I cared he was in trouble, there was a riot at his prison. Three screws got put in intensive care, one of em a woman and all, all over the news it was. These blokes in balaclavas, bits of wood in their hands, grinning like maniacs under the hoods you could just tell. Fires lit and all. Something to do with the bread rolls being stale or something he told me. He weren't one of em, so he told me, but they restricted things in there for all of em then, not just the ones who did it. We all stands together in here, he said, well, most of us. Pity he didn't see our marriage like that I thought.

But this copper was the first time I'd thought of him since, well, since all this stuff was going on with Luke. If Jase knew I'd had a jump with the copper who banged him up, well, one of the coppers who've banged him up over the years, he'd have called me from my hole to my pole. He hated coppers, Jase did. Not just cos they were the ones stopping his fun. I mean, he was hardly Goldfinger, our Jase. Might have had the looks to be a master criminal but his two brain cells left him about as confused as a cat when the clock's gone back. No, Jase, hated coppers right down to his bones. To be fair, a lot of people round by us did, even if the coppers were kids they sat next to in school. Lot of people here were me against the world. Gave them an excuse I spose. Mam told me no-one was going to give a girl like me nothing for free, but that just made me want to work harder. Not to blame it on everyone else. Don't get me wrong, no-one gave us a chance, but you gotta use that against the world in any way you can.

I hadn't given an owl's hello what Jase thought of me for longer than I remember, but I'm not gonna lie, part of me was glad when I recognised who he was. One bar of a gate back in Nina's column. If I slept with everyone he'd wronged, I'd have to open my legs from dusk til dawn.

It was two afternoons after when the phone went for me at work. We'd had a fella in to replace the glass in the morning, had made do with a piece of plywood the boss sent Taz to B & Q for the next day, replacing the mess of bin bags he wasted two rolls of sellotape on the night it happened. You could have flown a kite in here, the breeze coming in when the board was down.

'You're like Mary Poppins, Sal,' the boss told me. I

felt like Mary Menopause with the temperature up and down like a yo-yo. I wasn't sure if it felt hot when Taz told me it was a private call because of the bad feeling or cos I still had my cardi on, but either way, I wasn't feeling too special when he handed me the phone, his raised eyebrow more shaped than footballer's wife.

'Is that Mrs Tyler?'

I hadn't heard that for a long time. Hadn't used it since the minute he went away.

'Used to be. Who's asking?'

'This is Mr Jenkins calling from HMP Prison name. It's about your husband.'

'You're not catching on are you? I don't have a husband.'

I heard him tapping on a keyboard then, the pause filled with the patter of the plastic.

'Jason-'

'-yeah, I heard who you said. When I was married to him your balls hadn't dropped mate.'

'I'm sorry M-'

'-you don't know what to call me do you? It's Ms Carter. That'll do just fine.'

'I am sorry, Ms,' he paused, 'Carter.'

'Apology accepted. Now what's so important you've got to interrupt a busy business woman during the course of a working day.'

'It's regarding Jason.'

'My tea leaves told me that, darling.'

He didn't know what to say to that. Seemed like the prison service attracted as many geniuses as estate agency, present company excepted of course.

'Go on then,' I said

'He's in, there's no easy way to say this-'

'So say it.' Jesus.

'-he's in the critical care ward at the prison

hospital.

'Right...' I said.

'Right,' he said.

'How'd that happen then?'

'I'm not supposed to give out details over the phone, I'm-'

'Come on sweetheart. If you don't give me the particulars, how I'm supposed to know what to do about my darling ex-husband?' My words came with a shovelful of salt. My guts backflipping. I wasn't sure if it's because Jase was hurt or because I was right. Again.

'I suppose not,' he agreed.

'There we are.'

'He...'

'Yes...'

'He was found hanging by one of the officers at 7am this morning. They managed to get him down before he stopped breathing but he's not come to yet.' He told the secret like everyone does. A little quieter, a little bit pleased with himself, regardless of the circumstances.

'As next of kin, I'm informing you so you can come and visit. That's what the gaffer's told me to do.'

Across the desk from me, the boss had just sealed the deal on this old farmhouse we'd had on the books since last summer. Only 10k off asking price too. He'd been so worried that they'd be put off by the broken window he'd taken them to the cafe two doors down to do the paperwork but he'd forgot a declaration and they'd followed him in. He gave me two thumbs up and I winked back. I don't know why.

'Ms.'

'Yeah, I'm still here.'

I left it til the next morning. I didn't feel a need to rush to see a man who barely bothered when I was married to him, let alone all these years after. I'd wasted enough nights for Jase over the years and wasn't going to start again now, whatever the feeling in my belly.

The hospital was an hour away and my night was all planned out, last episode of a thriller I've been watching. Like life wasn't thrilling enough, hey? Work just about kept my mind off Luke, but the nights needed a bigger distraction. I couldn't very well spend it taking him grapes and a paperback could I?

I got the bus up first thing. Felt like it'd give me more time to think than tootling there in my banger. Cheaper too, petrol being what it is. I danced around the subject with the boss, but he cut through the crap and said 'if it's to do with that bloody brick, Neen, it's best you go get it seen to'. So that's what I was doing.

On the bus there, I tried to think of what I'd say to Jase. Mam always told me to be prepared for those big moments.

'Don't matter if it's the Boy Scouts motto,' she said, 'us girls need to follow it and twice as hard.'

Situation being what it was, I couldn't quite fathom if this was one of those big moments. For me, like. Wouldn't have been a week ago I reckoned, my ex old man getting it in the neck in nick. So what? He's lucky it wasn't me with the rope in the drawing room, all Miss Scarlet. But now there's been this brick through work's window and I gone and shacked up, temporarily admittedly but shacked up al the same, with the copper who banged him up all those years back. And all the while, the fella I think about every day- not the one who dragged me the down the aisle but the one I jumped on the job- is lying in a coma in a hospital bed ten minutes as the crow flies from my flat.

I'll let him talk, if he can. That's what I'll do. See what he's got to say for himself after all this time. I could do with a bit of comedy, he was always good for that, Jase was. If he's still fasto, Plan B, I'll play the concerned former betrothed. Mop his brow. Count to ten. See if I can catch the bus home before it turns back to town.

I had to dodge the hailstones when I got off the bus, nearly went a over t going up a kerb, bottom of my jumpsuit wet as a weekend in Barry Island. I'm not sure Jase would get the jumpsuit gag, wearing one to a jail. He was literal or lost, Jase. No chance I was asking for directions at reception, didn't want to mark myself out as Mrs Crim, not no more. I clocked the big map in the foyer and followed the trail along the floor to the ward, just like Gretel. I didn't feel like I was going to a gingerbread house, mind. For the first time in a long time, I just felt calm. No motion in the ocean.

When I got up to the ward, there were two screws I assumed, stood next to the reception desk, each with their hands together and held down their front, like a pair of altar boys about to get a bollocking. The phone stopped beeping as I walked up to the counter, the nurse sat on a swivel chair looking like someone ate her dinner.

'I'm looking for-'

'Mrs Tyler?' It was the voice from the phone.

'We've been through this already mate.'

'I'm sorry...' he said, leaving a gap where the name should have been.

'Fellas usually are, in my experience,' I said. The nurse done me a smile like the Mona Lisa.

'Where is he then? Let's get this over with.' The other screw piped up, the one from the phone concentrating ever so hard on something just over my shoulder.'

'Come with us'

'It's Nina,' I told him, couldn't cope with it anymore. How hard was it to get someone's name right?'

'Come with us, Nina.'

He had a moustache that looked like the inside of a Lambert and Butler, all silver and yellow and 9 carat gold. Then they came back, the somersault in my stomach.

'Actually, you know what? I don't think I will. I've come far enough in the pouring rain today to go a step further until you tell me what's going on.'

I slapped my clutch bag on the floor for effect. They looked at each other, the screws, talking with their shifty eyes. The nurse lost herself in a computer screen.

'It's Jason,' said the one with the moustache.

'I'd guessed that.'

'Yes, of course.'

He took a deep breath, his moustache bristling like a doss house bog brush as he did.

'He didn't make it. I'm afraid he passed away an hour ago.'

I waited for the cold floor, the trickle. But this time, it never came.

Outside the hospital double doors, I pressed the green telephone next to his name, or at least what I'd saved him as.

'To what do I owe this pleasure?' he said, sounding like he was in the middle of Piccadilly Circus at rush hour.

'I wouldn't call it that,' I said.

'I get it. You've fallen head over heels with me and want me to ask your old fella if I can make an honest woman of you.' He didn't skip a beat.

'No need to call a psychic in to help you with a case is there?' I said.

'I knew you were going to say that.' He chuckled to himself like a Bank Holiday turn on stage after three ciders.

'Am I on speaker phone? You better bloody get me off it if I am. I needs a private chat.'

'I might be able to read minds but I haven't mastered technology yet, love. Let me get out of here.' The sound of his bulk pushing and shoving his way through something and someone.

'Right, that's better. Just the two of us. Marvin and Tammi.'

'What?'

'Nevermind. What can I help you with? It's busy here.'

'I read all about that. Your mug's been all over the paper.'

'Well, I'm sorry you had to see it, but it's nice to find a kindred spirit who still gets newsprint on her fingers.' He was off again, chuckling to himself, morse code like air noises from the handset bumping against his chins

'I knew him you know.'

'Did you,' he said, 'knew who exactly?'

'Luke.' He paused before answering, the first time he'd done that.

'Well, well, well. You're another one who keeps popping up where I least expect it.'

'I need to talk to you.'

'You are talking to me.'

'I knows something. I knows what happened.'

Charlie

According to the app Ted had made me download, I'd had an hour and 45 minutes of deep sleep but I felt like Rip Van Winkle. In a good way. I'd written something other than a lesson plan or deleted tweet and I felt fine. The writing restorative. The colour of creativity flushing my cheeks. No need for make-up for today's TV appearance. Not that I'd get it today. The case study rather than the celeb.

A typical Monday at Thornberry started sedately. The steady hum of privilege. All flattened diphthongs and hand-me-down entitlement. Breakfast, served in a 16th century great hall, the wood beams of which had been plundered from a Flemish cathedral and was occasionally used as a film set for period dramas, was usually a sombre affair. Three quarters of the girls opted to skip the silver trays for an extra half hour in bed and it was probably the best decision most of them made all day. My colleagues knew better than to engage me in deep and meaningful at that hour, although Ted rarely got the fucking message.

'Any tips?'

'Don't try the porridge. It's like wallpaper paste.' He rolled his eyes. He was wearing a corduroy blazer I'd not seen before and his usual eager face. Maybe even more eager than usual.

'For the big interview I meant. Any pointers from a seasoned pro?'

'Watch it.'

'Meant with the most honourable of intentions. I'm a little,' he stopped to signal hello to the head girl, 'nervous.'

'Nervous?'

'You're used to this, the live audience of millions. I'm rather more at home with the past particular verb.'

'Was used to it. No more, Edward. I'm a just music teacher at an immorally funded private school-'

'-who played Glastonbury.'

'No, a music teacher-'

'-with a number one album.'

'Just an average music teacher-'

'-who needs to stop messing around and give me some advice.' I squeezed his arm, checking the girls didn't see. The gossip of a gaggle of premenstrual teenage girls might not be the Murdoch empire, but pick your battles, Charlie Ray. I wasn't just a music teacher. I knew that now. Alive again. Not just living.

My mind was back at a media training session Marcus had insisted I go to just before the UK album release.

'I know this buzz, Charlie. I can feel it in my stomach.'

I'd say I could too, but *Forever Songs* was the natural conclusion for my precocious talent. A flower about to bloom doesn't get butterflies. The session- that's what they called it- 'I thought this was PR, not John Peel'- took place in a converted loft in Soho. They'd set the space up like a mock TV studio. Sat me on a garish red sofa, firing questions my way in front of a camera. I wasn't even sure it was switched on.

'I'm pro nuclear war. So maybe viewers, that's the hidden meaning in *Forever Songs*. That there is no forever. We don't deserve it.'

The pretend presenter looked at Marcus for direction.

'This is silly,' I'd said, 'who the hell wants a pop singer's opinion on nuclear war?'

'You never know what they'll throw at you,' the presenter had said, the façade of interviewer-subject shattered.

'I think I'll manage.'

New adults were a rarity at Thornberry. Usually it was take your pick from a helicopter parent or investor. The woman walking towards us- long red hair, month salary shoes- could have been either.

'Charlie Ray. A pleasure to finally meet you.'

The voice from the phone. She offered her hand but I was holding a grapefruit juice. My left hand turned 180 to accommodate, offered like a paw. She laughed. Ted shuffled.

'And you are?'

'Her Mr 10 per cent.'

I laughed. Nerves made Ted actually funny.

'I'm joking. I'm Mr Headingly. Ted the head…of modern languages, that is.'

'Terrific. Melody Jackson. Head of Comms at Dunamis. Shall we grab a table for three?' She'd clearly never breakfasted here before. We followed her to a table furthest from the smell of bacon fat and stewed tomatoes, a Chinese student on the end of her bench oblivious to the high level strategy meeting about to take place.

'So, I'll start at the beginning. BBC Breakfast. One and a half million pairs of eyeballs.'

'I was already nervous,' said Ted, 'and now I'm imagining a population the size of Birmingham wondering if this was the right tie to wear with this jacket.'

'What?' said Melody, not used to her flow being interrupted, before catching on, 'it's fine, it's fine. Just think that's a Birmingham worth of people to make a good impression on. And we are of course. Doing great things in Birmingham, Belize, Buenos Aires. All over the world. It's just, in this 24/7 media landscape, everyone has an opinion to share on social media and people don't always see that. We're a big boy there to be shot at.'

'A,' I thought about what to call Luke, 'friend of mine took a shot recently.'

'Oh.' Her eyebrows, recently tattooed on, arched.

'Not at Dunamis per se, more hedge-funded schools.

'Did he?'

'Yes, Luke Harris.'

'Luke Harris.' I searched her face for a sign of recognition.

'Well, sounds familiar. The journos on the nats change so regularly these days, shrinking staff and all that. Ad rev, clickbait think pieces,' she drew two speech bubbles in mid-air with a pair of immaculate purple fingernails, 'Everything's black or white in Britain now. Good or bad. In or out. What we can do today is build up the grey area.'

'Sounds shady,' said Ted.

'I wish it wasn't but modern life is one big grey area. I wish my days were spent in Technicolour but at least that's something to aim for..'

'I'm not feeling any less nervous, by the way,' said Ted.

'How do we get a coffee around here?' said Melody, meercatting around the hall.

'Table service ended last month,' I said, 'cuts.'

'Very good.' She caressed the words.

'Of course you know we're sheltered from austerity here at Thornberry. In fact, Dunamis has actually invested £2m into facilities and services at the school over the past 36 months. But we need to harness that chutzpah on air this morning. Let me stop myself there. You know that more than anyone, you've performed all over the world. What's the small matter of a TV appearance?'

Those eyebrows again.

'Is this meant to make me feel any better?' said

Ted.

'Ted,' she locked onto him with eyes like lasers, 'you will be absolutely wonderful. I can sense it. You have a great, great energy.'

For once, Ted didn't know what to say. She pulled a Macbook out of her handbag and presented two pieces of paper on the table in front of us.

'Today's schedule,' she said. I didn't know if I was terrified or jealous of this woman.

'I don't see coffee in the dining hall in here,' said Ted.

'I don't see coffee,' she replied.

'The media briefing isn't due to start for 12 minutes but I suggest we move forward. You two are the stars of the show today. I can debrief Mr Pickles. Now, the overall hook,' she wiggled her fingers in the air again, 'for the piece is around how private industry is stepping in to save services in an era of apparent post-austerity politics. Now normally these pieces give people like us a kick-in, have got to think of the viewer over the corn flakes, but this time the angle is flipped. We'll get more than a fair hearing and it's a big chance to showcase the social good Dunamis can do.'

We were meant to feel reassured.

'But aren't our fees a little out of reach for the average viewer?' I said.

'Well, yes, but Thornberry has the most accessible bursary project in the whole private sector.'

'Does it?' I asked.

'Yes, that's a key message for today. Show as well as tell. That's why Nyah, that is how you say it, yes? Nee-yah. That's why she's one of our key case studies. You know Nyah I take it?'

We nodded. It was hard to miss the only black girl in the school. Saved from a refugee camp by a captain of industry trying to buy his way into heaven. One girl. And they were so very proud of her.

'Terrific. Now the piece will be made up of three smaller set pieces, all lives, split across the morning. Well, from 7.30 to 9. Each presents us with a platform to tell a different chapter of the Thornberry story...'

I looked at Ted. His eyes were glassy. I couldn't be sure if it was concentration or disinterest.

'Good morning viewers. It's a long time since I was in a school at 7.30 in the morning but in my new job as education correspondent I'd better get used to it.' I could see the reporter's toothy grin from the back of the room.

'But this school isn't your average one. You may have seen us report the alarming figures a few weeks back that modern language take-up amongst GCSE age students is at its lowest point in decades as parents push their children towards subjects like the sciences or computing. I'm here at the Thornberry School for Girls this morning, where, as you can see around me in these rather salubrious surroundings, language is alive and kicking.'

The cameraman, hair the colour of the boom mike, panned to a break-out zone where a specially selected group of girls spoke in Chinese Mandarin. Melody gave a thumbs up to no-one in particular.

'This is Ted Headingly, the head of new world languages at Thornberry. Ted, welcome to BBC Breakfast.'

'Huānyíng,' Ted said. The reporter looked stage shocked.

'I'm sorry.'

'Zǎoshang hǎo,' Ted said this time, 'that's good morning in Chinese, just one of the many languages the girls learn here at Thornberry.'

'Ah, zao shang how too,' said the reporter, still not quite right despite a morning of practice, sanity back with his toothy smile.

'So, Ted, language learning is down across the country but not here. In the age of Google translate and AI, do we really need our young people to waste time on languages anymore?'

'We most certainly do,' said Ted, in English this time, all mock indignation. He wasn't nervous. He was basking in the spotlight.

'In a turbulent world, the better equipped our young people are to communicate with empathy and able to talk each other's language, forgive the pun, then the better they'll be at working together to solve some of the biggest problems the human race has ever faced. That's the attitude we take here at Thornberry. The language is the enabler, the platform for progress.' The reporter nodded, his impressed agreement half a second out of sync with Melody's approving nod for Ted's performance, their heads like a pair of golden cat charms in the window of a Bangkok cafe.

The reporter moved towards a group of students, his questions and their answers just out of earshot from the back of the room. Ted stayed planted to the spot, mouthing 'can I move?' to Melody.

'How was I?'

'You were brilliant. A platform for progress?' I said, 'very neat.'

'Ted, you were terrific,' Melody swept in, planting a kiss on his blushed cheek.

'And now I can relax,' said Ted, the arms of his corduroy jacket raised in victory.

'Not for me,' I said.

'Yes, you're up next Charlie,' Melody said. The reporter joined us. His hair was parted down the middle in 90s curtains, the roots greyed like mince left in the sun. He was overly chirpy for this time of the morning, like a funeral guest filing the gaps with bonhomie, but the makeup caked under his eyes told a different story.

'Ted, that was fabulous, really,' he said, rubbing Ted's shoulder like an old friend. 'Does anyone know where I can get a posh coffee around here?'

'Now you're asking,' I said.

'Charlie, I'm Eoghan, spelt the Irish way,' he leaned in close, an overpowering musk swarmed my nostrils, 'I bet everyone tells you this but *Forever Songs* was such a big album for me. This is a little embarrassing,' he didn't seem embarrassed, 'but I serenaded my wife to it.'

He wore no ring.

'Anyway,' he looked around the room, 'we have met before, you won't remember-'

I didn't.

'-way back when the album first came out. Party in the Park in Manchester. Gosh, no, of course you don't remember.'

'No, yes, I think I do,' I lied.

'Well, it's an honour to meet you again. I don't think the education correspondent will get to meet many multi-platinum artists.'

A dagger through the heart but it beat again. No worry.

'And thank you. Right, coffee.'

'So think of your school at 8.30 in the morning and you probably get images of footballs flying around a playground. Parents jamming the pavements outside. Children gossiping about last night's TikTok trend.'

The reporter left two second of airtime dead, a wistful pause, my nod pushing the girls into action after

229

his wink, straight into the opening bars of *Forever Songs.*

'But not here at the Thornberry School for Girls in Dorset, where a,' he hesitated over the next word, 'former musical star leads this room of talented youngsters through one of my favourite songs of all time. Written by Miss herself...'

The interview passed by in a blur. Not a rock star blur. This one had a nobler purpose. The key messages. The what's next for Charlie Ray, will she ever again play. My eyes lasered down the line. Transmitting my sense, my soul all the way to Luke. Feeling down the feedback loop. A message to you, Luke.

Wake up.
It's me.
Let's get the bastards who did this.
Finish the chapter.
Post the article.
Sing the song.

Graves

Considering this started with someone being knocked off a pushbike, the body count ain't half piling up, Graves said under his breath, the stale dry of green tea causing him to half-wretch. But he knew it'd started way back, way before he'd rocked up late on a suburban street to a call he'd have avoided if the McDonald's queue had been two cars longer.

Now he had a city boy with a dodgy ticker, another dead in a London bath and some crim he banged up years back hanging from a waste pipe, not to mention the original hack lying cold soup in ward 10, still managing to tell social media something stinks about the biggest story of his career. And then the women. Wasn't it always? He'd wished it was, chance would be a fine one yaddy yadda. But there were two of them weaved through the whole thing like the gravity holding the house of cards together. Graves had always cheated at cards.

Then a third, flown in from Argentina- not on the public purse he wanted you to know- to blow the whole thing wide open, or that's what she'd promised. He didn't have the coin to fly over her junior sidekick, and anyway, three was a crowd. An ounce of prudence for once left him keen to keep at least some of his savings back in case that daughter of his decided she did want to see him again, although what she earned telling tales for the devil left his pot only worth pissing in anyway.

What did she know about all this anyway? What level of clearance did the head of comms for a dirty rotten corporation get? This spider's web of subterfuge and shit had got Graves in the groove again. 'Again' gave the impression this was at least a semi-regular occurrence. It wasn't. It might be like saying the Romans ruled the world again, or Vesuvio blew hot molten fear and beauty again. Both were perhaps a little dramatic, overegged. But

Graves was an emotional man, four big sloppy ventricles on a sta-prest sleeve, so allow him the hyperbole this crisp, autumn morning.

They still had no trace on the driver but Rabiotti assured Graves they were close. Should blow it all open, Sarge, he'd told him, but Graves knew in his bones the man behind the wheel was just another Jase.

Snook loved the sound of his own voice, but it seemed like millions of others did too, Graves thought. From a selfish point of view, he was glad it was Luke and not Snook lying in that coma, seemed like a much humbler bloke, the kind it was worth rediscovering your groove for. He didn't believe Snook though. Never take a journalist at their word. If the spotty kids at Central HQ could track down the whistleblower, you could bet all you had he knew who was sending those messages. It was only a matter of time before they found communication between the two. Honesty was the best policy when your digital footprint left more crumbs than Hansel and Gretel.

Did his daughter know who'd sent them, who was blabbing the state secrets to Luke? If she wasn't already in a huff with her old man, he wasn't likely to get back on her Christmas card list by stirring up a PR shitstorm for her to deal with. Or could the messages have come from Melody? He might not have been the best dad, but he raised his kid with a moral compass, her own strong will making her a formidable foe if she got even a sniff of wrongdoing. That's how he remembered her. Was she bringing down her bosses from the inside? Keep all the cards in the Cluedo envelope, that's what Smiler used to say. Funny how he ignored his own advice after a while. Graves was the ultimate anti-hippy but he couldn't help smile at the little coincidences that were getting thrown up. He'd dismissed his date's shock at seeing him again, 10 years on, pants off this time. Just the result of a small city and his wide net, but perhaps the cosmic order was trying to say something. Synchronicity, man.

It was the smell that got him. Cheap industrial detergent failing to mask an undercurrent of stale piss. That was the thing about being a copper. You led the pigs to the slaughter house but were spared seeing them turned to mince. Mostly anyway.

Graves hated screws. Failed coppers turned successful crooks, most of the ones he'd come across. He couldn't get a handle on the one stood in front of him though. Yet. Unsure if he filed him under good or bad so he hung in purgatory in his head, for now. I could give him the guided tour, he thought.

'So what really happened to him then?' Graves asked.

The man talked and Graves listened. He asked all the questions he was meant to- about his behaviour record, his history of mental health, his current state of mind. But what he really wanted to know was,

'Who gave the order?'

'Who got to him?'

'Was it you?' and, brain engaging mouth this time, 'How much did it cost to buy you?'

The screw stuttered for the first time, eyes searching for an answer, mind trying to keep up. Yellow moustache sweating. Graves went back to his filing system and kicked the man out of purgatory, down to where he belonged.

'Brother man, how goes it?'

'It's going,' Abdi replied.

'That's the spirit,' Graves laughed, a touch too maniacally for Abdi's tastes.

'And did you collect the precious cargo?'

'Which do you mean?' Abdi said. He pushed the paddle for cruise control, took his foot off the accelerator and eased the car into the left hand lane.

'In both senses, brother man, in both senses.'

Abdi had made a deal with Graves. He'd do a late night pick up at Heathrow only if he could stay overnight in the city and be back for midday. Graves had told him where to go and Abdi had hung up, answering only on Graves' seventh consecutive call. He'd explained. Graves had agreed. He'd had breakfast at the hotel, three plates worth, all paid for so fill your boots, and walked across town to be at the shop five minutes to nine, the journey timed on his mobile map. He could have spent all day glued to the glass cabinets but this was a special mission. A quick raid for an intricately hand-carved rook. The dealer thought it unusual but called the payee and took the card payment over the phone regardless. He could see how much it meant to the small Somalian man with a Welsh accent who he'd found waiting outside his shop that morning.

Abdi leaned over and opened the glove compartment. It was still there, 19 checks later. Thanks Graves. If I was going to miss my girls' smiles in the morning, I was going to give them an even bigger one the following night.

'Yeah, I can confirm that,' Abdi said.

'Stick me on speaker phone, will you?' Graves asked, 'I want to speak to her.'

Abdi fiddled with a button on the dashboard and Graves' voice switched from his bluetooth headset to fill the car.

'Buenos días to my star witness. Bienvenidos i Gran Bretana!'

Abdi turned over his shoulder.

'He's talking to you. Excuse the cultural

appropriation, he does it to everyone.'

'What was that, brother man?'

'Hola, Mr Graves.'

'Hola, Ysabelle. It's wonderful to hear your voice. Next date's in Buenos Aires, though right?' Abdi rolled his eyes in the mirror, Ysabelle not catching it.

'Okay, Buenos Aires is,' she paused, 'a bit different to here.' The car was on the stretch of motorway between Swindon and Bath. She looked out the glass to grey sky meeting grey tarmac.

She couldn't sleep last night. It was nothing to do with the bed, which was bigger and more comfortable than the one in her apartment. A combination of jet lag confusing her body clock for the first time and thoughts of Luke. Of seeing him again, same face, circumstances that couldn't be more different. Despite all of this, she was in London, a place she'd only seen on her madre's television screen, James Bond driving the city streets in an Aston Martin, looking as alien to the men of La Boca as a green man from Mars. She'd left her hotel and found her way to the south bank, the same moon above Luke had looked at for all these years, but much closer to him now, a crescent behind a cloud, illuminating her walk along the river.

She'd played the scene over in her tired head, how she'd walk into the hospital room, how the sound of Tom Jones playing from her phone would awaken him. How she'd say 'I told you not to eat madre's steak'. How he'd laugh and she'd lean down to touch his brow. She knew that was a dream, but as her abuela said, dreams have more power than she'd ever know. What she did know was that the shadow was darker than ever before. What she really wanted was justicia. That's what she'd came here to deliver.

In person, at the station, Graves' suspicion that

Ysabelle reminded him of the best and worst of Melody was confirmed. He was aware of the cliche. A lonely father looking for his absent daughter in any girl close to her age who showed him the kindness he'd missed. The shade of her eyes. Her determination to do the right thing. Her pigheadedness. All of these were on display from the Latin American lady sat in front of Graves in the downtown Cardiff station. One of the younger coppers would have suggested they do it by video phone but Graves knew this was no time for George Jetson. He did his best police work in the whites of the eyes. Looking at Ysabelle, he knew it'd be worth the trouble.

Graves thought of the last time he'd heard Melody's voice meant for him. He had a feeling he'd be hearing it again before too long. The big variable depended on how it'd sound. Graves had got one of the kids to print the pages off for him.

Dunamis Investments was involved in every type of business on every continent, inhabited or not. Education. Oil. Media. TV. Tech. Finance. Fisheries. Nuclear. Stocks. Shares. Everybody on earth knew this. His daughter had made sure of it. But the press releases told only half the tale. The private sector was a virus. Once it started it couldn't stop. Dunamis wasn't content with making billions. It needed to influence elections. Prop up sympathetic regimes. Whitewash human rights atrocities. Destroy rainforests. A list of politicians, officials and officers across the world on the payroll. Organised crime cartels to do the dirty work. Luke had followed the money. The illegal payments. The suspect transactions. The transcripts of bang to rights conversations. Whistleblowers on record, including Hamish, God rest his soul. The story of a lifetime. The death knell for a system that stank. The work of a poor hack lying in a coma whose name deserved to be known throughout the world.

Graves had left them at the bar. Tradition said the sarge in charge took the crew to celebrate when a case was cracked and Graves was only too happy to oblige. It was the first time he'd been in a boozer with a girl from Buenos Aires. She'd enjoyed herself, spent most of the night doing shots with the younger coppers, on the video phone to her accomplice back home, tequila being poured over the screen so he could join in too. Graves had stumbled home happy. The buzz back. Bigger than before. He fumbled for his phone in his jeans pocket, the light causing his eyes to squint. He searched through the contacts, hung on Melody's number for a pace of two and thought better of it. That could wait until tomorrow. He needed to be sober this time. His text was sent to Nina instead.

'We've got the bastards.' Maybe he'd see her again. Probably not. Probably for the best. Thinking what the literary detective would do, he considered pouring a solitary whisky when he got into his flat. More booze before snooze. He got under the covers and turned the lights off.

He was floating down an unknown river on his back, martini in hand, Weller playing loud, when the sound woke him up. His phone was at the foot of his bed, tangled in a pile of denim and boots.

'What?'

'Sarge, sorry to call this early but we thought you'd want to know.'

'What?'

'He's dead, Sarge.'

'Who?'

'The journalist, Sarge. Dead.'

Graves sat up, his taste dry.

'I'm on my way.'

Sadie

'Ouch.'

'Stay still.'

'It fucking hurts.'

The nurse decided against a response. My injuries hadn't warranted a doctor. A black eye and three butterfly stitches wasn't the worst diagnosis I'd been party to in a hospital these past few weeks. I had far more pressing concerns.

Hamish was dead. Sweet darling Hamish. I wouldn't be telling Stuart. It was not beyond the realms of possibility that he already knew. I always knew my husband had issues but had I missed the switch from socio to psycho? I was probably being hysterical, at least that's what Stuart would tell me. Even if he did know, he was surely too much of a simpleton to be a lone assassin. This was a wider conspiracy. He knew why Luke was in a coma. Perhaps I was being hysterical. You never hear of a hysterical man, do you? Purely a malady of female form. Maybe I was.

Ouch. This bump on my face fucking hurt but the dull ache would spur me on and steel my determination to execute the plan.

'Are you sure I can get away with this shirt?'

'Darling, it's a striped shirt. It's hardly haute couture straight from the catwalk.'

'Alright.' He wasn't sure.

'The British public is ready for a,' I bit my tongue, 'handsome organic food entrepreneur to beam into their pokey little living room,' I straightened his collar at the back, 'in a striped shirt.'

'Okay.'

The make-up man chattered away at another

guest, a bearded hipster moved to the country type who I picked up was at the 'vanguard of the artisan tequila movement'.

'But not the jacket?'

I moved in front of Stuart and looked him in the eye.

'Darling, you know how hot you get under the lights. We really don't want the world to associate Mooments with sweat patches, do we?'

'What's happened to your face?' he asked.

We'd been together for at least an hour.

'It's nothing.'

My make-up skills had all but hidden the evidence.

'But you've got stitches.'

'It's hard out there as a woman today, Stuart.'

'But-'

'And lots of little accidents have been happening around here haven't they?'

His eyes sank back into the excavated holes of his face. He looked to the other guest to see if they'd heard. I had turned the volume up.

'Look, you need to focus. Remember, three key messages.'

'Where's Dee?' he asked.

'Oh, she's here. Don't worry about that. Just a little tied up right now.'

'Are you Stuart?'. A girl in her early 20s dressed in a *Saturday Kitchen Live* branded t-shirt holding a clipboard entered the room.

'It's not me, darling,' I told her, laughing conspiratorially.

'Sure,' she said, laughing back.

'I'm Stuart.' he said, 'that's me.'

'Stuart,' she said, lengthening the last consonant in some sign of familiarity.

'How are you feeling?' she rubbed his arm.

'I'm great, yes, great. Never better.'

'Sure,' she said again, the arm rubbing over.

'Just make sure he has plenty of water on hand at all times,' I said.

'Sure.'

'It's a relaxing family show,' she said, 'just like having your best friends over for brunch.'

'It is so that,' the make-up man chimed in.

Stuart didn't have any best friends, or not ones that came over for brunch anyway.

'Darling, no health scares today,' I said, patting him on his balding head with as much patronisation as I could muster. He looked terrified.

'Toodle-o.'

I took my seat in the studio audience, close enough to see the sweat on Stuart's blotchy forehead. My fellow audience members were a strange combination of hardcore cooking programme fans, bused in pensioners, gay couples and tourists pulled off the street. Prime Mooments customers. The set had been manufactured to look like an aspirational weekend scene at the north London domicile of a trendy cabinet member. Stuart and two other guests sat around a round table to the right of an oversized island, all open hobs and faux marble top. The backdrop wall was bare brick, but from the edges you could it had been assembled from plastic.

'Welcome to *Saturday Kitchen Live!*'

A teenage crew member in branded t-shirt and oversized headset held up an 'applause now' sign. The audience obliged appropriately, particularly the hardcore fans, this the moment they'd imagined over and over on their provincial sofas, the spark plug that had kept them going through the four hour coach journey. The host took a slow walk across the set to Stuart and the other guests. He was ruggedly handsome, his outfit like he was a Liverpool Street commuter on a dress down Friday.

'And what a show we have for you today. Let me introduce you to our three delicious guests. First up, you may have been a fan of Mooments organic ice cream for as long as one of our other guests today but you probably only became aware of Stuart Winchester after footage of him on stage at the Good Food Show went viral. So, Stu, the man behind the Moo. Talk to me...' The presenter jabbed a finger in the air conditioned air towards Stuart. He could just as easily have been passing on a turn in a drinking game.

'Well, yes, good morning everyone.' Stuart fidgeted on his chair.

'So what have you been up to?' the presenter prompted him, his live TV experience kicking in.

'Well, apart from collapsing in front of millions,' the runners held up a sign asking for 'laughter now' but the audience beat them to it. They were that pumped. I looked across to Dee and saw her fists clenched in celebration.

'Get the first laugh in. Make them like you.'

'But you look a picture of health here today,' the presenter said.

'Well, a diet of Mooments of course,' Stuart said, relaxing now, smiling even at his own joke. Laughter again.

'And tell us what you're going to cook for us today...'

'Well, I know you usually have professional chefs doing this bit-'

'I trained under Raymond Blanc,' the presenter cut in, well-versed in the not-so-humble brag.

'Oh good' said Stuart, 'I'm more of a home cook

really.' I held back actual tears.

'You know, kids around the table sort of thing, so I thought I'd cook something really simple, something that takes me back to my childhood. West country pork chop and cider mash-'

'Cider? For the kids?' the presenter playing with him.

'Well, um, helps them sleep doesn't it,' laughs again from the audience, myself included this time.

'No, I'm joking of course, it's an old family favourite from our time down at the farm.'

'Great stuff,' the presenter said, mostly meaning it, keen to move the show on.

'And next to you, we've got...Dacey Dean. Give her a big *Saturday Kitchen Live* welcome!'

The audience really lost their shit this time, the runners not even bothering to reach for the prompt signs.

'Hiya everyone. Hiya nanna. She loves this show. Am I allowed to say that?' She played clueless as caricature, clearly the work of a Dee. Three weeks in the jungle had given Dacey's skin a deep tan, gym slim arms and questionable cleavage for this time of the morning, her body the canvas for a hideous camouflage vest.

'Dacey, my dear, you can say whatever you like,' the presenter flirted. Stuart tried and failed to keep his eyes on the camera.

'Tell us about the jungle...'

'I think the viewers know all about that,' Dacey teased, her tongue making love to every word.

'You're right, they will. So let me ask you, what the dickens does a cockroach stirfry taste like?'

The audience mock-wretched, real laughed. Someone on every row was replaying Dacey's best bits from the show on their phone for the person next to them, the sound still loud on most.

'Crunchy.'

'I bet.' The presenter was in love.

'And Dacey, I need to be careful here because his wife is in the audience, but you thought of Stuart a lot when you were in the outback didn't you?'

Stuart's bald patch turned beetroot. This was wonderful.

'I diiid.'

Stuart turned to her, his stare desperately trying to stay at eye level.

'Not strictly Stuart, was it? His wife can relax.' The audience laughed. Nobody knew who that poor woman was.

'More the Mooment wasn't it? The Banana Drama one.'

Dacey kissed the air, red filled lips immoveable.

'Made sure they had a tub for me as soon as I got out didn't I?'

'And might you be sharing a spoon with your fellow junglist Cooper?'

Her nails cut through the studio air. Stuart flinched.

'I wouldn't share that with anyone, ' the audience laughed, 'not even you Stuart, honey.' The audience oohed.

'Great, okay,' the presenter touched his ear, clear instructions he'd spent too long on this guest.'

'And what'll you be cooking for us today?'

'If you follow my Insta, you'll know my new macro diet 30 days to slim, trim and win is available now.'

'Yeah.'

'And I'm going to be cooking my no bake chocolate pecan paleo treat which you'll only find in my book. And here today!'

'Delicious. Right then...'

There was no need for duress to get the signature. Stuart had signed his death warrant with no small dose of relief. I hadn't even had to plant the seed that bore him rotten fruit. I'd have preferred to scratch my fingernails down a school board, but the year-end accounts meeting had become a necessary evil. In the start-up days, they'd largely been deep breath exercises around not losing all of the investment money from Stuart's former colleagues without damaging the vision. The money had inevitably always been there, the benevolent force in the background. But, like all his friends and kind, Stuart hated paying tax. Why pay for poor people to use services you never would? I'd gone along with it, of course. This was the efficient way to run a business. I believed it and I saw my chance. Stuart had a disqualification against his name. Some shady dealings from the old days had caught up with him.

'It's nothing, darling, a change in the regs is all.'

It expired in two years. Dee had helped cover it up. No journalist had bothered to search the Companies House records. Yet.

Stuart's password hadn't been hard to guess. I'd tried our wedding date and the boys' birthdays more to prove the rule than solve the riddle. Dunamis1234. You can take the boy out of the hedge fund. The sickness had separated him from his phone. It didn't take long to find what I was looking for. Luke was onto him. Emails exchanged with characters remembered from the annual family day. They hadn't been stupid enough to mention Hamish but the traces had been there. The one crime he hadn't tried to hide was the other woman, the adjective somehow suggesting I was his existing woman, which I hadn't been, not for a long time. If the messages were anything to go by, he'd been fucking Dee for the past six months.

If I'd written the script myself it couldn't have been sweeter. The solicitor said it was a simple case, but I knew it was anything but. Mooments was mine. Freedom was mine. The papers poked out of my clutch bag on the studio floor.

'Right then, Stuart. Let's find out if it's food heaven or food hell.'

'Do you ever think about the future?'
'That's a bit deep for 7 o'clock in the morning?'
'Oh, I'm sorry.'
'And I've only just met you.'
'There is that.'

The bus driver had given into the persistence of a boy with a haircut Britpop forgot in the front seat. A tinny tape of the NME's latest darlings punctuated the gaps in our conversation. I forget the name of the band.

'I meant politically, really,' he said, eyes stuck to the window, 'you know, if this march doesn't work out.'
'Well, that's still deep,' I searched for his name.
'Luke.'
'Luke, but the people need bread and war.'
'It's actually bread and circ-'
'-you get what I mean.'
'Yeah, I suppose I do.'
'And Britain has got the most stable political system in the world. Labour. Tory. Tory. Labour. We'll be alright on our little island.'
'Yeah, but that's not the point is it?' he said, turning from the window, the closeness of the seats making his response confrontational. He looked away, shy, sorry.

'What about the people we'll become, Luke? Have

you thought about that?'
    He looked at his watch.
    'What time did we get on this bus?'
    'About 6 o'clock.'
    'For the last hour, I've thought of nothing else.'

Ysabelle

'Buenos días,' he said, the accent gringo, the intonation all wrong.

'Good morning.'

'It sure is. And it wasn't a bad day yesterday. Cracking the case and, well,' he lay down next to me, 'this.'

'Where am I?' I asked.

'You're in Wales.'

'Yes, okay,' My head felt like a San Telmo dancefloor.

'We did drink a lot last night.'

He laughed.

'Yes, we did. Standard end of case stuff, but wow...last night. Last night.' He kissed me on the head. It was not unpleasant.

'Right, coffee. You're probably used to weapons-grade stuff and lucky for you, I think I've got the pod that will take you right back home.' He took his hand and pushed my hair out of my eyes.

'I'm Marco, by the way, Rabaiotti...in case you didn't remember.'

'Thank you,' I mouthed, and put my head back on the pillow, the cushions much softer here than the pequeño room the detective had booked for me. Maybe drunk me came back with this chico just to get some decent sleep. Jet lag was finally catching up with me. My eyelids felt like they were holding weights, but the one I'd carried on my shoulder all the way here had been lifted.

'Here you go,' he said, handing me the cup, 'it's a Patagonia blend, apparently.'

He had a kind, handsome face. Maybe it was more than just sleep. Another romance with a Welshman, but this time I was the one on holiday.

'I've got to drink up and get to work, I'm afraid,' he

said, 'turns out the journalist hasn't made it. Sarge wants us all in. There'll be a few hangovers in there this morning.'

I sat up against the wall. The shadow had prevailed.

'Oh shit, shit, I'm sorry. You knew him didn't you?' he said, shirt half-on, his face red and sweaty.

'I knew him.'

'Shit, I'm sorry,' he said, 'this is why they never put me on the door knocks. Were you close?'

I reached for my coffee and drank.

'I knew him.'

'Look, I've got to go...but you stay here. Relax. Sorry, not the right word. Take your time. Take a shower. There's no rush. And don't worry, we'll get them. Adios.'

'Thank you.'

He jumped off the bed into another room. Luke was dead. He'd been dead since the minute I met him. His shadow fell on my thoughts for years since, but maybe, just maybe now we'd both be free.

The coffee tasted like aqua from la Plata but I needed it. These Welsh drank a lot. My phone was at the side of the bed, tangled up in a pile of my clothes. The battery was dead. My hand stuck to the screen. I remembered now. I had called Bruce from the pub. The police had called me a hero but it was Bruce who deserved their praise. He had hacked into Luke's account. He had found his research, the interviews, the testimony of a man called Hamish.

'Give me ten minutes online and I'll work out the password of El Presidente.'

It was no surprise to a girl from La Boca that a big organisation was corrupt but globalisation seemed to have spread this sickness around the world. Nowhere was safe. The legal centre was collateral damage. I'd learned that phrase from the Arnie movie. Madre had a thing for Schwarzenegger. An unintended victim of the crime. We did so much good work, did it matter if the dinero came from a company we'd have taken down if on the other side of the courtroom? I thought about Medellin under Escobar, the spoils of crime and corruption keeping the streets safe, the people in love with their leader. Now we had corporations. A wave of nausea came over me. I didn't know what to think.

'If the world was black and white, why are the house of La Boca pink and blue?'

Abuela's words meant more than ever today.

'Platform five for the 12.15 o'clock service to Aberdare.'

I could just about make out the words the announcer said, the digital display confirming this train would take me to my destination. The train pulled in and the doors opened. I found a seat next to a lady madre's age. The green flowery jacket on her lap clashed with the green flowery shirt she wore. She pulled her glasses out of her pocket and turned to me, our faces a small distance apart.

'Helps me read Facebook, love. Only thing I need them for.'

I thought about sharing Bruce's trick to make the words bigger but chose a quieter life. The train was full of other passengers, most lost in their phones, some talking loudly about their love lives across the carriage. Two girls, both with bright red hair and eyebrows you could use to straighten a shelf, exchanged opinions on a boy who'd joined their office that week. It was clear he was going to cause them a lot of trouble. In that, this place was no different to La Boca. Their voices had a quality that made their words sound like song, the backing track the beeps from a gordo man playing a game on his laptop.

The train stopped at the universidad and groups of students entered. A group a few rows down from where I was sat, their faces full of the possibilities of youth, of the night ahead, the life ahead, spoke in Spanish. This was King's Spanish, not the language we spoke back home, all lisp and no grit. From the window, over the scrolling of my neighbour, grand buildings turned to graffitied walls to greenery and hills. The sun and shadow took turns in dominating the light, bridges and trees changing the mood. Sol. Sombra. Sol. Sombra. I knew the feeling.

I exited the station into a thin little street, small shops painted in pastel colours. It would make madre happy that Tom came from a place where they painted the houses like our forefathers did in La Boca. These people had mined too but now the shops sold antiques or kebabs, electronic cigarettes or two-for-one pizza. Two young boys stood outside a pub, smoking and play-fighting. They reminded me of the boys from the Facultad de Derecho. They took their hands off each other as I walked past and smiled politely. The smell of fresh chips overpowered the air, its source the open door of a cafe. I hadn't eaten since last night.

It came back to me. The policeman had told me we had to go to Chippy Lane. I'd laughed at the name but it was true. A lane full of chips and the drunk people who needed to eat them at two in the morning. He'd kissed me against the window of the chip shop, one hand on my ass, the other holding his cone of chips. People passed and cheered, some dressed as superheroes, one as Harry Potter. It was like we'd scored a goal at La Bombanera. He just laughed and asked if I wanted a bite of his sausage.

'You're disgusting,' I'd told him.

'What can I get you love?'

The woman who asked me had bleached blonde hair and purple eye shadow. She looked like Susana Giménez, a talk show host from the 80s madre cursed at every time she came on screen. I looked at the menu.

'This place is called Deli Delilah?' I asked.

'Why? Why? Why?' she said.

'I-'

'It's a joke. Yes it is, love. Deli Delilah.'

'I-'

'Big fan, are you, love?'

'My mother is.'

'Student are you, love?'

'No, no, I'm-'

'Missed out on 10% discount there, love, but don't worry, I'll give it you anyway.'

'Oh...thank you.'

'Now what you having?'

'Chips, please.'

'Chips,' she shouted over her shoulder.

'And what about to drink?'

'Tea.'

'Tea,' she shouted again, 'milk and sugar?'

'Yes please.'

I chose the path of least resistance. I was alone in the cafe apart from an old man, a flat cap on his head and an iPad on the table in front of him, canned laughter bouncing off the table. The cafe where I first met Luke came into my mind. It was both close and a million miles from this little table in a small corner of Wales. The tablecloth bounced brilliant red in the rays of the sun let in through the window, no sign of a shadow.

'Here you are, love. Enjoy.'

It had started to rain by the time I'd left the cafe.

Luke had told me the word for Welsh rain.

'Drizzle. That's not a word you'll learn in an Argentinian school or from American TV. Stick with me, you'll be fluent in all the ways we have to describe the weather.'

The road bent around to the left and the concrete opened up to a hundred hills and a thousand trees. A cat crossed the road towards me and followed my path towards the destination.

Our flag had a smiling sun, his grin hiding the hurt of generations. The Welsh people had suffered too. Their flag wasn't a collection of colours but a dragon. I passed a pub with the name and, despite the time of day, the windows shook with life. The sound of *Despacito* carried onto the street and the laughter sounded more like a Saturday night.

A man in a black suit and tie found his way slowly through the open door to the outside. His face looked like a map, a collection of lines and points of interest, sometimes close together, sometimes not. He looked to the sky and held his hand out like Oliver's bowl.

'Ah,' he said, 'turned out nice for him I see. He'd be happy with that.'

'Press the button that looks like Uncle Claudio's old Super 8 camera.' Madre breathed through her blocked nose, the sound as comforting here as her being in the bedroom next to me.

'Madre de dios, Ysabelle. Couldn't you just send a postcard? Fatima's son sent a postcard every day….from the Eiffel Tower….el, el, el…Venice….el, el, el…the grand bullring in España…' She snorted and searched her mind for landmarks she'd seen on TV.

I'd bought madre a phone from Bruce. I made him swear on El Jefe's life it wasn't stolen. He told me he was selling for an amigo who needed monedas pronto otherwise some of the barrios boys would do more than steal his smartphone.

'Unless you've turned into a road, I can't see you,' madre said. She hadn't mastered the technology yet. It took her 12 months after padre died to learn how to turn over the TV channel and even now she claims she can't.

'It's lucky it's on the right one for *Herederos de una Venganza.*'

I turned my phone around so madre was the right way round on the screen, but she did the same. We danced like this for a while, her bright orange hair turning over and over in my hand as the Welsh drizzle wet her face.

'Are you eating properly?' she asked me.

'Si, madre, si.'

'The food here is...look where I am...'

I turned the phone towards the house.

'This is the house Tom grew up in,' I told her, 'the house he went back to after the concert at the Top Hat where he met the manager who changed his name to Jones. The house where he lived with his wife Linda when they first met. The house he wrote *What's New Pussycat?* in...'

'Dios mio.'

I zoomed in on the door, the windows, the cladding chipping away from the front of the house. I turned the phone back to my face. Madre was crying. I cried too. I'm not entirely sure why. The tears ran down my face, diluted by the rain into something new.

'Hello, can I help?'

The front door of the house opened.

'Hello,' I said.

Nina

Deceiving an officer of the law, that's one way of looking at it. Wasn't expecting this one would throw the book at me, mind, and I was right about that at least. I don't know why I told him I knew what happened. My women's intuition might be one thing, but I ain't like Derek Acorah, communicating with the dead. Because that's what he was, Luke. Brown bread. Not like he'd be seeing Jase up there. Reserved a seat at very different bars that pair. More chance of the big lump sat opposite me being the next James Bond.

'If it comes in threes, who's getting a knock on the door next?'

'You tell me Mystic Meg.'

'Watch it.'

'Got me here under false pretences, telling me you knew the story on a live,' he fumbled for the word, 'case.'

'Murder case?'

'I didn't say that.'

'You can talk, with your late night texts.'

He wasn't embarrassed a bit. To be honest with you, I liked his balls.

'I thought you'd want to know we got the scumbags who did this.'

He took a sip of his tea, green one, wasn't expecting that, and sat back like Prince after a rib out.

'And you're sat here with me?' I said.

'False pretences,' he said, 'false pretences.'

'I could have told you it weren't just a hit and run.'

'The police have been known to employ psychics.'

His knee brushed mine under the table. I kicked him in the shin.

'Hang on.'

'Shut it.'

He started to protest, his gob opening like a sinkhole in the road, but thought better of it. We'd met in a cafe this time. Bottomless brunch o'clock according to the sales pitch on the table. The waiter had asked if we were here for the offer. He'd asked him if he looked like someone who went on the piss at this time of day and we both fell about laughing. He might be a copper but he cracked me up, fair play.

The place was full of prams, all the yummy mummies gassing away and ignoring their little terrors, left screaming in space age prams. He caught me staring.

'Never fancied it?'

'How'd you mean?'

'Motherhood. Early nights. Shitty nappies. All that caper.'

'How'd you know I never?'

He leaned in, his breath stinking of black pudding.

'Trust me, I know you well enough to know.'

It took me a beat.

'Give over, you filthy bastard,' I said, but it was a compliment I spose. He held his hands up like a robber from a silent movie.

'Serious though, not just a case of fancying it, is it? Not like switching the kettle on for a cup of tea. Might be for some women but not for me. There's always a reason for these things.'

He looked a bit stunned to be fair. First time I seen him like that. First time the bravado slipped, the always taking the Michael, always knowing what's next.

'I don't know what to say. I wasn't expecting you to say that.'

'Ain't your lot always preaching actions and consequences? What you expect, you ask a woman my age a question like that?'

'I'm sorry.'

He seemed genuine about it too. The silence just sat there for a bit, neither of us feeling the need to fill the gap, listening to the little voice in our heads. I could see he was, big eyes darting round the place. Looking but all the seeing was being done on the inside.

A double buggy tried to push through the space between our table and the next, two kids looked like Churchill bawling their eyes out, the mum all apologetic, stressed out by the screaming, banging the wheels into the chairs. All 'sorry, sorry, sorry'.

'Not your fault, darling,' he said to her. He waited til she'd made it out on the pavement.

'God, I know you're not meant to say but those two boys were ugly as sin.' I laughed so bloody hard at that, the other mothers looked more than once. It felt good to get it out.

'A good laugh's as good as a good cry, if you get me?'

'Isn't it the other way around?'

'Life should be about feeling something, shouldn't it? No time for bumbling along all dead inside. That's what I think.'

'I can believe that,' he told me, 'I can believe that. Guilty as charged here though.'

'How'd you mean?'

'Bumbling along. Spent too many years doing it. Putting nothing in, getting nothing back. That's all changing though.'

He looked like the dog with two dicks again. Happy as, but not smug with it. I was happy for him, funny as that might sound. I liked this bloke. Felt safe with him. Like he'd look after me, even if I hadn't asked him to. This wasn't what I was expecting.

'Did you mean that?'

'Mean what?'

'What you said earlier about there being a reason for it. It being-'

'Yeah, I knows what you mean.'

I took a sip from my tea but it'd gone lukewarm and there's nothing that's worse, cake next to it didn't stand a chance.

'The action and consequence thing wasn't just you. It was me and all. That's what happens to your head when you've had a Catholic childhood. Everything happens for a reason. Not just to tie the world up in a neat little bow. More like if something bad happens to you, you done something somewhere down the line to make it that way.'

I loved mam to death and I did and all but every now and then I don't half think she filled my head with nonsense and I might not have been so hard on myself all these years if it hadn't been that way. I'd keep myself up all hours all nights, racking back through my brain, weighing up every misdemeanour in case it was the answer as to why Tina and not me.

'Life's too short to talk like that,' he said.

'Yeah, there is that. I get you, I do. But I've been living this one a long time, that's how it feels anyway. I know we're just a dot on page 400 or whatever it is but I'm not reading that book. I'm trying to write my own story.'

'And is there room for another character?'

'Oh, there's been plenty, but you can believe that I'm sure. Not all of them hung around long enough to make an impression mind you. I suppose when it comes down to it I would've liked someone to love me back no matter what, unconditional love if you get me. I don't wanna sound like a dating ad but I've had a lot of love to give. I have. Just be nice to know you always had it coming back, you know?'

'You ever thought about getting a dog?'

Cheeky fucker.

'Man's best friend? No thanks. When's something going to be a woman's best friend?'

'Sounds like an Ann Summers ad.'

'I might have been better off with that. Might of.'

'The unconditional love thing ain't all it's cracked up to be anyhow,' he said. His face looked different now, sad almost. It was like seeing your favourite comedian doing a weepie. I wasn't expecting him to have the range.

'How'd you mean?'

'Love's supposed to make you a better person isn't it?'

'Is it?'

'You know, keep the standards up and you'll be rewarded. If you can do anything and still get rewarded, unconditional love, that's when things fall apart.'

I nodded. I got it.

'This is speaking from my very limited experience, but it turns out the unconditional love comes with conditions, or at least when it's incoming.'

'Your daughter?'

'My daughter.'

'You spend fifteen years as a superhero and the moment they want you to treat them like an adult, turns out they can't deal with you asking the same.'

'Every girl puts their old man on a pedestal. Even me...and mine was more familiar with the inside of a bookies than his own house. I won't ask what you done.'

And he didn't tell me. We sat there in silence again. The cafe had emptied out now, all the prams gone to the park round the corner probably. Sun had her hat on for the first time in a while.

'Can I get you anything else?'

'No, I think we're done here,' he said.

'Last time someone took me on a date in the park, I was 15 and there was a bottle of vodka nicked from his old man's bureau involved.'

'Who said this was a date?'

I didn't need to answer him.

We'd decided to walk off the cake in the flower garden round the corner from the cafe. He didn't need to say much, not after that. I don't remember too much about school, past the bullying, but we had this science teacher who wore this wig for the first three years. Then one day, she strolled in without it, first time she'd strolled in her adult life by the looks, sat down in front of a class of 30 naughty kids with less hair on top than Bobby Charlton, the collection of dead people's curls she'd carried around for years left next to the hairbrush and bedside mirror that day. The kids gave her stick, one boy in particular, but she had this look on her face like she couldn't give a flying fuck. It stayed with me, that look. I knew I was wearing it in that park. She'd told us about magnets, how the north in one attracted the south in another, if they were the same, then it didn't work, they repelled each other. But if one was positive and the other was negative, that's when you couldn't stop it. Nothing you could do about it, try as you might. Can't fight science.

That's how I felt about it now, in that park, his arm next to mine. Not touching, yet, but close enough to know they were being pulled together, into each other's forcefield, and there just wasn't anything you could do about it.

Charlie

'I've made a special playlist, you know?' Ted said. He was driving me there in his Fiat Punto, convincing me easily enough that a taxi would spunk the appearance fee and carrying a guitar on First Great Western would only draw attention.

'Imagine if Hot got hold of that.'
'It's Heat.'
'Heat!'

It wasn't like I needed a tour bus. Marcus would have insisted on something completely disproportionate to the budget. That's a measure of how I was badly advised and why a platinum best seller was working as a music teacher in a school for girls.

'And I'll be a bit sad, thinking of you in the train carriage all on your todd, some Herbert trying to take a surreptitious photo of you on their phone.'

'They would have put me in first class.'
'Still.'

He drove along for a bit, moving from the left hand lane into the middle, passing a caravan, waving and returning back to where we were.

'Beep beep, beep beep, yeah!' Ted sang out of tune with the stereo.

'See, I told you it'd be fun.'
'It's like the Mötley Crüe autobiography.'
'I only vaguely know what you're talking about,' he said. The butterflies in my belly did a backflip. I closed my eyes and counted down from ten.

Luke was driving that day. He hated it. Said he spent everyday in a car driving between doorstepping grieving relatives and covering the county fair.

'And whose fucking fault is that?'

No answer.

'And for the record, I still don't want to go to your ex-girlfriend's fucking wedding.'

'She's not my ex-girlf-'

'Touched a nerve?'

'Fuck you.'

It hadn't been fair. I knew that then but neither was dragging me to Devon for the wedding of some Hooray Henry to a girl he knew from uni who was clearly still in love with him. I was in love with him. Then at least. Just had a funny way of showing it sometimes. Sometimes winning the battle was the bigger objective. Fighting over the next hill. One nil up when no-one was keeping score.

There would be no more car rides now. No more road trips. Not for Luke. Where was he now? The big nowhere. Fade to black. I had him to thank for this journey. That thought of him, a few weeks back, fleeting at first, took over, encompassed all. Turned the music teacher back into what I was. Where I belonged.

'Beep beep, beep beep yeah,' Ted sang, 'available for backing vocals, just so you know.'

'Ladies and gentlemen, she may have been away for a long, long time, but her voice never left our hearts. The one, the only, Charlie Ray!'

Jools Holland stepped back into the black, the fingers of his outstretched hand wriggling through the studio air, his rat-a-tat delivery setting me up for the biggest three minutes of my recent life.

The words tumbled out. Year after year of notebooks filled with hangman and doodles. Shopping lists and burn books. These words were meant to be outside of me. To be sung to a world waiting to listen, even if the muse wasn't of it anymore. My first songs needed a

Marcus to make it out into the world, but things were different now. Warhol's words alive through a million bad bedroom singers. But I had the profile. Once. The social media followers still sat there, waiting without ever really knowing it. The benefit of working at a posh school paid for by a corrupt hedge fund was that the recording facilities were first class. The studios had been empty all week, the kids caught up in exam hell instead of making a racket to my slow hand claps. I'd had to teach myself how to set up the studio and record the sound for my lessons. It was easy enough. I'd sat in the booth and sang. Like I used to. A simple strum pulling the words together.

>'Synchronicity
>coming back to you
>to rediscover me.'

I'd polished it up a bit over the next few days. A trim here. A fade there. A much more stress free approach than the aborted second album session, Marcus off his chops arguing with the big name producer about the levels on a song which wasn't even there anyway.

Previously I'd fret about the posts. Each word. Each snark. These were obvious.

'For Luke.'

Send.

It didn't take long. The notifications pinged. Slowly at first, then metronomic.

>'Bloody hell, Charlie Ray is back.'
>'Thought she'd died tbh.'
>'OMG get in my ears.'
>'This is actually amazing.'
>'Charlie RAY!'
>'Big 🤍 Charlie.'

'Damn I missed this girl.'
'Still got it.'
'Absolute heartbreaker.'
'Lucky Luke.'
'New album anyone?'
'Love this.'
'Synchronicity. I feel ya Charlie.'
'Her voice is still so good.'
'Finally, I can stop listening to *Forever Songs*.'
'This on repeat'
'Who's this Luke then?'
'FIT VOICE.'
'Get this to number one.'
'Who's Luke?'

The attention of others pulsing life back, but this time the body was different.

It carried on like this for a week. Back then, interview requests had to be fielded by the PR team, each carefully considered as part of our awareness strategy, aligned against key demographics in core markets. My old email address, the one that pre-dated Team Charlie Ray, pre-*Forever Songs*, was still live. I'd thought about changing the out of office reply one hundred times.

'For interview requests, contact', 'for booking requests, contact' to something more real.

'Charlie Ray is on a permanent hiatus. Go find and fuck up the next big thing.'

It didn't take long.

'Charlie, Hannah at Blue Note PR says they're no longer representing you. I'm not sure if this email still works but we'd love to speak to you for insert name of every music magazine around.' Delete. Delete. Delete.

It was about the song. Not me. About Luke. Not

me. But then...

'Hi Charlie, it's Dawn here from Jools Holland. We'd love it if you-'

My finger hovered over the DEL.

'I saw you on Jools Holland, you know...'
'You did.'
'I did.'
'That's,' I wasn't sure what he'd wanted me to say. I was his live-in lover. He didn't need to woo me, 'great.' My tone rose like a character on *Neighbours*.
'That was when I knew, you know.'
'Knew what?'
'When I knew.'
He grabbed me by the ears and pulled me in.
'I was blind drunk on red wine in a hostel in Argentina, crowded round the TV in the communal room, and you sang. I didn't have a hangover the next day. That was when I knew.'
'That was when I knew nothing,' I told him.

'Charlie Ray, ladies and gentlemen...'
Polite applause rose from the audience, rising to an occasional whoop.
'We missed you!' A lone voice. Female. Older. Shouting above the collective.
'We missed you indeed,' said Jools, taking a seat next to me at a small table for two, the kind a mobster and his moll would have set aside at a cabaret. Jools smelled of Ted's aftershave. I wasn't sure who I judged, what it said about either man.
'So, Charlie Ray. We've not heard that voice in too long and what an absolute pleasure it is to have you back on the show.'

'Where have you been?'

'In hiding.'

'Ha,' he laughed, one shrill sound.

'But you really have-'

'I've been living life,' I paused, 'out of the spotlight.'

'Because you were very much in the spotlight, weren't you'

'Yes.'

'Hands up if you had a copy of *Forever Songs?*'. Jools turned to the audience, the dry cleaning tag sticking out from his velvet jacket.

I didn't turn. I knew what I'd see.

'Round of applause for *Forever Songs*, ladies and gentlemen. One of the albums of the century, I think it's fair to say.'

Applause and whoops.

'We've got a clip. Let's have a look at the last time you were here...'

A video played on a small screen. The Ghost of Charlie Past. Hair longer. Eyes emptier, if you knew what you were looking for. Jools looked the same. His fingers boogie woogying along to my guitar,

'What a performance,' he smiled, proud dad style.

'And now, new material.'

'Yes.'

'Tell us about *Synchronicity*. How did it come to life?'

Deep breath.

'The tune had been playing inside me for a long time. It just took a while for the words to follow.'

'And what wonderful words they are.'

'Thank you.'

'The dedication...'

'Yes...'

'It seems like a deeply personal song?'
'Yes.'
'That's all we're getting, ladies and gentlemen. Ladies and gentlemen, Charlie Ray!'

Graves

'We doing stake-outs now are we?'

'Does it matter if the meter's running? Think of this as your contribution to a greener economy. Cash still coming in but without the fumes.'

'I didn't have you down as Extinction Rebellion...'

'You better believe it, brother man. The world's turning and we're not learning.'

'I'll tell you to walk next time you call my cab then.'

'One step at a time, brother man, one step at a time.'

Abdi flicked through the radio stations searching for a sound that sounded about right. He'd thought about using the downtime to catch up on his podcast, an episode with a Somalian archeologist in the download bin, but experience told him his passenger couldn't go five minutes without sharing a piece of cod psychology.

The thick metal gates of the house opposite, eight foot tall and topped with decorative spears, gave the outside world the impression of importance behind the lock. A local sports star, a businessman. Certainly not old money, the mock Tudor windows saw to that. But it was none of these that was marched out into the waiting patrol car, even if he did show entrepreneurial tendencies. The cuffs weren't necessary, not on one of their own. An old unwritten rule. But Graves had insisted.

'Not smiling anymore are we, Smiler?' Graves said out loud, that exact expression spread over his own freshly shaved face like his mirror hadn't seen in a long time.

'Who's he then?' Abdi asked.

'Worth a £55 fare that, was it? I'd have gone to the opera instead.' He'd taken his girls to see Hansel and Gretel at the Millennium Centre, the pair of them hiding behind hands when the performers had jumped out of a gigantic mouth.

'A salutary comparison, brother man,' Graves said, leaning back when he'd usually be arse on end of seat, craving his driver's full attention.

'The fat lady has just taken a bow.'

He spread the newspapers all over the breakfast bar, the dining table he'd bought on an ambitious whim, leaning in flatpack behind the bedroom door.'

ALARM AT DUNAMIS: CRIMINAL CHARGES NEXT

HEDGE FUND TRIMMED

CHARLIE RAY SONG SQUEEZE DEAD

CORRUPT TO THE CORE: GLOBAL OUTRAGE AT DUNAMIS

LUKEILEAKS:HACK HACKED, DUNAMIS WHACKED

The driver had been a mug. £500 all it took to knock a stranger off his bike and into a coma. A Jase Mk II. Jase didn't make it because he knew too much, despite what he'd said on the record. Best to be sure. That's how they worked. Nothing left to chance. Rub him out. Stop the rot. But they couldn't. It was everywhere. Once Ysabelle and her sidekick and cracked it open, it was over. It was the best few hundred Graves had ever spent.

Graves took a slurp of his green tea, swilling it around his mouth and enjoying the cleanse of the hurt.

'Fuck.'

He'd left the iron on top of a cardboard box of books, brown marks scorched onto a charity shop copy of Camus' *The Outsider* that had sat on his bedside table for at least a year before he put it away unread and asked it to stop judging him.

'Fuck.'

He ironed the creases out of the white shirt, saved for best, a small Guinness stain on the tail, a victim of Melody's graduation all those years back. He didn't have many occasions to wear his best white shirt. He dabbed the marks left by his newsprint from his fingers with a sponge from the sink, seeds from his toast mixing with the fibres. He'd thought about asking Abdi to stop at the drive-thru on the way back but that was how this whole caper began.

Graves left the house without his big coat. The weather played no portent of today's engagement. No sun through the clouds. No dark and stormy sky. Just the usual Welsh drizzle, a comment on nothing other than the usual. Pathetic fallacy hadn't made it to Wales, Graves thought. Sounded like a band that'd open for Weller in The Style Council days.

'Lovely service.'
'It was.'

A there-we-are face and stare into the mid-distance. Graves wasn't playing that game today, however touching the sentiment, however conciliatory the eulogy. This wasn't the natural order, two fat fingers to the plan. A cosmic strategy gone wrong. But still.

She was there. The artisan ice cream heiress. Lipstick to match her dress and a thousand yard stare. No sign of the business partner. Must be all part of the recovery, Graves thought. He'd liked her, enjoyed their duals. Didn't take him too many leaps of faith to see her in the dock for doing her old fella in. She was far too clever to get caught.

Sadie saw him staring at her, the overweight officer. Under other circumstances she'd had teased him. A wink, the tongue tracing the lips, but today her mind was on other matters. The stomp of Dr. Martens on a march. The late Liverpool sun. The missed opportunities. Her future, without him, without her husband.

Nina stood towards the edges, unawares, her heels sunk half an inch into the give of the ground. She'd practised what she'd say, the forms of words for a relative or close friend. Just a well wisher. Saw the story. Wanted to pay her respects. Like people used to. She needn't have learned her lines. Queue out of the doors like the wedding of a local big cheese, except everyone was dressed more sombre.

'There he is,' she said, 'there he is.'

The press were there, long lens flashing light and heat from across the cemetery. A police press officer, force-branded waterproof over civvies, stood by their side, new in the job and unsure of the law, pleading with them on the grounds of decorum.

'One more shot and we're out of your hair.'

Charlie Ray was the big prize. Picture editors sat waiting for the money shot for tomorrow's front page, the rest of the roll going up on the sidebar of shame without much of a touch up.

'Charlie Ray looked demure in a black full-length dress, a splash of colour through the peacock brooch on the shoulder.'

'Lucky bugger,' Graves said to Rabaiotti, elbowing him in the ribs like an older relative at a family party.

'Taking tango lessons, are we?'

'It takes two, Sarge. You should know that.'

Graves knew that only too well, deep down behind his beer gut into the slightly bruised, the slightly battered soul that still burned inside him, brighter today that it had done, despite the surroundings.

'Lovely service.'

'I wouldn't know.'

'Because?'

'Because I just turned up. Busy morning, believe it or not.'

'Right answer. I'd hoped it wasn't because you'd lost all concept of loveliness.'

'Never change, dad.'

Graves laughed, not a funeral laugh.

'Coffee?'

'Green tea, actually.'

'You have changed.'

'Shall we?'

'I've got nothing else to do.'

Then they walked off like that, Graves and Melody, a hearse driving slowly towards them, this time another unlucky one laid out flat in the back.

Printed in Great Britain
by Amazon